A Matter of Revenge

Elizabeth Baroody

aka

Christy Demaine

Order this book online at www.trafford.com
or email orders@trafford.com

Most Trafford titles are also available at major online book retailers.

Printed in the United States of America.

ISBN: 978-1-4907-4085-0 (sc)
ISBN: 978-1-4907-4086-7 (e)

Because of the dynamic nature of the Internet, any web addresses or links contained in
this book may have changed since publication and may no longer be valid. The views
expressed in this work are solely those of the author and do not necessarily reflect the
views of the publisher, and the publisher hereby disclaims any responsibility for them.

Any people depicted in stock imagery provided by Thinkstock are models,
and such images are being used for illustrative purposes only.
Certain stock imagery © Thinkstock.

Trafford rev. 06/26/2014

 www.trafford.com

North America & international
toll-free: 1 888 232 4444 (USA & Canada)
fax: 812 355 4082

WHO CAN RECOGNIZE
THE FACE OF AN ASSASSIN?

Across at the cemetery, he saw an old lady gently placing flowers on a grave; a dump truck full of rubble from the asylum came rumbling by, causing him to think momentarily of the girl he had met the night before; two college students pedaled by, paying him no attention whatsoever in their ride to classes. It was an average Middletowne morning, peaceful, ordinary. Who would have ever guessed that in the little green house on this sunny street sat two of the most fanatic men in the United States, so clever in their deceptions that not even the CIA knew they existed?

CHAPTER ONE

From her window she could see the full moon rising, pale apricot, like some ethereal balloon being pulled slowly upward by invisible string. This was the perfect time, when streets were wet and trees glistened black in the season; the first small buds were hardening on the twigs. Outside the window, Middletowne lay sleeping in the flicker of the colonial street lamps. Nothing stirred; not even a cat crossed the cobbled streets.

Hurriedly, the woman dressed in a heavy twill coat and tied a scarf around her head. She selected a camera from the three lined up along the top of the bookcase, screwed a tripod into the base and picked up a canvas tote. Swinging it over her shoulder in a gesture that suggested long practice, she went out and down the narrow steps that led from the apartment to the street. Her feet knew every irregularity in the bricks of the sidewalk.

A light green Rover turned slowly into the street—Middletowne Security on its leisurely night patrol of the shops and the restoration area. She waited, motionless in the shadow of a goldenrain tree, until the Rover had passed. The driver was Colby Dance, full-time cop, sometime friend, and he was sure to want to know where she was going at this time of night. Twelve o'clock was late for a small town.

The moon was climbing quickly, and she silently cursed this delay. She started to run. The bag hit painfully against her side. She held the large camera out in front of her like a cudgel.

The ruins of the old insane asylum lay ahead, a rubble pile of fallen chimneys, shattered glass, twisted wire that had covered the windows, and rusted pipes from the "calming room," where the disturbed ones had once been sedated by warm baths. There, too, were the cribs, those awesome adult-sized cribs with their high iron sides that had been pulled up at night to keep the restless, mindless creatures from wandering in the dark. Over these remnants, reflecting the memories of three hundred years, hung a luminescent moon. What a fantastic shot!

She snagged her coat on a No Trespassing sign as she crawled under the fence into a restricted zone where demolition of the old building had already begun. She squeezed her bag through a gap between two metal gate posts and stood up. Stumbling in the soggy earth, the heels of her boots sinking into the muck with each step, she plowed up the hill. The picture would have to be taken from slightly downhill, in order to get the outlines of the ruin silhouetted against the full moon. Focusing, her eye picked out the gaunt iron cribs, and she quickly snapped a couple of shots. Once, these relics had sat in lavender and pink and blue rooms—pastel cells where adult bodies had vacantly peered out through the cribs' iron bars. All were gone now to the new compound far across town, out of sight of the tourists. The woman sighed. The editor of *Weird Stories* wouldn't be interested in the cribs, but he'd be crazy himself if he didn't like the moon shot. And it would net another hundred in the bank for her. It was free-lance work that paid off, not her regular job, working for Jack Wise on the local weekly.

Assignment completed, twelve frames of solid material to select from, she turned and started down the hill. Ignoring the slickness of the footing, she tried to find the opening in the fence where she had crawled in. Too late, she spotted the gaping black tunnel leading underground to the boiler room of the old building and, unable to catch herself, she plummeted down into it. Even as she fell, she managed to hold the camera upright. *Photographer right to the damn finish,* she thought grimly as she fell backward into the stinking moldy residue of leaves that lined the bottom of the concrete passage. The last thing she remembered was the full moon, smiling down in cold splendor just above the mouth of the tunnel.

A sleek gray beast suddenly appeared slavering at the mouth of the tunnel, whimpering with excitement at the sight of the woman's figure lying below. Curious, it picked its way down to stand over the still form. It sniffed the body, then licked at the hands and face, wondering.

The woman opened her eyes. A scream stuck in her throat as a large, rough tongue caressed her cheek. She lay unmoving, terrified.

"Here, Wolf. Here, boy! Damn it, you better come out of there! You know it's off limits!"

The voice sounded angry and was coming closer.

"Help! Help me," she managed to call faintly. The dog looked down in surprise, then raced to the opening and barked once, sharply. He paused just long enough for the man to see him, then returned to the side of his discovery.

She heard footsteps coming; then they stopped directly above her head. She heard an intake of breath.

"What the hell?"

The man paused with uncertainty, then scrambled down and brushed the leaves from her body. Without much effort, he lifted her in his arms and carried her up to more solid ground, staring at her with curiosity. The big dog jumped around in an ecstasy of excitement. He was a born scavenger, and this was by far the best thing he had found in his three short years of life. He barked at the man, bursting with pride.

"Good boy, Wolf," grumbled the man, with amusement in his voice.

"Yeah… good boy, Wolf," echoed the woman faintly. Her voice came out unsteadily as she held her head in her hands to stop the world from spinning.

"How did you get down in that culvert?" he asked, setting her down by a walnut tree. "Don't you know this place is off bounds to everybody except the demolition crew?"

Without trying to answer, the woman got groggily to her feet. She touched her camera; miraculously, the lens cap was still in place. *What a dumb thing to be concerned about when little red lights are exploding inside your head,* she thought numbly. She smiled briefly in the direction of the man's voice and decided she owed him an explanation.

"Yes, I know I'm not supposed to be here, but can you think of a better spot to shoot a cover picture for a horror magazine?" She touched her camera again.

"Frankly, no!" The man laughed. The dog, sensing all was well, placed himself happily between the two of them, his tail wagging against their legs.

Suddenly she sank to the grass, as a wave of dizziness swept over her.

"Can I help you get home?" he offered. "My car is just a block from here. I live in that little green house across from the cemetery."

"That's OK. I'll need a minute to get my head straight, though," she protested.

"No trouble. You just take it easy! Be back in a second. Come on, Wolf." The dog hesitated, glanced back reassuringly and bounded off after the man.

Within minutes he was back, driving a dilapidated, light-colored Volkswagen. She got in, gave him her address, and silently they drove the few short blocks to her apartment.

"Well, this is it. Number Nine, St. George. I live up there, over the barber shop. See, where the red geranium is in the window box?"

"Let me help you up the steps with your bags," he said. "Hey, that's heavy!"

"Yes, my job is in that bag—film, extra lenses, a notebook. But really, you don't have to help me further. You've been very kind," she demurred.

"It's nothing. I'll see you safely inside," he insisted. He jumped out and ran around to open the door on her side. Together they awkwardly climbed up the narrow stairs to her flat.

She unlocked the door and he followed her inside to the one large, high-ceilinged room that served as both living room and bedroom. Hastily, she picked up some clothing and newspapers and tossed them around the door into the kitchen. The man looked around the room with interest and smiled.

"Your place certainly tells a lot about you. All those books! And would I be correct in guessing that the photographs are your work?" He stood gazing at the pictures. "They're great. Who is the guy who rates a whole wall to himself?"

The woman didn't answer. She went into the kitchen and mixed two drinks, and by the time she returned, he was seated on one of her two couches. She handed him the cold glass with an apology.

"It's bourbon and ginger ale. It's all I've got."

"Fine. I've learned to like it since I moved south." He halted abruptly, then said quickly, "Hey, I don't even know your name."

"Sorry. I'm Andrea Wayne. I work for Jack Wise, right across the street there, at the Middletowne weekly. The paper's called *What's Happening Here.* We do some local stories and cover the area news for townees and tourists."

"Oh, yes, I pick it up every week. Good little paper."

He took a swallow of his drink and then gave her an incredulous look. "Don't tell me you are Andy Wayne? I was sure you were a man!"

"We fool some of the people some of the time." She laughed. "Now you know my secret. Who are you—Superman?"

"I'm Paul Hunter. I… ah, take some courses at the college. Don't look so surprised. It took me a while to get to it. I spent eight years in the air force."

"Oh, I see. Vietnam?"

"No, in the Middle East," he answered quietly.

"Sounds like a fascinating assignment. Were you stationed in Turkey?"

"No." He volunteered no further information, quickly finished his drink and stood up to leave. Buttoning his leather jacket, he headed for the door.

"Thanks for everything. If your dog hadn't happened along, I might have spent the night in that tunnel, or whatever it is." Hesitantly, she extended her hand. He took it and held it, and for the first time, they stood quietly appraising each other. Suddenly he pulled her forward. Their lips met briefly; then Andrea pulled back in surprise.

"My reward for being a good Boy Scout." He laughed as he turned and went down the stairs. Andrea closed and locked the door behind him, smiling slightly to herself.

She crossed the room to the window and watched as he got into his car. Under the streetlamp, his hair shone thick and blond. His shoulders were wide, and he was very tall, well over six feet. She thought about his face, coming close as he kissed her—eyes dark blue, jaw rather square, a small scar on his forehead. *I wonder if he got that scar in the Middle East?* she thought. *Paul Hunter...*

An impatient yip broke through her thoughts. Andrea looked around the floor despairingly, pulled up the couch covers, looked underneath, then turned to the closet.

"Don't tell me you got shut in there again, Jade. You are getting senile!"

She opened the closet door, and a fat champagne-colored Pekingese rose stiffly and blinked in the sudden light. On bowed legs, it waddled into the living room without an upward glance and made for the kitchen, where the sound of water being lapped was followed by the sound of a body settling into a wicker basket.

"Good night, Your Royal Highness," said Andrea.

Andrea turned to the photographs on the wall—sharp, contrasted, distinctive—all mounted on black mats against the white wall. The man in the pictures showed the gamut of his personality, first grinning like a kid with a birthday cake she had made him, then sulky and petulant in the studio pose she begged him to sit for, then sexy and vibrant—the many faces of G. Patchen Wayne. She had consciously avoided looking at them in the six months since he had been gone. While she had been at work one day, he left, taking the van and all the savings she had managed to put in their joint account—only a few thousand dollars, but it was everything she had.

"Where are you sleeping tonight, Patch Wayne?" she mused aloud.

Why did a twenty-eight-year-old man suddenly get the urge to head for California "to find himself?" Had their two years together been so boring? The truth, as much as it hurt, Andrea suspected, was that she had married a big kid who found out that he had money and wheels, the ticket to freedom that he had never managed to get before. She understood, but it hurt. Oh

God, it hurt. She had thought about divorce but so far had taken no definite steps. And Patch's letters indicated that such a thing had not even crossed his mind. He wrote as if he were taking a long, wonderful vacation.

Andrea pulled out the sofa bed and threw some pillows in place. She swallowed three aspirins to quiet her throbbing head and lay back. Then she reached for a postcard that was propped against the lamp. It had just come in today's mail.

"Hello, darling," it said. "Here is where I am. X. I have a job on a ranch but could use some money. Why don't you come out here? Love you. Miss you. Patch." He had added an address.

Each message was from a little farther west. Sometimes there was a plaintive note: "I hurt my hand driving a tractor," or "This is the third flat on the van. Where did you buy those tires?" Mother Andrea, make everything right.

She tried to stop thinking and get to sleep. She was so tired. A vision of Paul Hunter kept drifting through her mind, and she turned to clutch the pillow beside her, but when sleep finally came, the name she murmured was Patch.

CHAPTER TWO

It was a beautiful day. Sun streamed through the windows of the kitchen. Behind the house, in the backyard, Wolf was investigating each bush and tree for any smells of trespassing night callers—man or beast.

Paul Hunter carefully wiped his cup, saucer, plate, utensils, and methodically put them away in the cabinet over the sink. He went into the bedroom and made up the one used twin bed. He had inherited his propensity for cleanliness and tidiness not from his slightly fey and beautiful American mother, but from his German father.

The house Paul was living in belonged to Omar Shaifi, and Paul wanted it to be perfectly neat when Omar arrived. Chores done, Paul went into the living room and settled in the easy chair, where he turned on the radio to catch the news on the local station. The announcer was droning on in that bored manner that comes from saying the same things every hour.

"Prices are up again this month in local markets, as inflation hits a new high. Washington reports an eight percent rise this year. Middletowne will host the president of Yugoslavia, his lovely wife and an entourage of twenty-four for an overnight visit. During their brief stop here at Marlborough House, they are expected to tour the town by carriage. In Washington the president awaits a meeting with Gerald Ford on Friday. In other local news, seven hundred dental technicians are meeting at the Hilton—"

Paul shut the radio off. What luck! A tailor-made situation! If Omar arrived in time, they could go down to Marlborough House, wait for the president and his party like hundreds of other tourists, follow the route of the carriage ride and then try to fit a definite piece into the puzzle that had brought Paul to Middletowne in the first place.

Omar arrived by car, having forsaken the death-defying old motorcycle he usually careened into town on. The car was a dirty, ancient black Ford, a sedate vehicle probably chosen in deference to the elderly man who was in the passenger's seat. Paul did not immediately recognize the man, but as he got out of the car and started up the walk to the house, there was something definitely familiar to his stride. Paul grinned as he opened the door and greeted him.

"You have aged even more since I last saw you, Mr. Gay. Hello, Omar."

"What gave me away?" asked the man anxiously, slipping furtively inside the door.

"You walked too fast for a real grandpa type."

"I must remember that. I must. You have no idea how many would like to catch me. The things I must do to protect myself! Ah, you would never understand."

"It must be a hard life, old man," agreed Paul. He winked at Omar.

Omar rolled his dark eyes, indicating he thought the older man crazy. Mr. Gay, pretending not to notice, turned and went through the hall to the bathroom, mumbling something about his kidneys being unable to tolerate Omar's way of driving.

Singing some allusive tune, Omar went into the kitchen and took down a small brass pot and the strong Arabian coffee he always kept on hand. Soon an aroma of the dark brew filled the house. Before Omar could retrieve it, the coffee had boiled over on the stove. Paul felt aggravation as it trickled down through the burner, then puddled in a dark spot on the kitchen floor. With pleasure, Omar sloshed the hot liquid into two tiny cups.

"I bet you not have *ah weh* since last month I was here, *habibe!*" said Omar in badly broken English. "This can still almost full. Look in the car. I forget to bring in the sweet. Ah, it's delicious, from New York. You gon' love it. You go get it. We eat." Omar placed the two cups and saucers on a tray.

Paul went out to the car and on the back seat found a heavy round metal tin with sticky waxed paper crackling around the edge of the lid. As he straightened up with it in his hands, he glanced around out of habit to see if there was anything or anyone in the street. Across at the cemetery an old lady was gently placing flowers on a grave; a dump truck full of rubble from the asylum came rumbling by, causing him to think momentarily of the girl he had met the night before; two college students pedaled by, paying him no attention whatsoever in their ride to classes. It was an average Middletowne morning, peaceful, ordinary. Who would have ever guessed that in the little green house on this sunny street sat two of the most fanatic men in the United States, so clever in their deceptions that not even the CIA knew they existed? And of this fact, Paul was certain.

Inside the house, Mr. Gay had pulled the drapes across the windows so that no one could see him sitting in the living room. He had brought a hard-backed chair from the kitchen and was seated where he could see both the front and back doors. When Paul came in, the old man was sipping a glass of milk. He looked apologetic.

"My ulcer, Paul. Hope you don't mind."

"No, of course not. If I had ridden over a hundred miles with Omar in that wreck out there, I'd probably have an ulcer myself."

Omar paid no attention to the old man but offered coffee to Paul. Paul took one of the small cups and sipped it slowly. It was strong enough to dissolve paint, but Omar was pouring himself another cup. He then took the tin from Paul and pried off the lid. With endearments, he praised the sweets in his own language, selected one dripping pistachios and honey and slyly offered it to Mr. Gay, who shuddered and held up his hand in dismay.

"All those nuts. It would kill me!"

Omar passed the tin to Paul, who took a triangle, in hopes of tempering the taste of the coffee. He then remembered the news.

"Omar, today the president of Yugoslavia will be here, and I think it might be a good opportunity to observe exactly what takes place. He'll also take a carriage ride around the town. What are you smiling about?"

"I know this. That is why I come."

"How could you know? Usually they release this kind of news to the press only the day before."

"My ears in Washington tell me such things. We will go see this president, like the curious tourists. We will watch not only his every move, but the ones around him. Those dogs, the agents, *ya il kalib*, those agents."

Omar half closed his glittering eyes and pushed another large piece of the syrupy pastry between his lips, licking them carefully. Paul could almost see his mind working. He knew that Omar's thoughts could sometimes be diabolical. At other times Omar seemed not to think at all, changing from one unrelated scheme to another, often dwelling on the opposite sex, to whom he seemed to be very attractive.

Paul stared at him thoughtfully. What made this man tick, anyway? He had long, curly black hair, olive skin, and teeth that were white and even. Six months of the year he wore an old navy knit cap pulled down level on his forehead, a habit he had picked up in his shortlived career at sea. Paul guessed Omar to be about thirty, although in the year he had known him, he had never asked his age. Thirty would be about right in relation to the other members of the Shaifi family Paul had known in the Middle East.

Omar was the oldest and the only son in the Shaifi family, and he had turned out to be a bitter disappointment to his parents. At nineteen he left the family home secretly to come to the States with an uncle. He went wild with the freedom he found here and married a teen-ager to gain citizenship. Less than a year later, he walked away from Melanie, his wife, and got a job on a freighter bound for South America. Melanie divorced him while he was at sea, a fact that threw him into an uncontrollable rage when he discovered she had given birth to a son, his son, six months after his unannounced departure.

When Omar returned from the sea, he rushed back to the house Melanie and the child were sharing with her parents and tried bodily to take his son away from her. As it happened, Sam, Melanie's brother, was home on leave from the marines at that time. When Omar attempted to take the boy, Sam beat Omar to a pulp.

That episode added to the instability of Omar's mind, always erratic at best. When he told Paul about his troubles, his eyes sparkled with hate and a cunning look appeared on his face. Later, Omar told a strange tale of how Sam had died on maneuvers in an open field on Parris Island. He had been stabbed repeatedly in the back and left to die in a pile of brush. Authorities never solved the case, but the answer was clear in Omar's eyes. Revenge had been oh, so sweet.

Paul thought about this and wondered again how the hell he had gotten mixed up so completely with Omar in the first place.

He picked up the empty cups, took them to the kitchen and put them in the sink. Omar followed him into the room.

"It is something of importance I have to tell you," Omar confided. "The visit of King Hassan may be soon. He speaks in his country of the oil still hidden, perhaps, beneath the sea off the coast of Uddapha, and he wants to make big deal with the United States, get lots money in the U.S. banks and buy the—*sha iss'ma*—how you say?—real estate?" Omar broke into a laugh. "Maybe he buy California, huh?"

"Some of the Arab countries are trying to buy an island off the coast of South Carolina as a resort area," Paul replied. "American Jews are raising hell about it."

At the mention of South Carolina, Omar became perfectly still and glanced out of the corner of his eye at Paul. "This South Carolina, it is a good place?"

"Some people seem to like it. But what were you saying about Hassan's visit?"

"Oh, exact time not settled yet. Our man in the palace, who tell man in the Embassy, say the time is not sure. But he coming, all right. Today, tomorrow, next year… we are ready, my friend. Our plan will succeed because we know how to wait. We will be here and know what to do when the time is right."

Paul looked at him carefully. Omar's eyes had taken on a particularly fanatical glitter. Nervously he threw his navy cap into a corner. He ran his hands through his tangled curls. Then, placing his hands as if to pray, he seemed to sink into a religious trance. "Allah," he whispered, "has sent you to us as an instrument of his will, my friend!"

"Cut that religious crap. You know I'm here only because of Yasmina."

A sob escaped Omar's lips, and he shook his head in agonized agreement.

"Ah, yes, my Yasmina… my Nedra… my little sisters! This is my reason too!"

There was a certain hypocrisy in Omar's suffering that was not lost on Paul. Omar felt guilty about leaving home and having been in the States during the Six Day War, when his tiny country fell to the Israelis and his entire family died defending their farm. His guilt had grown and grown until, obsessed with his own personal vendetta, he found an outlet for his hatred and fear. Omar had joined with a group of people in Washington to plot the assassination of King Hassan Ibn Fuad, monarch of the country that had refused to join in the war—a country whose presence might have been powerful enough to change the course of history and save Omar's country.

Paul's reason for becoming involved was also his love for the Shaifi family, and in particular Yasmina, who had become very dear to him when he was in the Middle East.

He saw her first one day when he had stopped his Jeep on top of a small hill covered with olive trees. Below were two very young girls tending a herd of sheep. He stared down, fascinated by the unreality of the scene. It was as if an ancient scroll had been unrolled at that precise moment for his own private showing—a thing too precious to be shared. The girls looked up, saw him and, giggling, covered their lower faces with thin, white head scarves, a gesture so far from the present that it caught him by surprise. Their shy laughter echoed up the hill like a hundred tiny bells. The older girl then dropped her veil and softly called out a greeting to him in French. The younger one, less bold, sat down among the flock until she was almost hidden from his view.

He descended the hill and talked to them in Arabic, halting every now and then to consult his language book. His efforts with some of the more difficult phrases had both girls laughing aloud. Then, a very short, dark-skinned old man came into the field and shook a stick at him. Paul retreated, but he was intrigued. Again and again he came back to the hillside, and finally the old man beckoned him to his house. That was how it began, his friendship with the Shaifi family.

Paul was jolted back into the present by the appearance of Mr. Gay.

"This is absolutely the last time that I am coming to this place!" he said, shaking his head disconcertedly. "Look at these wide streets and all those yards. One can be very conspicuous in a place like this. Look, grass, right in the heart of the town, acres of grass. Why don't they build on it?"

"It's called restoration, Mr. Gay. Like in the old days, before concrete and crowds took over. You've surely heard of Middletowne before."

"Yes, I have, but I didn't think it would be so… exposed, open."

"I think I know what you're leading up to. You don't want to go downtown with us to see the president today, right? But how in hell do you think you can do your part without at least a look around?"

"I cannot do it. I will have to rely on what information you bring me, and, of course, my past experience. Don't worry. I'm the best in my business."

"You'd better be. My life, not yours, will be on the line when the time comes. If anything goes wrong with the weapon, you're the one I'll be looking for, old man."

Mr. Gay clutched his stomach and shakily popped three pink tablets between his lips. He then straightened his old gray wig, adjusted the thick glasses on his nose and stared sadly at Paul. He looked like a sick Geppetto regarding his Pinocchio.

Paul turned with disgust and walked into the living room, where Omar was turning the bookcases inside out in search of his records. Things were crashing haphazardly to the floor. Unlike Mr. Gay, Omar left evidence of his presence everywhere. He loved special foods, like his coffee, and left black cigars of Turkish tobacco all around the house. And then there was the music, always the music—the high, monotonous wail of his idol, Oum Khartoum.

"Where have you hidden my records?" demanded Omar, scowling.

"Forget that stuff for now. We've got another problem. Mr. Gay refuses to go."

"Aiieee! I am bringing this grandfather of a mouse all the way for nothing!" Omar leaned close to Paul and whispered with some enthusiasm, "Maybe we have to get rid of him. We can find another one."

"At this point? Impossible. You know he's a genius and we need him. As soon as the mission is over, we'll never see him again, but right now he is indispensable."

Omar went into the kitchen and began to plead with, then curse at the older man. But Mr. Gay was more afraid of going out in public in a strange town than he was of Omar's displeasure. He refused to budge from his chair.

"Come on. Don't waste any more time on him. Bring your camera and we'll take pictures of everything we think may be important later. He can go over the angles from the film, and later tonight you can drive him around the area while it's dark. He ought to be able to calculate the firing distance," said Paul impatiently.

"That son of a jackass! Why he is scared? He has never even been fingerprinted."

"Maybe that's how he has managed to stay alive. His fear makes him cautious."

They left the house together, noting that Mr. Gay had snapped the lock on the door before they reached the sidewalk. Only a slight twitch at the edge of the drapery indicated that there was anyone inside. Wolf jumped the fence from the backyard and followed happily along behind. Omar wore a Nikon camera dangling from a shiny metal strap around his neck. It added to the illusion that they were just two more tourists out for a stroll with their dog. They turned into the busy street that led to Marlborough House and blended in with all the other people going to see the president of Yugoslavia. No one noticed them. But then again, who ever recognizes the face of an assassin in a crowd?

CHAPTER THREE

The telephone was ringing. It was right next to the bed, and the pillow over her head didn't quite drown out the sound. Groggily, she pulled the phone off the hook.

"Hello, Andy, this is Gage. Jack says to remind you that you are due downtown in half an hour to cover the visit of the president of Yugoslavia."

"Oh, God, can't you do it? My head is killing me this morning." She covered her face with the bedspread to keep the bright morning sun out of her eyes.

"Big night, huh? Gotta lay off the hard stuff, baby. It'll getcha every time!"

"You won't believe this, but I fell in a hole."

"If you think Buddy's Bar is a hole, you ought to stay out of there."

"Funny."

"You want to trade with me and work tomorrow, Andy?"

"What's the assignment?"

"Two Middletowne kids are entered in those dirttrack races out near the airfield, and Jack insisted I go after it." He yawned into the phone.

"Dirt races? When did we start covering that small stuff?"

"Since Hamilton's kid took up bike racing."

"Uh, well, 'nuff said. You go mingle with the youthful rich. I'll take the visiting biggie any day. Tell Jack I'm on it."

"Will do. Andy, how about meeting me later at the Hilton for a drink and dinner? Who knows what might develop later on. How about it?"

"Hang in there, Gage. One of these days I'll say yes and scare the hell out of you."

Laughing, Andrea hung up before he could reply and reluctantly got out of bed. That Gage, always pretending to be on the make, or was it pretending? She decided his marital situation was as bad as hers. He was married to a small, dark-haired woman who was active in the church, in the Girl Scouts, Middletowne Audubon Society, the Spring Hills Garden Club. Natalie Gage was active just about everywhere except in bed. Despite her lack of energy in this matter, she had managed to produce a son, who was now ten. Her husband was a blustery redhead, going slightly bald, a damn good reporter. He led a life, though, of constant frustration between Natalie, who served every need except the one he desired most, and Andrea, who considered his ardent pursuit a thing of humor and pity, like an old joke told too many times.

Andrea stumbled into the kitchen and put water on for a quick cup of coffee, then jumped into the shower. She wished she could just stand and let the tepid water ease her aches and pains, but there was no time.

As she sipped her coffee, she thought about the events of the night before. The bruises on her hip where she landed had turned blue, and her elbow was scraped raw. But out of that physical misery, one bright spot had emerged. Who was that big, gorgeous guy who had brought her home? Thank God, he had picked that time to walk his dog. *Maybe I should send him some little thing, just to say thanks,* thought Andrea. *And remind him of me —"*

Suddenly Jade barked, interrupting her daydream. The Pekingese was hungry. Andrea went to the refrigerator, brought out a brown bag and held it up temptingly.

"Somebody gave me a steak bone with lots of meat. From the Inn, you lucky dog!" She cut the meat into small pieces, placed it in a bowl she then put down for Jade and hurriedly dressed for work.

She threw on green pants and a matching pullover, added a scarf for color and searched the closet for another coat to replace the one torn last night. The twill coat lay in the bottom of the closet, a bundle of dampness and mud, a challenge for the cleaners. One sleeve was ripped out at the elbow, hardly worth saving.

Jade, now full to the point of bursting, waited impatiently at the door to be taken for a walk. Andrea clicked on her leash and hurried out to the alley between the Antique Shop and Ye Olde Fabrics. She undid the leash, and watched as Jade bounded to the corner lot behind the old white house. There were still oases of grass and trees in this wealthy little city with its high real-estate prices. It was an excellent restoration of the eighteenth-century town with its open space and unpainted buildings—a carefully nurtured genteel antiquity that generated an enormous appeal.

Andrea whistled, and Jade appeared dragging a greasy box of fried chicken.

Quickly, Andrea dropped the box in a nearby can and raced the dog back to the apartment.

She then grabbed a camera and bag and, locking the door behind her, knocked on the one other door on the same floor. "Matt? George? Anybody home?" she called.

Oh, well, she thought, if neither college kid was home, she'd just have to come back and check on Jade herself. Matt and George usually took the dog in with them when she had to work late. It was kind of an agreement they shared.

Matt and George were like brothers, young brothers, to her. She gave them aspirin when they had colds, free copies of *What's Happening Here,* and let them use her telephone to call home when they ran out of money in the middle of the month. They seemed to know just when she was feeling particularly alone and blue after Patch left and would show up with wine and cheese and sesame sticks from Le Fromage, a shop across the street. Some Saturday nights they sat up and watched old horror movies until two in the morning; other times, they respected each other's need for privacy—an ideal arrangement.

It was only a short walk to Marlborough House, and already Andrea could see crowds gathering along the fence and across the street in the open, parklike area known as the Green. Security agents walked beside the fence, keeping an eye on the more aggressive tourists who insisted on leaning up against it. Their walkie-talkies crackled with messages.

Other "press" people were huddled together in their usual privileged spot next to the gate, but Andrea didn't choose to join them. She sat down under a tree and checked her camera to make sure she had a full roll of film. The heavy lens hung awkwardly against her chest as she pinned a plastic press card on her coat. She had covered about a dozen of these visits in the last three years—former Secretary of State Rogers, Moshe Dayan, a Russian poet, the shah of Iran—but the excitement was gone. She knew the ritual now by heart. When "Mr. Big" came through the gate, she would walk across the street and snap a couple of "greeting the public" shots—kids shaking hands, his getting into the carriage, waving to the crowd. Then she would sprint across the Green and wait until the carriage passed some quaint building and take a couple more shots. She would then look for her story—catch phrases, personal details. Her stories were special and had brought job offers from major dailies in the area. But she loved Middletowne, liked working for Jack Wise, and so she stayed. Besides, when Patch came back, as she knew he would, he'd look for her to be here.

Movement around the press group alerted her that the president of Yugoslavia and his entourage had come out of Marlborough House and were now walking down the sidewalk to the street. The president was flanked by his own personal aides and Yugoslavian security, his hosts from Middletowne, U.S. government hosts, and, of course, secret-service agents, conspicuous in their inconspicuous dark suits, white shirts, and striped ties.

Some of the entourage entered the carriage. Several slow-moving limousines followed behind the trotting horses. The sightseers tried to keep up with the carriage, but the driver, a large black man in a gold coat and green knee breeches, slapped the reins, causing the matched pair of horses to step lively enough to leave the crowd behind. The driver drove capably, up through the town, past the old church, then around and down past the courthouse on the other side of the Green.

Andrea got her shots as they passed by. Her camera was out of film now, so she put it away and started back to the office. It was then that she saw him, his head above the crowd, his blond hair gleaming in the sunlight as he hurried along, trying to keep the carriage in sight. Next to him was a dark man in a blue cap who was trying to take pictures. He looked vaguely familiar, too, but she couldn't remember where she had seen him. As they reached the edge of the far side of the Green, Paul Hunter turned in her direction. She smiled and waved. He looked startled, then turned hurriedly away and began to walk in the opposite direction. The other man was close behind. Could she have been mistaken? Was there another man who looked so much like Paul Hunter? After all, he was at quite a distance and she had only seen him a short time the night before. But no, it was Paul, for there was his German shepherd, Wolf. Why had he pretended not to have seen her?

Puzzled and slightly upset, Andrea walked slowly back to the office.

CHAPTER FOUR

"Who that girl is, the one who smile at you? She wears the... brown coat." Omar had hesitated. Unfamiliar with the word *tan*, he substituted *brown*, and then he continued, "I see her smile at you. She smile at you!"

Omar glanced back suspiciously. The girl in question had disappeared, but then he caught a glimpse of her walking on the other side of the Green. His face tightened with distrust, and he scowled at Paul's back, pulling on the edge of his jacket to slow him down. Paul shook him off angrily, but Omar persisted.

"Why she wave her hand to you? I think you know this one."

"I don't know what the hell you're talking about. If somebody waved, she might be in one of my classes, or maybe she thought I was someone else. Get off my back."

Paul was floundering, but he was damned if he would tell Omar about Andrea. She was a separate part of his life, one little episode that had nothing to do with them, and he intended to keep it that way. He smiled ironically to himself. *You liar,* he thought to himself. *You know damn well that girl hasn't been out of your mind more than ten minutes since you picked her up from that culvert!* Lying helpless in his arms, she had felt so small, almost as childlike as Yasmina. But there the resemblance ended, for Andrea had changed upon regaining consciousness. She was strong, self-assured, feminine, but with none of the old-world docility of Yasmina. Still, he liked it; he liked her.

He liked her too much. He hoped he would never see her again. All this time he had lived here, alone, avoiding friendships, waiting—waiting for the day when King Hassan would come. He would make the hit, and if it was successful, he would stay in Middletowne until all suspicion was past. Then, in September, when the lease on Omar's house ended, he would leave. He would have enough money to go anywhere, do anything he wanted.

Angrily, he stalked ahead, his long strides leaving Omar behind. Wolf had no trouble keeping up with him and ran ahead, so that he was waiting back at the house when the two men reached the cemetery.

The dog barked imperiously at the door, and Mr. Gay, waiting just behind the door, edged it open. He remained hidden from sight until Paul and Omar entered.

"Did you see the president?" he inquired excitedly.

"As close as I am to you," said Paul. "I hope Omar got some good pictures—good enough for you to work with, anyway. I'm going to develop them now and make a contact sheet. You should have forced yourself to come along. Looking at the area secondhand, you might say, is not the same as actually being there." Paul walked away without saying anything more.

"Well, I just... You see, I..." stammered the old man, ill at ease.

"You fool! That's what you are, fool! That kind life you lead, always scare like this? All the time hid? Did you ever kill anybody?" Omar leered with disgust at Mr. Gay and spat on the floor close to his shoes. He took out a long knife and began to clean his fingernails, wiping the dirt on the chair that he was sitting in. Luckily, Paul had gone into the little half bath he had rigged up as a temporary darkroom.

"I am the one to be a fear. I got plenty reason the police look for me. Nobody look for you, old man, so why you be scare? You big fool, that's all."

The old man seemed to swell with unaccustomed anger and struggled to defend himself against Omar's attack. His eyes narrowed as he leaned across and grasped Omar's knee to get his undivided attention. His gnarled fingers dug into Omar's flesh with surprising strength.

Omar's knife paused in midair. He noticed that the old man was flushed and trembling.

"I have killed no one, but my guns, my work, have killed at least sixteen people. I never pulled the trigger myself, but my guns, they have killed people you would know in a minute if I dared to say their names out loud. Famous people."

"Kennedy? Martin King?" asked Omar breathlessly. He leaned forward, thrilled. The knife dropped heedlessly from his fingers. He looked at Mr. Gay for the first time with open admiration, seeing him as a hero, a man of strength beneath his cowardly exterior.

For a moment Mr. Gay basked in the wonder of Omar's eyes. Then he shuddered, sat down suddenly and covered his face, remembering. "No names, please, no names! It is enough that at night I see their faces when I try to sleep. I lie there and they hover near my bed. It's horrible. They have no eyes."

Mr. Gay shrank; a haunted look appeared in his eyes. As if remembering something, he then reached out and ran his hand lightly under the table. Omar watched the movement with interest and laughed.

"This house is clean. If there were bugs anywhere here, Paul would know. No one hear you confess this story about sixteen dead people. Don't worry yourself!" A sly grin crossed Omar's face. "Only me, my friend," he whispered. "Now I know."

He picked up the knife again and resumed cleaning his nails.

Pale, Mr. Gay rose and tottered into the kitchen, where he attempted to fix himself a cup of hot tea. He needed something stronger but was afraid to have it because of his stomach. What had he been thinking of? He had never revealed the extent of his involvement to anyone before—and now, to that Omar! He stood like a beaten man, his thoughts racing wildly.

It had begun so many years ago. The first job was agony, a time of doubt and trepidation, undertaken for a friend as a one-time thing. But then another came along, and he was offered so much money that he made that gun, too. With that fee he bought stamps, special stamps, and was broke again. Then it began, the job and the money, and then another. He would design and construct the gun, test it, receive his fee and spend it, as he added to his growing collection of rare stamps from all over the world. Because of the danger involved, he had turned himself into a nonperson—no friends, no relatives, only temporary business acquaintances as anxious not to be seen with him as he was with them.

He set up a new identity. In his private life he ran an unsuccessful import business in lower New York. He sold ugly china bric-a-brac, moldy firecrackers, and pottery ashtrays, mainly to buyers for fairs and carnivals. He could hardly stand the shoddiness of the junk himself, but it did make a good cover for his many unexplained, sudden business trips. In that atmosphere of worthless trivia, who would ever suspect that nearly a quarter million dollars in rare stamps lay hidden among the pages of old books in his living quarters upstairs? Certainly not the teen-age punks who regularly ripped off the plaster animals that gathered dust in his show window.

Standing in this tidy kitchen, Mr. Gay was struck by the vast difference in his surroundings. Outside the kitchen window, he could see Paul's dog romping in the backyard. Nearby, a crab-apple tree dropped its pink blossoms gently in the wind, and the laughter of a young girl floated on the air from another yard across the way. He watched the old lady who lived in the house behind Paul's shoo a cat out from under her azalea bush and chase it with a broom. Wolf joined her, barking furiously. Mr. Gay could not stifle a sigh of self-pity as he thought of his dirty rooms over the import store.

"What's the matter? Ulcer bothering you?" said Paul, coming into the room to hang some film over the sink to dry. It hung there, slightly curled, like gray flypaper, from the metal curtain rod.

Mr. Gay observed the many distinct images shadowed on the negatives. "No," he said. "It's not my stomach this time. It's just a silly feeling, like homesickness, for a place I never had. See, I told you it was silly. I was looking in the yard, so nice and green, and a woman laughed. How can I explain?"

Paul nodded his head in agreement. He knew the feeling. He had had it himself ever since he came to Middletowne. Call it a desire for roots, or whatever. It made him feel twice as much alone.

For a moment the two men stood together silently, lost in their own thoughts, while from the living room came a long solitary wail, encompassing all the joy and pain of an ancient people. There was a pause, then one more agonized, drawn-out note. Omar had found his Oum Khartoum records.

"The film will be dry shortly," said Paul. "I'll make the contact print for you to study. Most of the visits are similar to the one today, and the house the king will occupy will be either this big brick one or a smaller house on the same street. I think we can count on the brick one. You'll see it has no windows on either side."

"Very commendable, but it's hardly a fortress," said Mr. Gay with a smile.

"It's well covered front and back. Open, yet somewhat contained by its grounds," continued Paul, with a feeling of annoyance.

"How long will it be until you can make the print? I'd like to be back in Washington tonight."

"I have to wait until the film dries. In the meantime, how about some lunch? Can you eat steak?" asked Paul, looking in the refrigerator.

"If you broil it," replied Mr. Gay with some enthusiasm.

"Good. It'll be ready shortly. Meanwhile, why don't you go in there and see if you can manage to sit on that damn record?"

After they had eaten, Paul processed the pictures. Mr. Gay then spent two hours poring over them with a large magnifier, asking questions about distances between points and making cryptic little notes on a yellow pad. When he had ingested all the information to his satisfaction, Paul burned the prints and negatives in the fireplace and ran the ashes through the disposal in the kitchen sink.

"Well, what you think? This going to be piece of pie, no?" asked Omar.

"No," said Mr. Gay. "I saw at least two police units in the background, not counting the Middletowne Security and the Virginia State Patrol unit. They were some distance away, perhaps a hundred yards from the edges of the crowd, ready to 'come in.' This means that if the hit is not clean, it will be harder to get out free during the confusion. You could get caught inside that circle."

Mr. Gay had just put his finger on the point that had been giving Paul a lot of sleepless nights. Much would depend on the element of surprise and the efficiency of the weapon.

"What about the gun? Have you figured that out yet?" he asked.

"There's no way you can use a regular weapon. It's going to have to look like something very ordinary, no case, no long-range type that needs assembling. There is no way to carry one like that into a crowd without raising suspicion. The top Feds can spot a bulge in a jacket at forty yards. Even an umbrella is subject to scrutiny."

The old man shook his head at the two waiting men, and Omar suddenly became very agitated. He sprang from his seat and shook his fist under Mr. Gay's nose.

"You are making the impossible! Nothing must stop us. Have you both not taken the money from my people to do this thing?" he stormed furiously. He didn't want even a moment of pessimism to mar the plan. He had helped to initiate it, had rented the house months ago with the idea of bringing someone here to be in place when the king came, had convinced Paul that killing the king would not only avenge the death of Yasmina but would give him enough to start fresh anywhere he wanted to go. Now this old fool was trying to tell him it was impossible.

"I didn't say impossible, just more difficult. It will take some thought."

Paul rose to his feet and looked down on the phony wig on Mr. Gay's head. To think his own life rested on the decision of this weird old bird. Good God, why had he ever agreed to come here with Omar in the first place?

"You'd better think clearly. When the time comes, it'll be me down there, my life on the line, and I want to walk away alive," Paul said seriously.

Omar turned on the record player again and the wailing began even louder than before. Slowly, he seemed to go into a trance. He began a weaving, stomping dance, his boots clumping heavily on the rug as he snapped his fingers in time to a distant drum. His eyes were closed, and he had detached himself from the situation. He did this when things weren't going his way. The other men watched his gyrations without expression.

Finally Paul spoke out angrily. "Why in hell don't you play a different record? It's driving me crazy."

"This one different record. I got four records," he explained, singing along. "Num mi num nummmm. Is not my fault they sound the same to American ears. This woman… ah, she is best singer in whole world." Omar crooned on, circling the room and stopping to beat the tabletop like a drum.

Unable to take the performance any longer, Paul opened the front door and went out, slamming the door behind him. He called to Wolf, who jumped over the fence to join him, ready for anything his master wanted to do. Paul patted his head.

"Come on, boy. You're the only one around here that has any sense at all."

They crossed to the cemetery, a quiet place in the late afternoon, and walked silently among the wreaths, some real, some artificial. On many lonely evenings, Paul had sat by the window and watched the rabbits invade the cemetery at dusk to feed on the flowers.

Paul stayed where he was until he could no longer hear the music from the house. After a few minutes of silence, Omar came out on the porch and looked around. He was wearing his hat again. His hair spilled out below the navy wool. His face looked sad and very foreign. His arrogance had dropped away now that he thought no one was observing him. He looked rather pathetic, even vulnerable. It was at such times that Paul recognized him as Yasmina's brother.

Paul crossed the street as Omar came toward him.

"We are going," he said. "Do not be mad, my friend! Mr. Gay is thinking good all the time you are gone."

Mr. Gay came out of the house and, with a polite but hurried good-bye, climbed into the Ford and sat as low in the seat as possible. Omar waved, said he would be in touch again soon and got into the driver's seat. As they drove off, Paul noticed that the car had Alabama license plates. Another stolen car! My God, thought Paul, how could he take such chances! He knew, though, in Omar's mind stealing was not really a crime, not if you took the item back after using it. Omar always took everything back— cars, trucks, television sets, clothing. His stealing was just a matter of selective "borrowing."

Paul went into the house and looked around in disgust. A cigar smoldered on the coffee table. There were ashes on the rug, bits of mud, and a sloe-eyed lady of middle age stared up at him from a record cover lying on the floor. It was obvious that Omar had visited, but of Mr. Gay there was not a sign.

Paul picked up the record cover and started to put the record inside. Then he hesitated and placed it back on the record player. He turned the volume down low and stood listening for a long time, trying to understand the music. It reminded him painfully of the Shaifi family and how they used to huddle together listening to this singer on the portable radio he had given them. No one in the house was allowed to speak during her concerts, and Paul discovered to his surprise that that adoration was not confined to families like the Shaifis. In the cities, businesses closed early so that employees could go home and listen to their idol's voice.

Thinking of these things made Yasmina seem close again, and yet, in the cold reality of his surroundings, Paul knew she was gone forever. He wondered fleetingly whether she had been wearing his ring when she died, a gold band from Damascus, carved with flowers.

He took the record off and put it away with finality. He felt desperately alone. He went to the phone book and flipped through to the Ws. There was a G. Patchen Wayne listed on St. George Street. He dialed the number and let it ring ten times. There was no answer. He hung up, dialed again, and it rang again with a hollow sound.

He switched on the television and settled into the chair across from it. So lost in thought was he that the picture flopped over and over on the screen, unnoticed, until the dog barked softly outside the door, reminding Paul it was his supper time.

CHAPTER FIVE

"I'd like the contacts on the president of Yugoslavia's visit. Are they where you can find them, Mr. Fischer?"

"But Mr. Wise has already made his final selection for the next issue," the elderly man replied with authority.

"Oh, I'm not going to change a thing. I want to check out a little detail on one of the pictures to make sure my cutlines are correct."

"Very well. Here you are." Hesitantly, he handed them over. "Be sure to return them to the file when you are through, Miss Wayne."

Andrea took the pictures back to her desk and began to go over them carefully. Mr. Fischer watched, as if she had stolen them. She might have taken the pictures, but when they reached Mr. Fischer's desk, they became his property, no longer of any importance to the photographer, except for severe criticism when they weren't up to par.

Mr. Fischer was about seventy, efficient, smart. He knew every aspect of printing and developing that had ever existed. He was never wrong. And what's more, everyone in the office was forced to call him Mr. Fischer, not only out of deference to his age, but because they couldn't figure out how to shorten his first name, which was Mordecai. You couldn't call a man who still wore a pince-nez "Mordy." Even Jack Wise, who called everybody nitwit, addle-brain, dummy, never applied those epithets to Mr. Fischer.

He glanced up as Andrea returned to his desk. One frame was circled.

"Can you run me a glossy on this shot of the crowd scene sometime today?"

"But Mr. Wise has made his selection," the old man reiterated emphatically.

"It's for me, not for the paper."

"Well, I suppose I could work it in. It will be sixteen cents. Paper and chemicals cost money, you know. After all, we are not running a developing service here."

Andrea fished around in the bottom of her bag, where she threw any extra change, and extracted a quarter. She laid it carefully on his desk. Mr. Fischer picked it up and took it to the petty-cash box, which was in the desk of Bernadette, the secretary. Carefully, he counted out four pennies and a nickel and handed it to Andrea. She dropped it in the bottom of her bag.

"Thanks. I'll pick the picture up later."

Behind his typewriter, Gage laughed and winked at her. Bernadette was looking in her desk drawer as if the quarter might climb back out and roll away. She never quite understood what was going on in the office, anyway. Working there was like being an earthling stranded among Martians. They were all so strange, so unpredictable.

Bernadette closed the drawer and turned to the typewriter. It was something she understood and truly loved, those neat rows of keys that never changed, never demanded decisions or original thought. She typed eighty words a minute, clean, precise, other people's ideas, other people's words. She turned her blue eyes to the copy on her left and began. Only her hands and eyes moved.

Jack Wise looked through the glass of his disordered cubicle, a soundproof haven from which he presided over the press room like a benign gorilla in a glass cage. He glanced at Bernadette. What a beautiful, dumb little broad. Good typist, though. Why, he thought, was a cute chick like that still living at home with her mother?

He caught sight of Andrea leaving the office, her leather bag hanging from her shoulder. She was off to interview a new group of musicians starting a gig at the Ramada Inn. Now, there was a woman he could go for in a minute if it were not for his wife of thirty years. Andrea made him feel strangely young. Whenever they sat close in his office discussing a story, his palms began to sweat and stirring deep inside came feelings from his youth. He watched Andrea leave, then picked up pages of copy from his desk and began wielding his blue pencil, reducing some of Gage's best prose to nothingness.

Outside in the parking lot, Andrea got into one of the Datsun station wagons that were shared by the office staff. They were the cheapest transportation Jack Wise could get, but Mr. Fischer, who also designed signs, had lettered "What's Happening Here, Middletowne, Virginia" on the front doors. The single word "PRESS" across the back, in gold paint, gave the cars a note of distinction.

Her destination was the other side of town, but she found herself passing the ruins of the asylum. Then noticing the gates of the old Pine Grove Cemetery, she slowed down to look at the houses on the other side of the street. The one painted green had a small front porch and, on the left side, a wide window completely covered by drapes. There was no sign of life. Of course, he might be at the college, or maybe he had a part-time job somewhere. She really didn't know why she had come, anyway. She shrugged and made a sharp U-turn, narrowly missing the green Rover cruising behind her. It sounded a warning siren, and she pulled over. This was going to be one of those days.

Colby Dance walked over to the Datsun and grinned at her wickedly.

"I got you that time, Andy, dead to rights!"

"Look, I'm on my way to a really hot story, Colby. You don't want to halt the wheels of progress, do you?" she smiled sweetly.

"If it was a real hot one, I think we'd know about it down at the station. How about going out with me Saturday night? It could make a difference." He tapped the book in his hand and looked at her. She gritted her teeth silently and held out her hand for the citation.

"How about Saturday?" he insisted.

"I'm working. The concert at the Palace."

"Man, you're always workin'. I'm beginnin' to think you don't like me, Andy. By the way, when is old Patch coming back? You and me ought to get together before he comes back. You tell me a time, anytime. I'll get off to suit you."

"Bug off, just bug off, Colby!" Angrily, she put the car in gear and pushed his hand off the door. The Datsun took off down the street, and he jumped backward.

"I ought to ticket you for that. You could of killed me!" he yelled loudly.

The policeman stood in the middle of the street, staring angrily after the disappearing car. What the hell was wrong with that girl? He wondered who was warming her feet while old Patch was gone. And why did Patch Wayne go off and leave a piece like her, anyway? He must be plumb crazy. He shook his head in amazement.

Andrea drove across town within the speed limit of twenty-five miles per hour, which was rigidly enforced in Middletowne. She looked frequently in the rearview mirror, half expecting Colby to follow her, but the Rover was nowhere in sight. She sighed with relief.

It was not only Colby, it was the questions about Patch that had upset her. How could she explain to other people, when she couldn't understand the situation herself. Most of her friends had avoided mentioning Patch after a while. But not Colby. He was the absolute opportunist. He showed up at the apartment two days after he had heard Patch was gone, bearing a fifth of Jack Daniel's in one hand and a clean uniform in a plastic bag in the other. While Andrea watched in amazement, he stashed the bottle in the kitchen and hung up his suit in the closet. He then tried to take her in his arms, but she shoved him away and told him to get out. They struggled, and Jade flew into action, sinking her teeth deep into his leg. He kicked the dog off into a corner, but she rushed back and bit him again. Andrea opened the door and told him to leave or she'd call the police. Reluctantly, he took his whiskey and uniform and had started down the steps when he suddenly remembered something. He came back up.

"Goddamn it! I *am* the police! Come on, Andy. Let me in."

Andrea laughed now at the memory of the whole experience, but it didn't seem funny at the time. In fact, she had had another lock put on the apartment door.

She approached the Ramada and saw that its marquee already announced the new act, "The Happy Hippoes, Shows at 9 and 11." She parked and entered the tastefully furnished lobby, while Mr. Witherow, the manager, offered her coffee or a drink, which she declined. He led her back to the performers' suite.

Seated inside the room were three of the largest young men she had ever seen. They had long hair, beards, rosy cheeks, and small shiny eyes, a family resemblance heightened by the fact that they all dressed alike. They wore plaid shirts and gray denim Levi's with matching jackets. Andy wondered where they had found gray denim. One was practicing on a flute, while the other two pored over a menu. A lunch order lay between them on the table, but they put it aside and turned their attention to her. Andy took out the yellow pad on which she had outlined a few questions, and when she looked up, they were giving her expectant smiles.

"How did you decide on the name for your act, the Happy Hippoes?" she asked very seriously.

"We read it in a children's book," they answered.

The one with the flute added, "We always try to be cheerful to promote the happy image." He gave a little trill on his flute, which sounded like "Here Comes Peter Cottontail," followed by "Over the Rainbow." The others smiled broadly in appreciation.

They answered all her questions. Yes, two were brothers. Tom was really a cousin, but they had grown up together on the same farm in Idaho. And on and on. Andrea wrote diligently. After a while people all began to sound the same even though they looked different. She knew that in a couple of weeks she'd be back here again asking the same questions, but to another group. As she had passed through the lobby, she noticed a sign saying that the Three Jumping Beans from Old Mexico were next to appear. *Better brush up on my high-school Spanish,* she thought. She sighed and turned back to the Happy Hippoes.

"Have you had a chance to see anything of the town yet?" she asked brightly.

"No, we haven't had the chance—" began number one Hippo.

"—to see the restoration yet," added number two.

"But we plan to take the carriage ride tomorrow," finished the last Hippo.

She smiled at the three huge men. Over two hundred pounds each, maybe even as much as three. They were fat, fat, fat.

My God, I must warn the horses, thought Andrea as her pen flew across the pad.

CHAPTER SIX

Every day the weather became more pleasant. The crab-apple tree in Paul's yard was red with leaves, when he suddenly realized that there were only about three weeks left of college. He wondered what he would find to do when school was over. At least it filled his days. The cold months had not been too bad. He had made a couple of casual acquaintances among the students and had joined the Chess Club, which met once a week in the Campus Center. He saw all the movies in town, and then there was Wolf. But the restriction of no friends, no attachments, insisted on by the group in Washington, and agreed to out of a desire to preserve his anonymity, made life almost unbearable at times. He hoped that his mission would be over soon.

On this day in late April, he decided to go down town to Le Fromage and get some blueberry croissants for his breakfast. If one got there early enough, the pastry was still piping hot from the oven. He would then grab the bag, and he and Wolf would jog home to get there while the croissants were still warm.

Calling Wolf to come with him, Paul began to jog down the street. Birds were singing, and masses of azaleas and tulips spread a riot of color in the neat green yards he passed by. Wolf was delirious with the warm air and fast pace. His black ears stood alert, his tongue lolled from his mouth, his lips curved up in a smile as he ran along not stopping for a single sniff anywhere. They paced faster and faster, and when they got to the corner of St. George, they were both panting.

Wolf looked for the puddles of water left by the merchants who washed down their sidewalks each morning. He found one, and Paul stopped to let him drink. As he stood there, he saw someone standing in the alleyway between the two buildings. He felt a tingle of recognition. She stood as if waiting for someone, facing the open lot at the end of the alley. He pulled Wolf away from the water and started walking toward her.

Andrea heard footsteps and turned to see who was coming. A smile started to form, but before she could say hello, a small, tan bundle of fur shot past her and confronted the surprised man and dog. It snarled with a ferocity beyond its size.

"No! No, Jade!" screamed Andrea, but too late. Jade was past hearing anything.

The irate Peke, bent on defending her territory, rushed the German shepherd with wild abandon, barking, circling, nipping fiercely at his heels and throwing bushels of grass behind her as she emulated a mad bull, pawing with her back feet. Wolf looked at her in amazement, lowering his huge head the better to see this canine dervish whirling about his feet. He looked at her with curiosity mingled with pain, shifting his feet as her sharp teeth snapped at him again and again.

Paul stepped in front of Wolf, causing the Peke to rush around and attack from the rear. Wolf tried to jump away from the nipping jaws, but made no attempt to attack the smaller dog. Finally Andrea was able to grab Jade, snap the leash to her collar and forcibly drag her aside. Horrified, she attempted to mumble an apology.

Exhausted, Jade lay down on her side in the grass, her big brown eyes rolled to one side, watching Wolf. Now winded, she expected him to come in for the kill. She waited, all fury spent, resigned to her fate. Wolf walked to her side, while Paul held his collar tightly, not knowing what would happen next. Almost indifferently, Wolf stopped to lick the blood from his ankles. Then, his long, rough tongue reached out and licked the heaving side of the other dog. Jade seemed to hold her breath, then rolled over on her back. Wolf sniffed her all over, then turned to look up at Paul with a foolish smile on his lips. He had been smitten. He was in love.

Jade flipped over on her stomach and lay complacently in the grass, somehow realizing she was no longer in danger— not quite understanding why, but accepting it. Carefully, Wolf moved in and lay down near her, Andrea and Paul turned to each other, laughing with relief.

"She comes here every day, and I guess she thinks this lot belongs to her. Is your dog all right? I'm so sorry this happened."

"You can't hurt that big old goof." Paul smiled. "Look at him now. He's forgotten all about the attack. They seem to have reached a truce."

Paul and Andrea stood awkwardly, not knowing exactly what to say to each other, and then Paul explained why he had come down to St. George Street. "I like those hot croissants over there at Le Fromage, and Saturday is blueberry day, which is my favorite."

"Oh, the almond is delicious, too!" said Andrea. "Come on, let's hurry over there before the college kids buy them out."

They dragged the dogs along and hooked their leashes to the cement planters full of flowers outside the shop. Together they went inside.

"We'll take six blueberry," ordered Andrea, thinking four for him, two for herself. She knew how much a big man could eat, and Paul was bigger than Patch.

The lady behind the counter was flustered—two of her best customers together! She liked them both and was pleased at the sight. Her husband, the baker, came out of the kitchen as Paul and Andrea crossed the street to her apartment.

"Look!" she exclaimed. "Andy and the blond man. Look! Going up to her apartment together!"

"So?" replied her husband. "Good for them. They aren't children, Hildy, so mind your business."

The baker gave his wife a pinch on her large derriere. She pushed him away, giggling. When he returned to the kitchen, she went to the door for a better look.

Andrea unlocked the door, and they all trooped inside. Suddenly the room seemed more filled with life than she could remember for a long time. Paul sat on the sofa, with Wolf on the floor at his feet. Jade made straight for the kitchen and her water bowl. The fight had tired her and made her thirsty.

Andrea put on some coffee, and they sat by the window, talking about the town and making general conversation. Both carefully avoided anything personal. Each studied the other with intensity, and looked away whenever their eyes chanced to meet. When their fingers touched as they both reached for the sugar at the same time, they each pulled back nervously. Something terrible and wonderful was happening. There was a feeling of fear, yet excitement. When their cups were empty, they sat together in silence, prolonging the time together as long as possible.

Finally Paul stood up to leave. "Thanks for the coffee. I like yours much better than mine."

"It's just instant."

"Well, it's very good."

"I'm glad you liked it."

He stood in the doorway, reluctant to go. He was thinking of the night he had brought her home and how much he had wanted to come here again. "Do you live here alone?" he asked hopefully.

"Yes." She offered no further explanation.

"I live alone, too," he said. "Well, thanks again. Good-bye."

She closed the door and listened to his footsteps going down the stairs. She then gathered the cups and saucers and took them into the kitchen and let the warm water run over them for a long time. She was lost in thought.

He's so different. But he is young, handsome, and alone. Why? She was so drawn to him, right from the beginning, that her feelings frightened her. *I don't want to get involved again,* she thought. *Why am I standing here memorizing his face. Oh, Lord!*

She crossed over to the bookcase and took out a large photograph album. She turned to the back page, which held the latest picture. Mr. Fischer had done a good job on the blow-up of the crowd scene at Marlborough House. In that picture, near the fence, stood Paul Hunter, his blond head above the crowd. The tip of his dog's nose appeared about at his knee, while to his left was the dark character with the Nikon. Andrea took out a magnifier and studied the face of the second man, trying to remember where she had seen him before. She slowly flipped back through the album pages, and there it was. It had been taken last summer. The secretary of state was coming out of the courthouse, and there was the same man, sitting on an old Harley Davidson motorcycle. He watched the secretary intently. She remembered it had been a long shot; she had had the big lens on. He probably didn't even know she was taking his picture. She closed the book as a knock sounded on her door.

It was Matt, one of the boys down the hall, with her mail. He had placed the blue envelope from El Rancho Motel right on the top of the pile of letters.

"Looks like a message from the happy wanderer. Can I read your *Book Digest* when you get through with it?"

"Sure. Why don't you take it along now and bring it back later? I'll be out on assignment all day, anyway. Weekends are story time."

"Yeah, lots of *turistas* in the street today. Thanks for the mag!"

He vanished down the hall, and she turned to the mail with resignation and tore open the letter from Patch. It started with the usual complaints.

> **Dearest darling,**
>
> **I am staying here a few days. The axle broke on that damn van. Next time don't buy such a piece of junk. I was in the desert and hit a rock, pow, that baby was gone. A good old boy is letting me work at his service station until I get it fixed. If you could send me a couple hundred, I could get out of this place. Or bring it in person, honey. I sure miss you. At the above until next week. Please come.**
>
> **Love,**
> **PATCH**

She folded the letter and put it back in the envelope. What a situation. He walks away, then it's darling, honey, love Patch. Just keep on loving Patch. She no longer knew what she felt about him. His letters reminded her of a kid away at school. She took out her checkbook and wrote a check for one hundred dollars to G. Patchen Wayne, put it in an envelope and addressed it to El Rancho Motel. She looked at the small, irregular handwriting on the blue envelope. Love doesn't just die; it eats away a little at a time, leaving a big, empty hole where something wonderful once existed. And one day there would simply be nothing. She could look at his pictures and the pain would be gone.

The telephone interrupted her thoughts.

"Hello?"

"Hi, it's Paul. Paul Hunter. Ah... there's a movie you might enjoy, playing at the Middletowne—*Harry and Tonto*. I believe Art Carney won—"

"—the Academy Award, yes," she prompted, waiting.

"Would you like to see it? Either show, the seven or the nine? Can I pick you up?"

She hesitated only a minute. "I have to go to a dedication ceremony at Seaport this afternoon. Can I meet you at the theater just before the nine o'clock show?"

"Great! I'll see you then. Good-bye."

"Good-bye."

Her hands were tingling when she put down the receiver. She laughed at herself. She had turned down Gage, Matt, and George, practically used karate on Colby Dance, and now she was going to date a perfect stranger—well, almost a stranger. She knew almost nothing about him, but maybe tonight, she could find out more—why he lived all alone, why he had settled in Middletowne, and was there a girl in his life?

She got out the album and sat looking at his picture.

CHAPTER SEVEN

Downtown, the lamplights gleamed palely along the almost deserted streets, and few cars passed. Omar looked up and down the streets, his agitation increasing with each passing moment. He walked back to the house across from the cemetery, pausing, to look back toward town, but no one appeared to be coming that way.

"Where he is?" demanded Omar to himself. First he had called and found Paul not at home this morning. The telephone rang off and on for an hour or more. Now he and Mr. Gay were here and still no Paul! Where could he be all day and night?

Under the streetlight, he consulted his watch. Twelve midnight. It was a good thing he had a key to the house or Mr. Gay would have insisted on returning to Washington. As it was, the old man was sitting inside in his straight chair, trying his best to stay awake, which at his age was nearly impossible.

Omar strode angrily into the house and started flinging off his clothes, until he stood there naked except for a pair of briefs and his wool cap.

"I going to bed. I take Paul's room, you take the other. We must stay to tomorrow. Where he is I don't know, but I find out. Don't you worry."

"But I brought nothing to sleep in," protested the older man.

"Don't matter, no women here. You sleep, and tomorrow we talk."

Omar stomped through the hall and slammed the door behind him. Mr. Gay got up and cautiously peeked into the extra bedroom and decided it might be safe for one night. Fully clothed, he lay down on the bed, his feet sticking out over the edge. He heard an owl hoot far away, then the dog in the backyard rattled his chain; then all was quiet. Mr. Gay slept.

As the church tower pealed one o'clock, Paul came whistling down the street, but he stopped when he saw the old blue Plymouth parked next to his Volkswagen. He knew it could belong to only one person, so he let himself quietly into the house. He stumbled over a bundle of clothing, denim pants, a dark sweater, strewn carelessly on the floor. The smell of stale cigar smoke hung in the air. The exhilaration of the evening with Andrea left him quickly as he sank down on the couch in the dark, plunged back into the reality of his situation. Despondency settled over him like a dark cloud.

He heard Omar snoring from his own room. Unable to stand the sight of the hairy body in the other twin bed, Paul pulled some covers from the closet and bedded down on the couch. He tossed, half sleeping, half awake, the rest of the night.

That was where the rumpled Mr. Gay found him in the morning when he tiptoed out of the bedroom in search of the bathroom. He stared at Paul. What a strong, but innocent face Paul had, he thought. He never knew what kind of person he would meet in a business like his, but of all he had known, Paul was different, a breed apart from the usual killer.

When Omar Shaifi had first contacted him to design the gun and work with the group to plan the assassination, he asked what man would do the actual hit. Paul Hunter was described as having had at least three prior jobs as an assassin within the last two years. But there was a difference. To the outside world, he was attached to the air force. His real job was in security throughout the Mediterranean area. He sought out informers, drug suppliers, smugglers who were suspected of endangering the United States through subversive dealing. His job was to track them down and get rid of them, anyway he could, but permanently. His last job had been in Turkey, tracking the middlemen who got the drugs out to the ports in France. The key man was found one morning floating in the Seine, his neck and back broken. Shortly afterward, Paul was given a formal discharge and returned to the States. He thought it was all over, but then someone in Uddapha remembered him—a tall, blond person in a country of dark people, who disappeared suddenly after two men were shot to death.

The two descriptions of Paul didn't match. The informers in Washington who checked him out said he was a dedicated assassin, primed for the job since childhood, when he spent his days in his father's munitions factory. He had been chosen for the top security position when he was only nineteen, trained for it, psychologically programmed for it. He did it willingly, without fear, without guilt.

Then there was the Paul Hunter of Yasmina's letters, gentle, kind. He had been known to carry a sheep in his arms for miles so that he and Yasmina could nurse it to health in the warmth of their kitchen shed. He had sat on the Shaifis' dirt floor and played his harmonica while Father Shaifi danced. He had made Mother Shaifi laugh.

Mr. Gay gently pushed Paul's shoulder. Paul awoke instantly and reached automatically for his left armpit, then smiled at himself. He no longer wore a gun to bed.

"You must be used to a shoulder holster," guessed Mr. Gay, amused.

"I forget sometimes, but I carry nothing now. It's an old habit."

"May I make myself some tea, and coffee for you?" he asked.

"Eggs in the fridge, bacon, bread in the box," offered Paul, shaking his head groggily. The couch was not too comfortable; his legs hung over the end.

"Never eat much myself, but I'll fix you something."

"You ever been married, Mr. Gay?" asked Paul, curious.

"No, I've always been alone. No wife, no children."

"You never find woman crazy like you!" Omar said, laughing as he emerged from Paul's room to go to the bathroom.

There were sounds of water running. The toilet flushed. Then they could hear Omar brushing his teeth. *I hope he's not using my toothbrush,* mused Paul. He lay sleepily back on the couch.

When Omar's naked brown body passed down the hall and disappeared into the bedroom, Paul got up and looked inside the bathroom. A soggy towel was on the floor, soap foamed inside the sink, and *his* wet toothbrush lay beside an oozing tube of toothpaste. Angrily, Paul thrust his brush under a stream of scalding water until the overhead mirror steamed up. Then he grabbed the towel and mopped the paste and soap from the sink. He flung the towel into the hamper.

As he shaved, his thoughts drifted from Omar, the terrible slob, to Andrea, the beautiful. He had used the movie as an excuse to be with her again as soon as possible. Everything inside of him told him it was wrong—wrong for him, dangerous for her—but he did it anyway, thinking he could terminate the relationship at any time. They had met at the theater, and the movie turned out to be better than he expected. They had spent most of the time looking surreptitiously at each other in the dark like two kids on a first date.

After the show, she suggested that they go over to the Ramada for a drink. He didn't have his car, so they went to the parking lot behind the *WHH* building and borrowed one of the Datsuns. At the Ramada, everybody seemed to know Andrea. The manager insisted on buying them a second drink, and people kept coming over and sitting down at the table. Paul had been conscious of their curious glances, but Andrea had simply introduced him as a friend, even once as a very old friend, strangely omitting his name. "Hi, Dottie, this is an old friend of mine," she had said. Then nothing, almost as if she were anxious not to have them know who he was. In a crowd like that, it was passed over. People thought they must have heard a name, then forgotten it, but she actually never gave it. As the night wore on, Paul felt desperate, hemmed in, looked at, all the things he had tried to avoid since coming to Middletowne. The feeling grew, and he suggested they leave the busy lounge, explaining that he had an early appointment. She seemed to sense something was wrong but said nothing, and they drove back to Andrea's apartment in silence. She had offered to drop him at his house, but he refused, saying that he would like the walk. He was glad it had worked out that way when he saw the battered car in front of the house and realized it must belong to Omar.

The three men ate breakfast in the kitchen together. At first Omar just sat there, giving Paul a very suspicious look, which Paul ignored until he could stand it no longer.

"Where you gon' last night?" said Omar, breaking a piece of toast in two.

"I went out to the movie."

"The movie show, it don't last so long. Where you gon' after that?" he continued.

"Stopped for a drink. What is this—an inquisition?"

Omar wrestled with the unfamiliar word, gave it up and pushed on.

"You agreed to stay... cool? No women. I think you find woman."

"Why don't you lay off this stuff?" asked Paul, pushing away from the table. He felt his anger rising.

"So soon you forget my little sister, hardly cold in the grave?" Omar said acidly.

"Why do you think I was out with a woman? It could have been a guy, or I could have been alone. It's none of your damned business as long as it doesn't interfere with my reason for being here. Don't worry! I never forget that. Never!" Paul exploded. Incensed, he turned on Omar sarcastically. "Look who's talking about women. You raise hell if you think I'm just seeing somebody, yet you go out and sleep with anything female that happens along! What's the damn difference, Omar?"

"Plenty different for me. I love lots women. You like one woman. You that kind."

"Well, leave the subject alone. This has nothing to do with the job."

"You leave the woman alone, my friend. Now! Afterward, you get all women you want. For now, you are the... like the priest." A scowl etched deep lines on Omar's face, making him appear much older than he was. He bit viciously into a slice of toast as he fixed Paul with a penetrating stare.

Paul met his eyes and waited, unwavering. A calm had descended upon him.

"Well, who she is, this one of you not to speak?" The words were serious but so chopped they were almost unintelligible.

Paul turned and walked out of the room.

Mr. Gay, tense now himself, got up and began to stack dishes in the sink. Cups clattered, plates teetered. Not even the warm water he ran over the dishes could take off the chill that shook his shoulders. With men like these, he always felt uneasy, fearful. As a sharp pain twinged in his abdomen, he tried to relax.

"Don't bother Paul about this little... nothing. It's not important. We are all in this too far for Paul to take chances. He's no fool, Omar! So what if he goes out one night for a little fun, a little female companionship? Even I, old as I am, sometimes still feel the need. I go down to the girls on the street, and ten dollars later I am feeling much younger." He laughed coarsely.

"Whores!" Omar spit the word out contemptuously. He had never paid a woman in his life. Women had always gone with him and done anything willingly.

"Paul does not take the whore like you, old man. Remember my sister. She was the love of him before she die. And she die a virgin. She clean to her grave. I would swear on the name of Allah! But Paul, he is not us. If a woman has come, we cannot take it—*sha iss'ma*—too easy?"

"You mean, we must not take it too lightly."

"Yes. You ask him who this woman is," Omar commanded.

"Why? After all, some things are his own business. He's not a hermit."

"It is not good he get close to any person here. As the time draws near, we are in most danger, and no woman can be the trust."

"Please! Just say no more to him. He knows what his situation is. You must trust him to watch out for himself. We came here with more important things to discuss, like the special weapon. Without that, the whole mission is nothing."

Mr. Gay had succeeded in distracting Omar for the moment by mentioning the gun. Slowly, the anger receded from Omar's face, and he replaced it with a false smile.

Omar followed the older man into the living room. Paul was reading the paper, and the radio was on.

"We have decided on the gun," said Mr. Gay softly.

"Well, you better hurry up with it. Nobody seems to know when the king is definitely coming, but I need the gun at least two weeks before I use it. It has to be checked out to see what firing range it has. I want it in my hands to feel it, test-fire it, see what it will do."

"We are making the weapon inside a camera."

"Inside a camera? What kind of range can you get with something that small?" Paul sat forward, alert, frowning.

"Not just any camera," explained Mr. Gay excitedly, "but a large one, a single lens reflex, weight about four and a half pounds."

He hurried to his overnight bag and carefully removed two identical cameras. Somehow they already had a deadly look about them. He placed one in Paul's hands. Paul whistled in appreciation.

"Is it loaded?" he asked, looking for a hidden safety somewhere.

"They're both... well, just cameras. Today they take only pictures, not lives. I will take one to my shop in New York for alteration. One you will keep, and use as is. Let people see you using it. It will then be a familiar object—an ordinary, usual part of you. There is one problem in converting, though. We need space for the silencer. It will have to project out of the camera itself. The firing mechanism will be attached directly to the shutter. A larger lens won't work because the lens area would be partially covered, and any photographer would notice that in a minute." Mr. Gay paused.

Paul thought of Andrea. She'd certainly be curious. She couldn't be easily fooled.

The three men sat looking at the lenses. Mr. Gay seemed almost apologetic as he continued. "You see, the cameras were numerous in the pictures Omar showed me. Almost every tourist had one. It is the most natural thing to carry. Besides, it has a sight of its own—a trigger."

"The idea is good," said Paul. "Did you try removing the lens? Oh, no, I see. It would be immediately obvious without the glass, even for a short time."

"The space inside is too small by itself, even with the film and holder taken out. And the film numbers would be missed if anyone got too close, so we're going to leave the film in."

Again Paul's thoughts turned to Andrea. She would notice if there were no numbers to indicate film, maybe even offer to load it for him. He shuddered slightly at the thought. Then he remembered something funny about the way she carried her own camera at times—that odd tripod with the handle on one side.

"Have you got a tripod, Omar? A thing to hold your Nikon steady?" he asked.

"I don' got one, I think. My hand already steady."

Mr. Gay grasped the concept immediately, as Paul knew he would. He smiled with a glint in his eyes and clasped his hands together as if anxious to get to work on the new development. He picked up one of the cameras and turned it over in his hands. On the bottom was a round screw hole to attach a tripod. He nodded.

"That's it," he said. "The extra space we need. And the legs of a tripod, I believe, are mostly hollow tubing. There's also an adjustor knob to turn the camera in any direction. That knob can be the barrel, with the silencer on the end. Of course, it will have to be firmly attached, not movable, to connect to the firing mechanism inside the camera itself."

As the old man talked, almost to himself, Paul could see the ultimate weapon being created right before his eyes.

"You should be in my business," said Mr. Gay to Paul. "This thing had me stumped. But now, it's clear. The answer never was in the camera itself, no matter how hard I tried to put it together."

He jerked to his feet. He was no longer interested in anything here. He wanted to be in New York, at work, with his hands creating another instrument of destruction. Paul understood.

"You can pick up a tripod anywhere between here and Washington. Even drugstores have them."

"Would it attract attention in any way? Is it used outdoors?" asked Mr. Gay.

"Yes. Anytime you need something steadier than your hands to shoot at slow speed."

"Shoot at slow speed... but not in this case, eh, Paul?" The old man chuckled.

Omar had been watching Paul intently, more than interested in this conversation about the tripod. He smiled faintly, remembering the girl on the Green. He recalled her carrying a camera much like the one in front of him. Paul had tried to pretend it wasn't she who had waved at them that day, but he had lied. She must be the one. Ah, yes, Paul could not fool Omar.

Slowly Omar went over to the telephone book and leafed through it. Of course, Paul was too careful to write anything down, not even a small dot near a name. Omar had not really expected to find a clue in this way, but there were other ways. He noticed Paul watching him and smiled.

"It is small place. In Washington we have many books for the telephone, one yellow only for the business," he mentioned, as if suddenly interested.

Mr. Gay and Paul looked at him curiously.

"If we have no more business here," said Mr. Gay, "I'd like to be on my way. Paul, I'll have something for you when we come again. I promise you'll have it in plenty of time."

"The camera was a good idea. I'll begin to carry this one around with me and familiarize myself with how it feels and how it works. Will the sight be the same?" he asked, raising it to eye level and squinting slightly.

"The same. I'll work the other trouble out."

"It only has to fire twice. If I can't get in and get it done in two shots, I can't make the hit and move out in time. Two good shots, one for the head and one for the stomach," he reflected coldly, as if discussing the stock market. The victims of his past suddenly flashed through his mind. Some had been close enough to look into his eyes at the moment of contact. They had looked surprised, as if life had played a dirty trick on them. Usually, it had taken only one shot, never more than two.

Seeing into his thoughts, Mr. Gay patted Paul on the shoulder with admiration. "You've got the guts to do the job. I'm glad I don't see the dying. But then, all of nature is in the process of eliminating itself one way or another."

"Don't rationalize, Mr. Gay. We're killers. Face it," answered Paul, without feeling.

Mr. Gay shook his head and held up his hand as if to ward off the effect of the words. There was nothing more to say. Paul spoke the truth, and he knew it.

As the two men prepared to leave, Omar took a bundle of old bills out of his pocket and put it on the table without explanation. Paul put it in a drawer. He followed them to the door and watched until the old car was out of sight.

Omar turned when he got to the corner and started toward town, away from his usual route to the highway.

"What are you doing?" asked Mr. Gay, alarmed.

"I'm going to drive around this place," said Omar flatly, slamming into low gear. The look on his face was almost catatonic as he gazed about, searching for something important.

"But why? We did all this before, don't you remember?" He looked at Omar for some better explanation, but Omar ignored him completely.

Omar's eyes darted from side to side, studying every female figure that passed. If she were here, he thought he could recognize her again. She was rather small with dark hair, not as curly as his own, but curly. Light skin like Americans.

As they combed the streets, Mr. Gay shrank farther and farther down in the seat and pulled his old felt hat low on his brow. He hated Middletowne.

Much to his relief, Omar finally gave up and turned toward the highway. For today, he would give up the hunt. *But I'll come back alone,* he thought to himself, *and I'll find that girl.*

CHAPTER EIGHT

The following Saturday morning was fair and warm, a pleasant change from the rain that had marred previous weekends. Andrea awoke early.

Matt and George had been out to eat breakfast at the restaurant down the street and had stopped to pick up their mail at the box in the hall. They picked up Andrea's, too, and knocked on her door. Matt handed her an envelope with the small, irregular writing.

"Looks like that guy again. He doesn't give up, does he? None of my business, Andy, but what are you going to do about him?" asked George, lounging against the door.

"Why don't you come on in and have some coffee? I'll read you the latest."

"Nothing doing. Forget it. It's your business," protested George vigorously.

"Oh, come in anyway. Pot's on. I know you two; you're just trying to help."

"OK, but we don't want to hear anything. Where's the ugly mutt?" asked Matt as they entered.

Jade, recognizing their voices, emerged from the kitchen and jumped immediately on their legs, pulling out tufts of denim with her long toenails. Matt picked her up in his arms and sank down on the sofa, while George went into the kitchen and began to search the shelves for cookies, potato chips, anything edible. He was always hungry. All he found was some RyKrisp and a box of stale Rice Krispies. "You sure need to go to the store, Andy," he muttered, disappointed.

"Yes, I know," she acknowledged.

She went over to the chair by the window and looked at the letter. He was still in Arizona. Would he ever reach California, she wondered. She opened the envelope.

> **Dear darling,**
>
> **I got the check and thanx, but I did say two hundred. Send the rest if you can get it. The man I work for let me fix the van here, but I need to pay him for the parts, and it is only fair you send the dough because it is half your van. His daughter talked him into letting me have the parts. She is real nice and cute. You would like her. This is going to be short because we are going on a camping trip with some of her friends. I saw one of your pictures in** Natural Living **this month, so you can probably send the rest of the money. Let me hear from you soon.**
>
>

Love,
PATCH

Andrea put the letter back into the envelope and stared at it thoughtfully. He'll never know it's really all over between us until I take the first step and literally spell it out in so many words, she thought. She realized that it was she all along she had needed to convince, and now she was sure. *The service station man's daughter is cute and nice. I would like her. I'll bet,* she thought grimly. *Going on a camping trip. Two could have a lot of fun in one of those double sleeping bags.*

She put the letter in a drawer and slammed it shut. The boys looked at her expectantly.

"How's Patch doing?" asked George.

"He's doing fine. He'll always do fine, wherever he goes."

She walked to the window and looked down at the people in the street below. How could they walk, talk, laugh, eat ice-cream cones? Couldn't they hear the death knell of her shaky marriage? "You guys are law students," she said quietly. "Who is the best lawyer in town for divorce cases?"

Both boys stopped munching on their crackers immediately.

"Are you sure this is what you want, Andy? Isn't Patch coming back at all?" George asked.

"I really don't know whether or not he will come back. It's over. It was over when he left; I just didn't know. Oh, I had my pride to consider. Nobody likes to be abandoned, but I should have had the sense to see the signs long ago."

"Hey, listen, it was never your fault—" began Matt defensively.

"Oh, yes, it was. I handled the whole marriage scene badly from the beginning. He should have been the strong one, looking after me. I should have leaned on him, made him feel a sense of responsibility to me. Instead, I took over, paid the rent, gave him spending money while he pretended to go to school. He never did actually sign up; he just sat in on a few classes. I don't know what he did with the tuition money."

"We didn't know that. You never said anything," said Matt.

"No, I never said anything to him about it, either. There were other things, too. Being in love with him made them somehow not as important as they really were. Can you understand? I loved him. I really did."

Without warning, tears spilled down her cheeks. She put her hands up to her face, and as she did, her fingers shook with the effort to hold back all the pain and anger bottled inside.

The boys were embarrassed by this emotion. Matt fidgeted, not knowing what to do. George went into the kitchen and took a long time running a glass of water. By the time he came back, Andrea had pulled herself together.

She sat holding the little dog, staring through swollen eyes out the window. She accepted the glass of water without looking at George directly. "I'm sorry. I didn't mean—"

"Ah, that's all right," said George. "Look, when you get it together, we're down the hall. I know a great lawyer. I've been researching some cases for him. He'll help, if it's what you want."

"Thanks. That's what I want. Make an appointment for me sometime this week."

She followed them to the door, still holding the dog tightly in her arms.

"I'm sorry. I never cry. I don't know why I started."

"Hell, it's good for the soul. Let it all hang out," said George. "I'll let you know when Mr. Adams can see you. He'll treat you right."

"Thanks, George. You too, Matt."

She closed the door. As the boys started down the hall, she heard Matt ask furiously, "What was in that letter, anyway? I could kill that guy!"

Nothing, replied Andrea silently. *Nothing and everything.*

She drew a hot bath and climbed into the bubbles and fragrant vapors of Chanel bubble bath. She allowed Jade to lie on the bath mat while she tried to soak the aches away, tried to assemble the remnants of her life.

She could begin by setting aside old falsehoods concerning Patch, such as the lie she had been living about not being able to leave Middletowne. Patch wasn't going to be returning to Middletowne now. What was left for her that really meant something? As if on cue, the telephone rang. She climbed out of the tub, grabbing a towel.

"Andy, get over here and get some of these kids out on assignment," said Jack. "It's Saturday, you know, and things are hoppin'. You and Gage are to go over to the hotel. There are about seventy Pakistanis over at the Hilton, and none of them speak English. Who are they? Why are they here? Nobody seems to know. There are ladies in those dresses with no tops—"

"You mean saris, Jack," she interrupted.

"—and rings on their toes. Get a picture of their feet. I want feet!"

"I'm coming! I'm coming!"

She hung up and dressed quickly, powdered her nose and put on a little lipstick.

She checked out two cameras and grabbed her coat, then hurried down the hall and knocked on Matt and George's door. Matt answered and looked at her with surprise.

"Yeah. Whatcha need, beautiful?"

"I'm working. Can you check on the pooch for me? I may be late."

"Sure, Andy."

He breathed a sigh of relief. Looked like things were almost back to normal.

As she crossed the street to the office, an old motorcycle pulled slowly into St. George Street and paused at the corner. It headed down the other side. The sound of its engine was muffled by the cars and voices of people on the street. Andrea didn't even turn her head, but if she had, she would have noted that it was an old Harley Davidson, painted black and silver. The rider wore a battered helmet, also black, like the curls that pushed out beneath it. The rider stared at Andrea as she entered the building. With difficulty, he read the sign over the door. From the look on his face, he did not comprehend the business that went on in the building. But he did know the girl—Paul's friend.

He wished he had seen which doorway she had entered the street from. He parked his bike and looked in the doorways, noticed the mailboxes and carefully copied down all the names belonging to women. It was a laborious task, but now he would find out her name. She lived in one of these places.

Rolling the cycle into the parking lot behind the stores, he walked over to the drugstore. A sign on a wire rack outside caught his eye. "What's Happening Here." That name was the same name as the building the girl had entered. It was the newspaper. He took a copy, hurried inside and pored over all the names he could find, matching them with the names from the mailboxes. He checked again and again, but none matched. He sat back, discouraged but undaunted.

After a while he went back to St. George Street and hung around for more than an hour, but the girl never came back out. He headed for the house across from the cemetery. Paul would be surprised to see him. He had not told him that he was coming.

Paul was trying to study. He had an exam on Tuesday, but he was finding it hard to concentrate. He kept thinking about Andrea and wondering what she was doing. He had tried to put her out of his mind, but thoughts of her slipped in unwanted. She was well known, popular, practically a friend, or at least known, to most of the entire town, and he couldn't afford to be seen with her. Why couldn't she have been some college girl that would be gone by summer? But no. She was a personality and was here to stay.

He cast aside his caution and dialed her number. It was still ringing when he heard the unmistakable sound of Omar's motorcycle just outside the door. What the hell was he doing here again this weekend? He answered the heavy knock on the door.

"What are you doing in Middletowne again so soon? Do you think it's wise to be seen in a small place like this week after week?"

Omar tried to find an excuse that would sound plausible. "I come to tell you," he said, entering, "Mr. Gay, he is working very good now. You help with the trouble. He gon' have the gun to you before long."

"You came all this way to tell me that? What's wrong with the telephone?"

Omar ignored the sarcasm and made his way to the kitchen without further explanation of his visit. He took down his coffee and put the pot on to boil. "You forget. This is my house, too?" he leered as the water hissed on the stove.

"You want it back? I can be gone by tonight and we can forget the whole deal. You and your little group of fanatics can get yourselves another boy!" snapped Paul.

"Not now. Is too late." Omar looked at him angrily and, taking a small, curved Arabian knife from his pocket, began to clean his nails. It was symbolic, a symbol that Paul would understand. The knife was crescent-shaped and deadly. It could be used to scoop out a man's eyes, or tear out a wagging tongue. Paul had seen such knives in every bazaar in the Middle East. Arabs, Syrians and Turks wore them under their robes. Paul had been called upon to defend himself against one in an alley in Marrakesh, and only the fact that his arms were longer than the other man's had saved him from a gory death. He had been able to come in and break his opponent's nose with the heel of his hand. It was nice to know things like that in a place like that. Because of that incident, Omar's trick with the knife now amused him.

Omar laughed self-consciously and put the knife away in its enameled sheath. "Why should we fight together? You are like my brother, no? I just make the test on you, but nothing is change! My house, your house. What's the difference, eh?"

Paul felt a sudden regret that this little threat hadn't ended in a showdown. Each day he felt more and more convinced that it had all been a mistake, becoming involved in this intrigue. And the longer he stayed in Middletowne, the less the whole thing appealed to him. It was the waiting. It postponed his entrance into a new life, dimmed his chances of ever being able to forget his old career. He wanted to start clean.

The coffee was boiling out of the pot, having been forgotten in the heat of the conversation. Omar yelped with pain as his fingers grasped the thin metal handle. He plunged them into the butter in the refrigerator.

The telephone rang, and Paul went quickly to answer it.

"Hello, it's Andrea. Paul?"

"Yes." He hesitated, unwilling to acknowledge her name aloud.

"I hate to bother you, but I'm down at the Hilton trying to talk to some Indian performers who speak no English. I was wondering if you had any experience in the language—Hindustani or something like that? It sure would help," she asked.

"No, that's one I missed. How about Turkish, Greek, or Arabic?" he offered.

"Don't think that would work. Oh, well, here goes the old sign language. Thanks, anyway. Sorry to have bothered you, Paul." She started to ring off, then heard him speak.

"Uh…" He tried to think how he could word it without arousing Omar's suspicion. "I'd like to see you," he ended bluntly. He knew Omar was listening from the kitchen.

"All right. I see my partner giving me a sign to hurry. I'll call you later," she promised.

Gage hurried up to the booth and triumphantly showed her a notebook covered with notes and quotes. She looked at it in surprise.

"I found a student from the college who speaks French!" he announced.

"So—French?"

"Yeah, the leader of the dance troupe speaks perfect French. The rest of them are singers and dancers, and guess what? They're in the wrong city. They're due to perform at Chapel Hill tonight, but somebody brought them to the wrong college."

"Good grief! That's three hundred miles from here. What are they going to do?"

"I don't know. Move fast, I'd guess. Let's get the pix and get out of here before they find out the bad news and all start crying at once. Get a shot of that luscious chick with the emerald in her nose! God, I never saw so many brown bellies before."

"Ever been to Miami Beach?"

"Yeah, but it ain't the same, honey."

"You stare all you want. Jack wants feet pictures. They really do have bells on their toes. This is fantastic!"

Andrea and Gage wrapped it up and checked in at the office. It was past one, and Gage suggested they go to lunch together. For once she agreed. They went out the back door to the parking lot, commandeered one of the Datsuns and drove to Seaport.

Outside the front of the building, a motorcycle cruised slowly by. The rider searched the street and nearby buildings, but the dark-haired girl was nowhere in sight. He could wait. She would have to come back to her apartment sometime.

CHAPTER NINE

The sun was just beginning to rise as Paul lay awake in the second bedroom, listening to Omar snore in the back room. Cautiously, he got out of bed and crept down the hall to make sure Omar was actually sleeping. Then he dressed quickly. He picked up the camera Mr. Gay had left for him to use and went outside. Softly, he whistled for Wolf, and together they ran down the street to the next block, where he had parked his Volkswagen the night before. Wolf jumped into the back seat, and within minutes Paul was in front of the apartment on St. George Street.

He knocked on the door for several minutes before he heard her voice answer, unclearly and with a definite tinge of annoyance. Jade began to bark as he heard Andrea moving around, probably putting on a robe.

Down the hall, a door popped open and Matt stared at him with suspicion.

"Oh, sorry. I thought it was our door," he mumbled. A sleepy grin passed over his face as he looked at Paul. "Going or coming?" he asked mischievously.

"I just got here," confessed Paul.

"Tough luck! Well, see you around."

Matt shut his door as Andrea opened hers a crack.

"Good morning. Can I come in?"

Wolf was trying to force his big head through the crack, while Jade tried to bite his nose.

"Guess you'd better. These two dogs will wake up the whole neighborhood. Hush, Jade! Listen, I look a mess, the place is a mess... Oh, come in," she groaned.

Paul stepped inside and smiled hesitantly at her confusion. She was wearing a pale-pink robe which barely reached her knees; her hair fell in tangles, and her face was free of makeup. She looked like a sleepy little girl, and, as if it were too early to cope with anything, she flopped back into bed and curled up with a sigh. He sat down awkwardly on the edge of the bed. She sat up and looked at him with still half-closed eyes. She glanced at the clock on the table.

"Why are you here at seven o'clock in the morning? Why?" she asked.

"You didn't call back yesterday. You're never at home when I call you. Is there some reason why you don't want to see me again?" he pleaded, surprised at the note of desperation in his voice.

"No, I just forgot to call. We were busy and..." Her voice dwindled off uncertainly.

"What is it?" he asked.

"I thought maybe it was you who didn't want to see me again. I mean, you were pretty anxious to terminate our date the night we went to the Ramada. You began to act bored and restless almost as soon as we arrived."

"I don't like crowded places. Never did," he admitted. "Can't we spend the day together, just you and I? Please, anywhere you say."

He stared at her, and they were both suddenly aware of the bed, their closeness.

Andrea pulled her robe tightly around her. "I have to get dressed now."

"I'll take the dogs for a walk. Think I can handle Jade?"

"Probably. But about today. I may have to work. My boss may call."

"Dress quickly, then, so we'll be out of here by the time he does." Paul then thought of the man sleeping in his house. "Hurry," he added.

"But how shall I dress? Where are we going?"

"Put on anything, as long as it's casual. I had in mind a beach I found one day. It's secluded, with driftwood, gulls. It's very pretty. You can show me how to use my new camera. It's much like your big one, there."

"Sounds like fun," said Andrea. "I'll hurry and dress before Jack Wise catches me."

Paul called the dogs and put on their leashes. Jade gave Andrea one baleful glance before she scuttled out of the door. Wolf pranced on ahead, delighted.

Paul paused at the door a moment. "The photographs of the man, they're gone. Is the man gone, too?"

Andrea nodded. "He's been gone a long time actually. I just wasn't aware of it," she replied.

As Paul went out, she reached for a letter on the table telling Patch of the divorce action. She put it in her bag to mail as soon as possible. She then got up and began to dress hurriedly, went into the kitchen and filled a bag with cheese and a long loaf of French bread she had bought from Le Fromage the day before. The telephone rang, but she ignored it. *That's one for you, Gage,* she thought merrily as she locked the apartment door and ran down to the street.

Paul stood at the corner looking into the window of the photo shop. He was actually looking into the reflection, watching the street behind him out of habit. The two dogs were sharing a partially eaten ice-cream cone they had found in the gutter. Jade gulped the biggest part, her eyes fixed on the larger dog.

As Andrea passed the restaurant, a man who had been sitting far in the rear turned to the proprietor and asked casually, "Who that girl is? She very pretty, don't you think so?"

"That's Andy. Andy Wayne. Yeah, she's a doll."

"She works across the street?"

"Yeah, that's her."

Omar was suddenly very hungry. He ordered pancakes, eggs, bacon, and coffee with a feeling of satisfaction. He didn't have to follow her any longer. He now knew her name and where to find her. She would cause no more trouble. It was lucky he had heard Paul whistle to Wolf this morning. Omar had had a hunch Paul would lead him to the girl.

He attacked the plate with gusto, his eyes glittering with excitement. Paul had been up there in the girl's apartment maybe thirty, forty minutes. And what had they been doing? Omar put a large piece of pancake in his mouth and chewed noisily. *I need a woman,* he decided. *I must find one soon.* He looked at the bacon and put it in his mouth. He was not supposed to eat bacon, but he loved it. *Allah, forgive me,* he intoned silently and reached for a second piece.

Paul and Andrea squeezed into the front seat of the Volkswagen, with the dogs sharing the back seat. Every time Wolf tried to sit down, he sat on Jade's tail. And each time he did, she gave him a warning nip in the side. He decided to stand, back pushed against the roof of the car, with his head hanging out the window.

Behind the wheel, Paul felt a chill, a feeling he had known in the past—a sort of warning signal when danger was near. He cased the street, but he detected nothing unusual in the few people who were out at that hour on a Sunday morning. He searched the doorways and store windows, but there was nothing.

Andrea turned to him and smiled, and the chill subsided. They drove off.

"I brought bread for the gulls, too," she said, smiling.

Paul smiled back and looked at her closely. *After today, I'll leave her alone,* he thought, *but today, I've got to have this day. I've never wanted a woman as much as I want this one.*

On their way out of town, they passed incoming tourists on their way to spend a quiet Sunday in Middletowne—a place of wide, tree-lined streets far from the hustle and bustle of the big cities.

"Would you mind stopping at the next store on the left? I want to get some wine. Would you like anything else?" she asked.

"No, but the wine will be hot. I'll get some ice," he added.

Paul was amused and secretly pleased. They were going on a picnic. It was the most ordinary, middle-class American preoccupation he could think of. And it was somehow incongruous—Paul Hunter with a girlfriend, two dogs, and a picnic. He laughed aloud, and Andrea turned to him questioningly.

"It's nothing. I was just thinking how this car must look with Wolf hanging out the back," he improvised.

"You mean we look ridiculous. I agree. We need a station wagon, at least. Well, it's not much farther, I hope."

They turned off the main highway. After about a mile more, Paul drove the car up to the shoulder. They got out and, toting the food and an old blanket, headed down an overgrown path until they reached the beach.

It really couldn't be called a beach. It was more of a sandy strip that would be nearly covered with water when the tide came in. Now it was about ten feet wide. Driftwood had come in on one side, making a shelter. Undisturbed by visitors, sand crabs had made a thousand gritty hills near their holes on the beach. It was a pretty little cove, bright in the sunlight.

They sat down on the blanket, while Wolf rushed for the water and plunged in. Jade, after getting her front feet wet, retreated and came back to the blanket. Wolf was paddling happily in the water, biting at floating sticks.

"He's getting soaked. I sure hope he dries out before it's time to get in the car!" laughed Andrea.

"He usually doesn't. Smells like hell, frankly," admitted Paul. He stood up, stripped off his shirt and shoes and lay back in the sun. Andrea sat watching the dog, then took off her sandals and went down to the water. Seeing her coming toward him, Wolf swam to shore and shook himself, soaking her to the skin.

"Oh, you beast! Now look who is going home wet! Look what your dog did to me," she protested, trying to shake dry.

Her halter was clinging, and her shorts sagged in front. Even her hair was dripping. She tried to pull the wet fabric away from her body.

Paul watched her, laughing uproariously, until she threw one of her sandals at him. He caught it and teasingly held it aloft before burying it in the sand. "Now you'll have to hop all the way home, dripping wet, through crowds of gawking tourists. Your reputation is shot, lady!"

"You're nuts! Your dog's crazy, too. Come on, Jade, let's leave the two nuts together."

As haughtily as possible, wearing one shoe retrieved from near the blanket, she strolled to the end of the beach. Jade waddled along behind. Wolf followed discreetly, and when Andrea and Jade sat down, he sat down, too, just a few feet away. Andrea tried not to laugh. She stared out over the water, ignoring Paul and the elaborate maneuver he was attempting. He would drag the blanket closer, then stop, then a little bit closer, until he was only a few feet away. Wolf watched him curiously, but Andrea pretended not to notice. Suddenly he was behind her. His arms circled her waist, and he pulled her backward onto the blanket, laughing. She laughed, too, but only for a minute. Their eyes met; unconsciously, she raised her hand in protest. His mouth sought hers. She felt dizzy, suffocated, as he pushed his hand under her halter. Her mouth felt hot and bruised, and she twisted her head from side to side until he stopped. She lay under his body, unable to move.

"Stop. Stop. Oh, please," she begged hoarsely, pushing weakly against his chest. She pushed again, and he rolled over on his back, releasing her.

He lay there tensely, not looking at her, as sweat poured from his body.

She sat up, trembling, and tied her halter tightly, feeling her nipples press hard against the material. "I think we'd better go," she said almost painfully. She stood up and brushed the sand from her shorts.

He reached out and grasped her ankle to keep her from walking away.

"Please stay. Just stay with me. I promise I won't touch you if you don't want me to, but don't go. Just let me be with you, if only for today," he pleaded.

She looked at him, wondering. Why would he say something like that? She realized how little she really knew about him. But one thing stood out in her mind. She had never been so attracted to anyone before, not even Patch. When she had stopped Paul from making love to her, she knew she was trying to stop herself as well. All the old desires had come back, and she was frightened of herself. She wasn't ready to fall in love again. She was very conscious of his hand on her leg, and she pulled away but sat back down on the blanket near him and took his hand in hers.

"I'm still married. The man you saw in the pictures is my husband."

"Where is he? You told me you lived alone," Paul replied.

"He left me several months ago. Oh, he writes, just as if things had never changed. But, of course, they have. I've filed for divorce, but until then I don't want anybody in my life. It's too soon, Paul," she explained, "and I don't want to get hurt again."

"He must be a stupid son of a bitch," said Paul without malice. "If he comes back, I'll kill him." He was shocked at how easily the words had come out, as if he had the sure solution to every person who became an obstacle in his life. "Kill him!" had been his solution for a long time. But he was different now, no longer under orders. Momentarily his mission had been forgotten, but now he remembered. It was just the same as it used to be. Only the people were different this time. He rubbed his hands over his eyes, suddenly feeling weary. Andrea looked at him curiously.

There was an apologetic "woof" from Wolf, and they turned in his direction. Jade had her head in the bag of food and was pulling out the cheese with stealthy determination.

Andrea jumped up quickly. "Drop it, you bad girl!" she ordered. She rescued the cheese and then reached for the bread. "Do you have a knife? I was in such a rush I forgot it."

"No. I don't carry one." He almost added "anymore." "Here, let me show you the best way to eat."

He took the bread and cheese and broke it in chunks, giving half to her. He poured the wine into paper cups and added ice from a plastic bag, then placed the open bag upright in the sand. The dogs lapped from it and, when sated, sought the shade of the driftwood at the end of the cove.

The sun plus the wine they had drunk made Paul and Andrea sleepy, and they dozed on the blanket, their only contact, his hand over hers. After a while they awoke and watched the sailboats far out in the water.

"I had a sailboat once. We were on a little island not far from Skorpios. It was beautiful there, for a while," he told her almost wistfully.

"It sounds wonderful. Why did you leave such a place?"

"It was over," he said strangely. He had found his man.

"Oh, your tour of duty was over. I see."

He had become suddenly silent, drawing into that reserve that always seemed to linger beneath the surface.

"The sun is going, and we haven't had time to try out your new camera," Andrea said regretfully.

"I forgot all about it," admitted Paul, smiling. "It's been a nice day. Thanks for... everything. For staying."

"We'd better be going back to town. Thank heaven, your dog looks fairly dry," she said, standing up to leave. Then she hesitated, looking around the sand. "My shoe. Where did you bury my other shoe, Paul?"

All the sand looked the same. Together they began to dig around where they had first been sitting. The dogs joined in, not knowing what they were looking for but having a great time.

After a while, they abandoned the search. The shoe could not be found.

When they got to the car and were all ready to drive off, Andrea pulled off her one sandal and threw it out of the window.

CHAPTER TEN

Paul left Andrea at her apartment and drove home in a glow, happy but tired. Wolf, who finally had the back seat all to himself, had dropped into a deep sleep and was snoring loudly. As they drove up to the house, Paul was surprised to see Omar's motorcycle gone from the side yard where he usually kept it. There was a white card stuck in the screen of the front door.

Paul took out the card and turned it over, recognizing the scrawl that passed as Omar's handwriting. He frowned as he contemplated the message.

"Goodby. I am gon. You see me agn. yrs frend. omar."

What the hell is this note stuff? Omar had never left him a note before in his life. In fact, Omar avoided writing in English as much as possible. It was an almost traumatic undertaking for him, and Paul could not understand why he had bothered to take the trouble. He tore the card into several pieces and put it in his pocket to dispose of later. He was relieved that at least his house was empty again, rid of those cigars, the dirty clothes, and all those loveless traits that characterized Omar, *yrs frend.*

Paul yawned and let himself into the house. He felt a little sunburn beginning to tingle on his back. He thought of Andrea. *How will it be with her?* he wondered. Reluctantly, he shook off the thought, strolled into the kitchen and just stood there. Laughing at his own preoccupation, he swung open the refrigerator and looked inside. Man cannot live on love alone. He took out a couple slices of ham and threw them into a frying pan. As it sizzled, he put the coffee on the other burner and watched it come to a boil. *I love her. I love her,* he admitted to himself. *What can I do about it? Nothing. I would only ruin her life.*

The old Harley Davidson was cruising slowly down the highway east of Middletowne, when the rider decided to turn into the driveway of a rather run-down motel. Inside the motel office sat an elderly man watching television. His back was to the door, but he jumped up spryly as the rider entered. "What kin I do ya for, buddy?" He grinned, exposing old, yellow teeth.

"Do me for?" repeated Omar, hearing the phrase for the first time.

"What I mean is, need a room fer the night?"

"Yes, two, maybe the three days I am staying."

"Got any luggage? You gonna have to pay me in advance if you don't," cautioned the clerk, his smile momentarily disappearing as he noticed no bag in sight.

"I have money. Don't to worry, mister," said Omar, reaching for his billfold. "How much money you want from me? I pay you two days. Is all right?"

"No need to git huffy. I seen you was all right the minute you come in here, but the boss tells me, 'No luggage, git the money.' It's a rule, see? Oh, we do git some losers in this place sometimes. But they don't fool Calvin. That's me, Calvin."

He turned and looked through the keys on the rack behind the counter.

"I got a nice room all the way to the back. Number eight. Just fo'teen dollars a night. That's cheap around here, son." He glanced out of the window at the motorcycle in the middle of the drive and continued, "You can park your Cadillac in the back, around behind number eight, 'cause it's the last one on the lot."

Omar stood there speechless, trying to sort out the unfamiliar slang. Huffy? Cadillac for motorcycle? He decided it must be a joke. He pulled out some bills.

"That'll be twenty-eight and your tax. Government gits its, too, ya know?"

Omar threw the money on the counter and reached for the guest register, which the man had turned for him to sign. He wrote the name John Hopkins, a pseudonym he had picked, based on a big hospital near Washington. John Hopkins, what could sound more American than that? He took the key to the room from the clerk.

"Thank you very much. Hope you have a nice stay, Mr., ah, Hopkins."

After Omar had rolled the cycle toward the end cabin, the clerk grimaced and scratched his head as he glanced again at the register. Hopkins, hell! The money looked all right, though. He pushed it into a drawer, locked it and went back to his television program.

Omar took a small bundle of clothing out of a leather bag on the back of his motorcycle and let himself into the room. It was surprisingly clean and even had a tile bath. He lay down on the bed. He was tired but too keyed up to sleep. He tossed back and forth, his head aching with a multitude of ideas.

He needed a car, because his motorcycle was too loud and might attract attention. But he could not steal a car in a place like Middletowne. Washington was different. There were many people there—strangers, foreigners—moving fast about the city. No one ever bothered to look at him in Washington. There was also crime, lots of stolen cars. In Middletowne, though, life moved at a slower pace, there was less crime, fewer foreigners. *Good for them,* he thought, *but bad for me!* He held his dark hand up to the light that slanted down through the venetian blinds.

Angrily, he jumped up from the bed and went outside, restlessly looking around for something to clear his mind. Across the highway a red neon light beckoned, "Moody's Bar and Grill." He began to walk toward it. As he passed the office window, he could see the old clerk inside, watching the flickering shadows of the television screen. Omar stood silently and observed young Burt Reynolds standing over a corpse lying on the floor of an elegant apartment. It was an old *Dan August* rerun. Reynolds picked up the murder weapon by inserting a pencil into the barrel, then placed the gun carefully in a plastic bag. Omar smiled at the hero on the screen. Guns! Always in America, the guns! If one were facing one's enemy as a man should, the knife was just as sure, and if in the right hand, it was always as lethal as the gun, and noiseless, as well. Omar reached up the sleeve of his jacket and felt the knife on a leather strap just above his wrist. He sensed the stiletto blade on the inside of his right boot and then confidently moved on toward the sign across the highway.

The regulars at Moody's, seated at the long pine bar, barely bothered to look up from their beers as Omar sauntered in and took a table in the corner. It was an anonymous type of place, found over and over on the outskirts of towns everywhere. It smelled of stale smoke, beer, and oppression. The faces along the bar seldom smiled but simply peered suspiciously out from under old hats and plaid hunting caps. They expected life to deal them some low blow even as they sat there quietly nursing a brew and dreaming of better times and better women. They, too, were watching Dan August—handsome, suave, exciting Dan—a world away from Moody's Bar and Grill.

After a while a very short Korean girl came out of the kitchen in the back to take Omar's order. She wore a short white uniform, starched clean, that rustled when she walked. It did little to hide her bowed legs.

"What'll it be?" she asked, her eyes flicking over his face with interest.

"What kind san'wich you got here?" Omar smiled up at her. He stared openly at the round, flat face. She smiled back, showing even, square white teeth. Their eyes met.

"We got roast beef, chicken, hamburger, cheeseburger and hot dog." She giggled and leaned over to confide in his ear, "The hot dog is terrible. Don't order it."

"Maybe is better the cheeseburger?"

"The cheeseburger is OK. You want something to drink?" she asked, pressing herself close to the edge of the table.

Omar could smell her perfume, and from her glossy hair came the smell of incense from a far-away place. He longed to reach out and touch her, but instead he looked away, feigning disinterest.

"Glass wine? You have glass wine in this place?" he asked hopefully.

"Sure. It's a relief to hear an order for wine. All these guys drink is beer, beer, beer! Nice to have a gentleman ask for wine."

Omar remembered an old line from an American movie that had seemed to work for, who, Frank Sinatra, Spencer Tracy?

"What you doing in this place? You real nice girl for place like this," he echoed hopefully, approximating the cliche. He touched her hand softly.

"Oh! Oh! You really want to know? OK, I'll tell you. Long time ago my big soldier boy, he brought me to this country. Nothing work out and he get a divorce. I get Micky. He's my son. Look like me."

Omar's interest quickened with her last statement.

"Your husband, he don't want his own son?" he asked in disbelief.

"Like I say, he look like me, not him," she said defensively. Then, with a wistful glance backward, she hurried off to the kitchen.

So you are like me, little one. He tried to recall Melanie. Her face escaped him, but not his son's! He would think of him forever as he saw him last, a baby with black curls, his image caught in babyhood for all time.

He turned his thoughts back to the Korean girl, and when she came back with his order, he asked her to sit down and have a drink with him at the table. She refused.

"Moody won't let me sit with customers. It's his rule. It's not that I don't want to. You understand? You look like OK guy to me."

Her voice had dropped as she looked him over shrewdly. *He's not old and fat,* she thought. *It wouldn't be too bad with him.* Her mind flew to the tiny hoard of money she had been able to save as a waitress.

He paid his check with a new twenty-dollar bill, and she could see as she leaned over to put a napkin by the plate that there was more money in his wallet.

"You live around here?" she ventured cautiously.

"I am traveling man. I am staying at motel across the street for the couple of days. Very lonely, that place." He spoke carefully and added, "Number eight, my room."

"No wife with you?"

"I am single, and my bed gets too lonely sometimes."

She stopped smiling and moved away from the table, as if he had broken one of the rules of the age-old game by mentioning the word *bed*. Her face became closed, withdrawn.

Nonetheless, he was aware she was still watching him and felt his ego swell with the surety of his conquest. It had happened this way with many women before, and it would happen many times again. He was glad he had come to Moody's Bar and Grill.

Omar finished his meal, crossed over to the motel and let himself into his room. He undressed without turning on the light. He removed the dark knit cap last of all and threw it on the floor on top of the rest of his clothes, then stepped into the shower.

Later, when the expected knock sounded on the door, he went to open it. He stood just out of her sight as he let her inside. For a moment she was unable to see him and said cheerfully, "Look! I stole a bottle of Moody's best wine. He drinks it himself!" Her eyes adjusted to the gloom, and she stepped back as she noticed his naked body. "Hey! You come on pretty fast, don't you?"

Omar smiled and locked the door behind her. He unscrewed the cap on the wine bottle and, lifting it to his lips, drank deeply. He offered her the bottle.

"My name is Kim," said the girl, looking very young and afraid. She tipped the bottle and drank from it, looking inside it as if to find the courage that had suddenly deserted her when she entered the room.

"My name is John… John Hopkins," grinned Omar as he reached for the zipper on her white uniform. The dress fell to the floor, and she stood there shivering with fear and excitement. Her chest was small and bare, and she was wearing a faded pair of pink panties with a red heart embroidered on one side.

Her smile became a mask of resignation as she felt his hands on her breasts. His mouth found hers, then traveled to her throat, leaving a hot, wet trail. *Three hundred dollars more and Micky and I can go back home to Korea,* she reminded herself.

The dark man was strong. She could feel the muscles in his arms as he half pushed, half lifted her to the waiting bed. He fell on top of her, breathing heavily.

I'll see my mother, my father, she thought, as he pushed her legs apart savagely. *I'll see my little brother, my old Uncle Tamuri, and Auntie.* She felt the man enter her body and begin a slow, agonizing rhythm unlike any she had ever known. She tried hard to concentrate on all the people she remembered at home. Who else? Her memory failed her, and hot tears raced down her cheeks at the treachery of her body responding to this stranger. Her body rocked back and forth beneath the man. Her soft cry joined the triumphant animal sound of the man.

After a moment they moved apart awkwardly, and almost immediately Omar fell into a deep sleep. Kim lay quietly, then moved tentatively into the circle of his arm and laid her head on his shoulder.

In the morning he'll give me money, I'm sure, she thought.

CHAPTER ELEVEN

"Captain Gandy refuses to leave until the last minute of his last day," said Jack Wise, looking at a glossy of the fine old ferry captain.

"That's Captain Gandy for you," said Andrea. "He's always been the same about that boat run—dedicated, concerned. It's been a big part of his life, and now it's ending."

"Retiring at last."

Andrea picked up the file pictures and smiled at the captain's heavy white brows and his twinkling eyes that gazed out beneath the shiny black brim of his white cap. "The old ferry will never be the same," she added.

"Ah, there's Bill Smedley and young Jerry—he's a good kid—Captain Clark. They're all pretty good skippers," reminded Jack.

"That may be true, but Captain Gandy—he's special. Thanks for giving me the story. I'm going to take that last ride with him, and if I get sentimental about it, you'd better not blue-pencil a line."

"Keep out the fat and I won't have to. After all, we're only thirty-two pages."

"I'll keep it in mind, luv."

"I really should send Gage. The last trip ends at midnight on the other side of the river. It's late for you to drive back alone," said Jack thoughtfully.

"No, you don't! This one is mine, Jack. I'll manage."

Before he could change his mind, she grabbed her cameras, hastily checked her flash equipment, and then, stuffing as much as she could into her bag, she waved good-bye.

She stopped at her desk and dialed Paul's number. She had seen him only once since the day at the beach, one quick lunch between assignments, and she wanted very much to be with him again. As the telephone rang, she thought about him. God, he was handsome! He was so... likable? *The word is lovable, stupid*, she admitted to herself. And she knew she could easily fall in love with him, given enough time. It would be so easy.

Just as she was about to hang up, he answered sleepily.

"Did I wake you?" she asked.

"Andrea? I was studying, and it's pretty boring stuff. Guess I dozed off," he lied. Classes were over for the year. He hoped she didn't know.

"Then, come out with me for a ride on the ferry," she began hesitantly, unsure whether to disturb him.

"The ferry? That's me knocking on your door. I'll be there in ten minutes."

"Wait! Paul, I'm still at the office. Meet me in the parking lot. Good-bye."

"See you in a little while."

He hung up the phone and put down the camera he had been using when she called. He began to strip down the targets he had placed all over the house—the long shot, the close range, the length of the house. He really needed more room. He rolled up the targets, locked them in the closet, then opened the blinds in the kitchen. It was already night. He had been practicing with the camera since afternoon. No wonder his head felt slightly dizzy.

The camera had started to feel natural to his hands by this time. Of course, the other one with the firing mechanism would be heavier. Paul had driven to Norfolk and purchased a fairly sturdy aluminum tripod in the camera department of a large discount store. He had paid cash; the check-out clerk hadn't even bothered to look up as she handed him the package. If he had said to her, "I'm going to use this to kill somebody," would she have looked up then? Or would she have dismissed him as a nut? Probably. The world was full of innocents.

Sometimes he thought of the missions he had been on in the past and of what he was capable of doing in the future, and it made him afraid—not for himself, but for all the innocents who passed him in the streets each day, unaware, so vulnerably unaware.

He decided to take the camera on the ferry and watch Andrea as she worked with her own. Funny, he had always avoided cameras, with their all-seeing eyes, recording life, gathering evidence, catching moments that could come back to convict. The innocents liked cameras and readily offered smiling faces up to the lens, wondering only if they looked good. They had nothing to hide.

He slung the camera over his shoulder, went back to his bedroom and from the closet took a shoe box. He stared inside at the pair of red sandals, size six. That day on the beach when he buried her sandal in the sand, he had looked inside and noted that her size was exactly half the size of his own shoes. He had gone back to the beach and searched again, but he couldn't even find the one she had thrown away. The next day he bought these, but for some reason he had not given them to her. Tonight he would.

He had already decided never to see her again after tonight. It would be sheer hell to give her up, but lately his thoughts had been more on her than on the job he had come here to do. He would miss her quick laugh, her wit that made the most mundane situation humorous, her enthusiasm for everything, her determination not to let the situation with her husband destroy her love for life and people.

I love you, Andrea, he said to the empty house. She was so honest, so open, that if she knew the slightest thing about him, she would take him straight to the FBI and beg him to expose Omar's group. He shuddered, thinking of what they would do to her. They'd get her. All this ran through Paul's mind as he walked toward the office where Andrea awaited him.

She stood in the parking lot, trying to see her watch in the dark. There was barely enough illumination to see the dial, but she knew it was getting late, and she felt restless.

In the other section of the lot, behind some shrubs, an old dark-blue Pontiac was parked. Only the occasional glow of a cigar gave evidence that the car was occupied. Inside, Omar watched the girl through half-closed eyes, wondering why she was waiting instead of getting into the parked Datsun nearby. How long would she remain there alone? His knife made circles in the air as he cleaned his nails. He liked the feel of the blade running under his cuticles. He thought of the girl's throat. He imagined the knife sinking into her throat, her eyes widening with surprise. Such a pretty thing she was! No wonder she had Paul thinking of his balls when he should be thinking of the business ahead! It was a good thing he had found out about this girl before Paul did something foolish and ruined everything.

Omar leaned forward, his eyes searching the lot. Perhaps the time was now. It would only take seconds. But there was a light from the office she had come from, and a shadow near the window told him that someone, her boss man perhaps, still worked inside. If the man should decide to come out at the wrong moment, Omar would have to kill him, too. The man, probably a big shot, meant trouble. There was noise, police investigations when a big shot died.

Omar crushed out his cigar and carefully cracked open the car door, pressing the light button down. He was half in, half out of the car when he heard footsteps—heavy and rapid—coming toward the girl. Quickly he slid back into the car and closed the door as the girl's voice rang out.

"I thought you'd never get here! Ready for a very romantic boat ride in the moonlight?"

"Yes, I'm glad you called. I haven't been on a ferry for some time."

A thrill of apprehension ran down Omar's back as he huddled low in the Pontiac, scarcely breathing. Holy Allah! It was Paul. Omar squinted over the edge of the window just to make sure. The arrival of his friend was not totally unexpected, but it did come as something of a jolt to his plan. How could he get to the girl when Paul was around? But wait! That ferry was a big one, often empty late at night. The restrooms were on the upper deck, and maybe, just maybe, she would go up there alone.

The Datsun pulled out of the parking lot.

"What's in the box?" asked Andrea. "A midnight snack, I hope."

"No, it's something I owe you," Paul answered with a laugh.

"What could that be? Come on, Paul, don't keep me guessing," she begged.

"You can open it when we get on the ferry."

She looked again at the box, then reached over and squeezed his hand.

"You went back and found my shoes, the ones I left at the beach, didn't you?" She tried to open the box with one hand.

"Yes, I did try to find them, but I had no luck. It's hard to disguise a shoe box, isn't it?"

Suddenly she understood and looked almost embarrassed. She turned to him, a small, funny smile playing at the corners of her mouth.

"Oh, Paul, you didn't buy me another pair?" Her voice sounded strange when she spoke. "Those sandals were old ones. You really shouldn't have bothered."

For a minute they looked at each other. He longed to take her in his arms, to tell her how he felt about her, but he only smiled and looked away. An ache was building up inside.

"What the hell," he muttered gruffly. "It's only a pair of shoes."

"They'll always be special to me," she said quietly, staring ahead at the road. *Oh, Lord,* she thought to herself, *why did I meet this man? I am so conscious of him, I can hardly hold the wheel.*

"Darling—" he said suddenly. It burst from him and hung in the air between them. Paul was amazed at himself. What had made him blurt it out like that? Was he losing his mind? He had already determined that tonight would be it. There would be no more dates, no more anything after tonight, for her sake. But now that she was here, beside him, beside him…

Ahead of them was a deserted service station. A single light burned above the restroom doors to discourage vandals. Andrea pulled into its driveway.

"I want to see my new shoes. Now, not later on the ferry. I always was a rotten little kid about waiting for my presents. Used to drive my grandmother crazy." She was talking very fast, ignoring that "darling," as if it had never been said, fully aware, though, of the passion behind that single word.

Paul handed her the box silently, without meeting her gaze.

She grasped it, pulled off the top and looked delightedly inside. "They're red! Oh, Paul, they're beautiful, and the right size, too!" She took off the black pumps she was wearing and threw them in the back seat. She then put on her new sandals.

"They don't match a thing I'm wearing. Look, green and red. I'm a Christmas tree! And you know what? I don't give a damn. Thanks, Paul."

She leaned over and gave him a quick kiss on his lips. He pulled her closer and held her tightly without speaking. In a moment he kissed her, at first softly, carefully, then harder, forcing her lips apart. Her mouth tasted sweet and warm. He made the kiss last, unwilling to let her go. She lay against him limply. He pressed his lips against her ear, whispering, his hot breath on her neck.

"Let's go back... your place, my place, anywhere. Oh, Andrea... forgive me."

The last two words sounded strange to her, out of place. Forgive him? For what? For wanting her, for wanting to make love to her? No, it was something else, something she didn't know. She pushed him back gently and shook her head.

"I have to go to the ferry, and we must leave right away or we'll miss the last run. I have to be there. The oldest skipper is retiring, and I told Jack Wise that I'd ride the last run with him." Her words ran together. He noticed that her face was flushed, and that her hand was shaking as she turned on the ignition. The Datsun spluttered into motion. Paul sat back, resigned.

They drove the rest of the way to the landing in silence, each submerged in thought, engrossed in the complications of their unconsummated, yet desired affair.

The station wagon lurched onto the metal gangway, and they drove into the bowels of the lower deck to join the line of waiting cars on board. Chains were lashed across behind the car, and an attendant jammed blocks under the back wheels. They were the last car to get on.

Partway up the deck, in a second line of cars, Omar waited frantically. His anger turned to puzzlement as he saw the Datsun, at last, come on board. How did they get behind the other cars? When had he passed them on the parkway? There was only one road to the ferry. Where else could they have gone? He scowled, wondering, but here they were, after all. He would watch for his chance to catch the girl alone.

He took off his navy wool cap, placed it on the seat beside him and put on a new yellow poplin cap with a visor made of green plastic. The cap had a fisherman on the front. He had seen many tourists with similar headgear. He put on a pair of clear glasses he had bought at Woolworth's for $5.95, and laughed at his image in the mirror. *You look like a fool,* he told himself. Like Mr. Gay, with his silly wigs. It was worth it, though. He could take no chance of being recognized by Paul.

He looked out at the churning water, propelled away from the bow of the boat, and felt just a twinge of regret. The girl was so pretty, and Paul would feel sad. But it was his duty. She would only cause trouble.

In the other car, Paul was looking at the sandals skeptically. "But how do they feel? Do they fit all right?"

"Oh, sure, a little slickery on the soles. You know how new shoes are. I noticed it when I was driving."

"Slickery? What the hell is that? Some kid word?" He laughed, but his voice sounded harsh, almost derisive. It was something he could pick on, and he decided to work it into an argument once and for all—an argument to make her dislike him. He couldn't trust himself anymore. Every time they were together, he completely lost his head. He no longer was able to stay away but came back every time he heard her voice, like tonight.

She looked at him, noting the change in his voice. "Slickery isn't exactly a word, it's more of a feeling. You knew what I meant."

"Perhaps I did, but I really didn't expect words like that from an adult. It sounds pretty childish, and you call yourself a journalist?" he chided. He attempted to sound snide, even condescending, but the words almost stuck in his throat. The arrow had hit its target, and he could almost feel her bristle with indignation. He hated himself for what he was trying to do but felt that he must continue, as ugly and unfair as it must seem to her. He dug in relentlessly, now that he had piqued her attention.

"I've noticed a lot of childish mannerisms you have, Andrea. Don't you think this cute-little-girl act is pretty immature for a woman of your age?"

"Of *my age?* What do you mean by that remark?" she challenged.

"Well, you're no kid anymore. You've been around, been married, and all that."

She looked at him in disbelief and felt her anger rising. He had never been like this before.

"My God!" she blurted. "You sound as if I'm ready for social security, a rocking chair by the fire, and a cat for company—"

"Don't bother about the cat. That fat Pekingese will do." He laughed.

For a minute he thought she was going to hit him with her fist, a small, round weapon already clenched for action. "Say what you want about me," she said through clenched teeth, "but leave my dog out of it. She's been more of a friend to me than most of the people I know, and that *seems* to include you! Oh, what started all this, anyway? This whole conversation is just plain silly!"

He steeled himself for the next nasty remark.

"You're oversensitive, Andrea. If you were mature, you could recognize your own weaknesses and improve your whole personality. You tend to laugh and joke too much, and you use those kid expressions. Are you afraid the big bad wolf will get you if you let yourself grow up?"

"Paul! Paul! What's really wrong here? This is not you. I don't believe you're saying these things about me! One short half hour ago you kissed me."

"Well, you're a very cute broad," he began again, doggedly obnoxious.

Without waiting for another word, she grabbed her cameras and bag and jumped from the car. In the dim light her eyes flashed dark and angry in her pale face. Her mouth trembled, and he longed to go to her, to kiss away all the things he'd said, but he sat mute, afraid to trust himself to speak. She stared at him.

"You're not... on something, are you? A depressant, maybe?" she asked.

"No," he answered, suddenly sick and tired of the whole game. He turned away from her and studied a large hawser hung on the peeling white wall near the car.

She stood there a moment, then remarked flippantly, "Well, see you later, Grumpy. I've got work to do on the upper deck."

She strode across the deck, cameras clanking, the soles of her new sandals slapping on the metal. He watched her climb the narrow stairs to where Captain Gandy presided over the pilothouse. Paul felt very tired. He glanced at his watch. Forty minutes more of crossing time. He would try to get some sleep, if his conscience would let him. The insults and sarcasm had left their mark on both of them. He hated it all. He slumped down in the seat, and soon the sea air and the sound of the waves had lulled him to sleep.

In the Pontiac, Omar remained tensely alert to all that was going on in the other car. Paul and the girl seemed to be arguing about something, and then the girl got out, carrying some kind of equipment, and went up the steps. Omar noticed that Paul did not follow her. Omar waited a few more minutes, then slipped cautiously out of his car, keeping his face turned to the front. He stood in the shadow of the door to the engine room and watched Paul, who appeared to be asleep. Smiling, Omar crept silently up the narrow steps to the upper deck.

It was raining. A soft mist hung over the top deck. All he could see was the lit pilothouse and two feeble lamps near the doors to the waiting room. The lifeboats creaked gently in their berths.

Omar peered into the waiting room, filled with long rows of hard wooden benches. Life preservers, canvas-covered circles appearing never to have been used, were stored under the benches nearest the doors. There was no one in the room.

Omar crept full circle around the ship. Not a soul was on deck, the rain having kept everyone in their cars. He noticed the white railing, about three feet high, that enclosed the deck everywhere except where the lifeboats were. The open sea lay directly beneath them, and he could see the black water surge past.

At each end of the ship was a pilothouse. One was dark, its big brass wheel fixed in position; the other was lit up, and from it came the sound of voices full of life and laughter. He could hear the girl's voice and see flashes of light from her camera as she took pictures. He edged toward that pilothouse.

Two men were inside; one was the captain, a white-haired man in a dark blue uniform. The other had a cap like the captain but wore a red vest, evidently a crewman of some kind. There was also an elderly lady, slightly stout, with silver hair. And there was the girl.

Their faces looked sad, but the girl was making them laugh, moving about inside the small space and getting them to pose for her. Once she pointed almost directly in Omar's direction, but he drew back behind the wall just in time to avoid the flash. For a moment he thought she saw him, but then she turned and did something to the camera.

He couldn't stay there. To be safe, he went back and waited just inside the waiting room, behind the door, where he could see the pilothouse, without being seen. Pretty soon the second man came out and clattered down the steps. Omar looked at the clock on the wall. It said fifteen minutes to twelve. They would dock on the hour. Not much time. Where was that girl? Why didn't she come out?

As if in answer to his question, he saw the door open and heard her voice.

"Thanks so much, Captain, and you, too, Mrs. Gandy, not just for tonight but for all the trips we've made together on this old ship. I'll send you some pictures... enough for the grandchildren, too. Lots of luck to both of you!"

"Well, just because Cap's retiring, don't be a stranger, Andy. It isn't the end of us, you know. Come see us sometime when you're over this side of the river." It was the voice of the elderly lady.

"I sure will. Still in the big white house on the beach?"

"Oh, my, yes! Too old to move! We wouldn't know where else to go."

"I'll be dropping by one day real soon. Good-bye, now."

"Good-bye, Andy," the captain and his wife replied.

The captain's wife shut the door of the pilothouse. The deck was dark where the girl stood. Omar watched her, then pulled his knife from his sleeve. He looked at it, undecided. What if she should cry out? He put the knife back in its sheath. It wouldn't be necessary now that he knew the open sea lay just beyond the lifeboat. One good shove and over she'd go, weighed down by all that stuff she was carrying. A burial at sea! He grinned with enthusiasm. What a romantic, wonderful sound that phrase has, he thought—a burial at sea! Food for all the little fishes, and such tender meat it would be.

He heard her shoes scrape on the wet metal of the deck. He crouched low behind as her footsteps came toward him. He watched as she hesitated to adjust the heavy strap of the camera over her shoulder. She put a notebook into her handbag and then looked around for a light as she tried to see her watch.

She moved forward into the doorway, her back to him, and raised her arm toward the glow from the lamp. He knew it was his only chance. Noiselessly, he sprang from behind and dealt a stunning blow to the back of her head, just below the ear. She never turned or made a sound of pain as the slick soles of her sandals slid out from under her. He stared for just a second as she rolled under the lifeboat. The loud blast of the whistle signaled that they were coming into the dock.

Omar turned and raced frantically for his car. His heart was pounding in his ears. He pulled his cap low over his forehead, sprinted down the steps, and slipped into the Pontiac. His hand trembled with a combination of fear and relief as the boat's engine ground into action and the gangway clanked into place. He had to wait until the first line of cars unloaded; then it was his turn. He drove off the ship and careened onto a dark road. Laughing excitedly for no reason, he felt the need to urinate, suddenly, desperately. Angry at himself, he pulled far into the woods and relieved himself. His hands shook, and he fumbled with his zipper. He climbed back into the car and drove on, no longer laughing.

Back on the boat, a black man was shaking Paul by the shoulder. Paul awoke slowly and looked around in surprise. They were still on the ship. He looked at the man questioningly.

"What's the matter? What do you want?" he asked, stretching his cramped shoulders.

"All the cars have to leave, mister. You the last one on. Everybody else done long gone. This is the last trip t'night and you got to get this car off of here."

The ship sat high in the water, empty of all the cars and trucks that had been on deck before. Only the Datsun was left, and Paul could see just one lone attendant left at the gangway, waiting to see him off. Paul looked about anxiously. Could Andrea have been mad enough to leave him and take a ride with some friend she had chanced to see on board? He looked at the ignition, but the keys were gone. He recalled her putting them in her bag when she got out of the car.

"What's the matter, you drunk or sumpin'?" asked the black man. "I'd be glad to take you in my car, but we got to see all the cars is off this ship before we close her up for the night."

"Hell, no, I'm not drunk. I came with a lady, and she has the keys. She went up to see the captain thirty, maybe forty minutes ago. I went to sleep."

"Captain and his missus is gone. They been gone about ten minutes. Ain't *nobody* left on this ship except you and me, and Mr. Corbin. That him foamin' at the mouth down there, wantin' to go home. He got a young wife," explained the man.

Paul was wide awake and beginning to seethe. What kind of game was she playing—hide-and-seek? He felt angry but at the same time apprehensive. He jumped from the car and looked around, hoping that Andrea would appear.

"You look around down here. I'm going topside and see if she's still there, maybe sick or something. I don't know what's wrong."

Paul strode down the length of the lower deck, looking in the corners near the steps to the boiler room. The man at the gangway gave him a look of undisguised irritation as he passed by on the way to the steps at the far end. He went up two at a time, his long legs taking them easily, and paused at the top to peer down the long, empty passage. Nothing moved except the creaking lifeboat, swaying against the ropes. He glanced into the waiting room. The restroom doors hung ajar, disclosing two ancient porcelain toilets and minuscule sinks. He searched the pilothouses and found a film wrapper. He threw it down. It might not even have belonged to her. There was nothing else inside.

He crossed to the far rail. The scene was identical—the ropes, the fire extinguishers on the wall, the second lifeboat swinging. And there, on the deck, a handbag! The edge of her green notebook protruded from the top.

A pen rolled out of the handbag under the lifeboat. Paul stooped to pick it up, and saw Andrea hanging over the side.

"Oh, my God! Andrea! Andrea."

The strap of her camera had caught on a weight anchoring the lifeboat in place. From that slender piece of leather she hung like a battered doll, her body rolling with each list of the ship. He crawled under the lifeboat and grabbed her under the arms. Locking his feet around the weights, he drew her up onto his knees, then carefully dragged her backward onto the deck until she was lying beside him.

He sat up, still holding her tightly.

"Up here!" he shouted as loud as he could. "I need help!"

The two men raced up the steps, spurred by the urgency in Paul's voice. They stopped abruptly when they saw the figure of the girl lying on the deck. Then they moved closer. The black man stared down in surprise, his voice high with shock.

"It's Miss Andy Wayne. She and the captain is big friends! Is she dead, mister?"

"I don't know. No, no, she's not dead. She has a pulse. But I've got to get her to a hospital right away. Where is the nearest hospital?"

"Oh, law, there ain't no hospital for a long ways on this side of the river, but I can take you to a doctor. I know where he live," offered the black man.

"Listen, I got to get that car off," began the other man.

"For gosh sakes, Corbin, you worryin' about the ferry when Miss Andy Wayne is laying up here half daid? You're plumb crazy man. We gonna get that car off. I ain't worryin' about no car!"

Paul took the keys to the Datsun and threw them at Corbin in disgust.

"Here! Move the damn thing yourself." He turned to the other man. "Help me get her to your car."

"My name is George. George Watson," said the man, introducing himself as he lifted Andrea's feet. Paul supported her head and shoulders. Carefully, they negotiated the steps to the lower deck, crossed the gangway and entered the parking area at the edge of the dock. Paul held Andrea in his arms while George Watson opened the doors to a new station wagon. Paul got into the back seat and cradled her head in his lap.

He could feel her breathing. Her body felt warmer now than it had before, and it was losing some of its rigidness. He rubbed her hands and feet and noticed that her sandals had fallen off and were now probably somewhere on the bottom of the river. He shivered. If that strap hadn't caught and held, that's where she would be at this minute. *If she had died on the ferry, I would be under investigation,* he thought ironically. Then he admitted to himself that if she *had* died, he wouldn't care what happened. His life wouldn't be worth living that way. He reached down and kissed her.

She stirred and murmured something, but he couldn't tell what she said.

As they sped down the dark road, Paul tried to sort out what might have occurred on that deck. Did she slip? Damn it, she said the shoes were slick on the bottom! But how did she get under the lifeboat, the only place on deck that was not covered by the mesh railing?

The station wagon hurtled down the road. George seemed to know every bump and curve. After about two miles, he turned onto a dirt road. A colonial house appeared, set back in a grove of trees. Perfect setting for an old country doctor, thought Paul. But the man who answered George's frantic knocking was a young man with a lock of long hair over his forehead. He was probably still in his thirties. He wore large, dark-framed glasses.

"What's the matter, George? You run over somebody in your new car?"

"Now, Doc Evans, you know I'm a good driver. This poor lady had a bad fall on the ferry. She must of hit her head or sumpin'. She had a close call, and we didn't even know if she was breathin' there for a while."

"Bring her right on into my office," the doctor directed. He pointed to a beautifully furnished suite of rooms at the side of the house. Paul took Andrea in and put her gently on a long damask sofa. He propped her head with the extra pillows.

The doctor poured something onto a piece of cotton and held it under her nose. She gave a gasp as the ammonia fumes reached her sinuses and blinked awake.

She looked up dazedly at the doctor, who was holding her wrist. Immediately Paul took her other hand and rubbed it, reassuring her quietly. She turned toward him, trying to speak, but then her hand went to her throat and her eyes opened wide in pain and alarm. Tears poured down her cheeks as she tried to get up.

"Take it easy. Lie back, now," instructed the doctor, gently forcing her back on the pillows. "Let me take a look at that bruise on your neck. It seems to go all the way around to the back. There's a knot here, under one ear."

"She was caught by the strap on her camera. That's the dark circle. She may have hung by it—oh, maybe as long as ten minutes," explained Paul.

"Where were you? Are you her husband?" asked Dr. Evans.

"No, I'm a friend. It was late, you see, and I went along to drive home with her. I was asleep in the car on the lower deck when it happened."

"That's right, Dr. Evans. I woke him up when I seen this car wasn't making no move to leave the ferry. He went looking for Miss Wayne. She had the keys," added George.

"How did you fall? Were you pushed?" asked the doctor. He was looking at her injuries as if there were some doubt in their stories.

"Fall." She grasped her throat, painfully forcing the words out. "I... fall." She struggled to sit up again, pushing away the doctor's hands. She put her feet on the floor and sat, trying to get the room in focus.

"You're quite sure she was alone? That knot there looks like some kind of blow. A very dangerous, even fatal area if it had been a little higher." The doctor spoke to Paul, who nodded, understanding. He shook his head to the first question.

"There was no one up there when I got there. Even the captain had gone. All the cars had left. George, did you notice anybody leaving the upper deck?" asked Paul.

"Well, the truth is, I mostly stays near the front, so I don't see nobody using the back stairs. They could of been somebody... you know, the toilets is up there. Captain and Mrs. Gandy, they come down as soon as we docks. But they don't have to pass the lifeboat where Miss Andy was," explained George.

"I... go... home," announced Andrea shakily. She stood up, holding her hands out as if to balance herself. She pushed the doctor away and held her arms out to Paul for assistance. Her eyes pleaded with him. He held her tightly as she leaned into him, closing her eyes. He looked questioningly at Dr. Evans, who frowned.

"I think she'd better go to the hospital. I'll call ahead. She's got some abrasions on her elbow, and there's a scrape on the back of one leg. She needs X rays on that neck."

"No! Paul, I go... home!" she croaked. Her voice came with tremendous effort but with a determination that puzzled the three men. She held fiercely to Paul and looked up at him, tears flowing from her eyes. "You take... care of me."

"She doesn't want to go. That's that," apologized Paul.

"Well, there's no law to make her go, but it's the safe, the wise choice. If she insists on not going to the hospital, I won't be responsible for any complications later. She may have a concussion," argued the doctor. He looked angry.

Paul looked from one to the other, then decided to take a chance on Andrea. She seemed to be steadier now, coming around rapidly despite the ominous blue bruise beginning to color the entire area of her throat below her jawline.

"George, will you take us back to pick up Miss Wayne's car? I'll drive her home, and if she feels worse, I'll take her to the hospital in Middletowne." Andrea nodded in agreement. She squeezed his hand gratefully.

"You betta let me call my wife." George Watson laughed. "She ain' never gonna believe this story. She think I'm stoppin' off to see my girlfriend! Where that telephone at, Dr. Evans?" He followed the doctor into an office.

They could hear George speaking to someone in a loud voice. He ended the conversation with, "I see you in about fifteen minutes, baby. Wait up, now."

Dr. Evans wrote out a prescription for pain and put several capsules into a small white envelope with instructions to take them every two hours as needed.

"Pay... doctor," Andrea insisted, reaching for her bag. Dr. Evans raised his hand in protest, but she took some bills and pushed them onto the desk. He looked at them, then put two back in her bag.

"I'd rather bill you, Miss Wayne. You should check back with me tomorrow or the next day. At least go to your own doctor. You can never be sure in cases like this. An unexpected fall can have complications, especially if untended," he advised.

Paul helped Andrea out to the station wagon, and George roared off once more into the night. They found the Datsun, looking very small and alone, on the pier. Andrea shivered at the sight of the ferry and turned away.

Paul offered to pay George Watson for all he had done, but George raised his hand in protest. "Go along with you, man! I don' want your money. I tell you what, you want to pay me? Then, you help somebody else when you get the chance. That's the onliest way we gonna ever be brothers, right?"

Paul stood speechless as George Watson took off down the road in his new station wagon. You never know when the truth is going to hit you, thought Paul.

Getting into the car, Andrea turned to him with surprise and touched her throat carefully. Her eyes were round with wonder. Realization had finally come. "I'm alive... It was so dark." Fear made her voice ragged, frightened.

"Yes, darling, you're alive. We're both alive. I... love you, Andrea."

He kissed the tears, tasting dirt and salt on her face. He kissed her hands, covered with grime and the metallic smell of the deck. What had happened on that upper deck while he slept? Had she fallen in the rain? How?

Andrea lay back in his arms, and his words drifted over her like a warm summer rain—soft, healing. She relaxed against his shoulder, feeling his lips on her face. From a long way off, her memory dredged up their argument. Something silly. They had been arguing in the car. Then she had talked to the captain... It was raining. A bad pain suddenly. Then there was nothing, just the dark, dark, dark. He loves me. He said he loves me, and that's all that's important now. *I love him, too,* she thought, *but I'm so tired. I'll tell him later. He ought to know.*

Paul realized she had fallen asleep. Gently he propped her head against his arm and, holding her, drove carefully down the road, looking for any sign that would lead to a bridge. It was a long way, at least twenty miles, to the nearest bridge.

Finally they pulled up in front of the apartment on St. George Street. Paul carried Andrea up the stairs. Jade met them at the door but did not bark. She sniffed anxiously at Andrea's ankles, noting strange sea smells.

Paul undressed and washed her with warm soap and water. He avoided her throat. She felt his hands tenderly sponging her legs. He put her in bed. His voice came from a long way off, coaxing, insisting, as he raised her head from the pillow.

"Come on, take these pills. You'll need them."

Obediently, she opened her mouth and swallowed the pills. She was aware of Paul's eyes on her, on the lacy beige slip she wore. She wished vaguely that things were different. She sank back against the pillow again, her eyes drooping. "Paul, don't leave me," she murmured hoarsely.

He watched as she fell asleep, then turned out the lamp and lay down on the bed. Jade looked at him with curiosity and moved away to the kitchen, accepting him. Paul lay awake, holding Andrea's hand until exhaustion overcame him and he, too, slept.

During the night Andrea woke from a terrible dream. She sat up in bed, her eyes staring into the semi-darkness. The nightmare ran through her mind again, real and compelling in its horror. She was walking through an empty street in the rain, her feet not touching the pavement, kind of gliding along, trying to reach a streetlamp in the distance. If only she could reach that lamp… there was a big clock under it. But there was a shadow between her and the clock. It was faceless, menacing. Its arms, upraised, blocked the clock. *I'll never see the time, and I must see it or I'll die in this water.* The rain? *No, in the other water, down there, the abyss below.* Pain ricocheted up the back of her head. She was falling, swimming in the water. *I'll never see what time it is, ever.*

She began to cry silently. She touched Paul's back, reassuring herself of his presence, but the nightmare would not go away. The horror persisted until dawn. The outlines of her own furniture, her books, her pictures, comforted her in the pale glow. She lay close to Paul's back, her arm around his waist, and slept.

The door to the motel opened, and Kim cried out happily when Omar walked in. She had come there straight after work, wanting to see him, and when he didn't show up, the old man, Calvin, had let her into the room. Now she sat up in bed, her small, bare breast peeking over the top of the bedspread. She pouted unhappily.

"Where you been so long?"

"Business. Always I have business!" snapped Omar, angry at seeing her in his bed. He took out two twenty-dollar bills and the keys to the old Pontiac and tossed them on top of her white plastic purse, which lay on the dresser.

"Oh, thanks for the money! You're sweet, Johnee."

"Cut the sweet stuff. Twenty for you and twenty for Moody for the car," he said, reminding her of the deal.

"Sure, Johnee. I don't forget. You come to bed now?"

He didn't answer her, just went to the dresser and began to shove his few dirty belongings into the bag he carried on the back of his motorcycle. Realizing that he intended to leave, Kim threw herself at him. He gave her a rough shove back onto the bed.

"Oh, Johnee, it's too late tonight for you to go away. The room is paid for; what a shame to waste the money," she pleaded.

He turned to look at her, considering. She lay back and raised her knees. She watched him hopefully. She wriggled suggestively against the sheets. Omar felt tempted but turned back to the dresser. He could see her reflected in the mirror. Against his will, he began to undress, his clothes dropping off slowly.

"You'll be glad you stayed. You going to feel wonderful," she whispered. She sat up in bed and helped him unbuckle his belt. His pants dropped to the floor. His stomach was level with her mouth. Fleetingly, her tongue darted out and touched the inside of his navel. He groaned with surprise. Desire shot through his loins.

"In the morning I go!" he stated, hating to give in to her, yet unable to turn away.

He pushed the girl back on the bed and lay beside her. For a moment his thoughts returned to that other girl, the one he had pushed off the boat. She wouldn't bother Paul again, and Paul could now go about his work. Women were all a lot of trouble, only good for one thing. He turned to Kim and entered her abruptly.

CHAPTER TWELVE

Late in the morning Paul awoke to a knocking on Andrea's door and to Jade's barking. Snuggled close to his back, Andrea murmured painfully. Then she moved away and sat up in bed, as Paul went to answer the door.

"Oh… hi! I live down the hall." Matt looked at Paul with surprise.

"Come in, Matt," croaked Andrea.

After a moment's hesitation, Matt stepped into the room and looked at her in awe.

"Hey, what happened? This big lug beat you up?" he ventured, half smiling. He eyed Paul as if it might be a possibility. Matt approached the bed and stared.

"Don't try to talk, Andrea," said Paul. "I'll tell him what happened."

Matt sat on the edge of the bed as Paul told him about the accident, about how the camera strap had kept Andrea from falling into the river. As he talked, Matt grew pale and shook his head in disbelief. He clutched Andrea's hands tightly in his.

"You could have drowned, Andy! Wait until I tell George about this! Hey, what can I do to help? Let me get your groceries. I'll take the mutt over to our place. Tell me anything I can do," he begged earnestly. Andrea motioned to the Pekingese, who was already trying to climb into his lap.

"Could you keep her dog for a couple of days? That would help," said Paul. He had to get back to his own house and feed Wolf. He had completely forgotten him until now.

Matt tucked the dog under his arm and started to leave, then turned back suddenly. "I brought your mail, Andy," he murmured. He gestured almost apologetically at a long legal envelope on the top of the pile. "From Arizona. Probably you-know-who."

He glanced at Paul and looked back at Andrea.

"It's all right," she managed. "He knows about Patch."

"Well, I'll be over later if you need anything."

After Matt left, she opened the long envelope, noticing that it was from an attorney in Tucson. The words caught her by surprise. She began to feel confused and angry.

"I have been retained to act in the interest of my client, G. Patchen Wayne, to contest the divorce action against him, instigated by you on the fifth day..."

She handed it to Paul, indicating that he should read it. He did so silently.

"The bastard is going to fight the divorce. Where does that put us? He can't keep you, Andrea. What the hell is his game?" Paul crumpled the letter and threw it across the room. He felt an antagonism amounting to hatred for this man he had never seen.

"Why? Why won't he give up?" whispered Andrea. She sank back into the pillows.

"Let me get your pills, something, before I go."

She smiled up at him, holding out her hand. He took it and gazed down at her. There was so much left unsaid between them—things that couldn't be said, now or ever.

CHAPTER THIRTEEN

"This is your partner in New York calling. I am in a telephone booth; speak loudly so I can hear you. The merchandise has been received, but it must be tested at the other factory. When do you want the shipment in Washington?"

"Ah, so it is you at last, Mr. Gay." Omar grinned, intrigued by the codelike conversation. He loved anything conspiratorial.

Omar had been back in Washington headquarters for two weeks, and so far he had heard nothing from Paul in Middletowne or Mr. Gay in New York. He was getting very anxious. The group was anxious, too, afraid that Omar was spending too much time perfecting details that would slow down the operation should the king decide to come earlier. They had already decided among themselves that Meda, wife of one of the ambassador's aides, would do the job, sacrificing herself, if Omar's plan fell through at the last minute. She was rather hoping that she would get the chance and made frequent remarks on how slowly the plan was going. The others hoped Omar's plan would work, knowing that Meda would implicate them all if she were caught.

It was rumored now that the king's visit would be sometime in July.

Mr. Gay was speaking again, his silly talk, asking when to send the shipment. The sooner the better, figured Omar. They could take the gun down this weekend. That little development should shut up some of the members so anxious to get underway. The killer would have the weapon. What else did they have to worry about now?

"Deliver it the end of this week."

"You will have the five thousand dollars then?" the old man asked eagerly.

"Of course. You think we play games on you, old man? You bring this thing and you get the money just as we say in the beginning."

"Must I come with you while it's being tested? I swear it is perfect!"

Omar sneered. He knew how much Mr. Gay hated those trips to Middletowne, and his fear made Omar enjoy his discomfort even more. Besides, he wanted Mr. Gay with him.

"Of course you must go, you fool! How will Paul—how will we know whether it works until he has tried it out? When all is hokey-dokey, your job will be over. You get the money and we will never see each other again." Omar smiled with secret knowledge. *I will never see you again, old man.*

"Very well. I'll be in Washington with the merchandise on Friday night. You're sure of the money, all of it?"

Mr. Gay had a dealer holding a certain stamp from a stolen collection for him. The dealer was anxious to get rid of it. If Mr. Gay didn't come up with some money, the dealer was going to send the stamp out of the country and Mr. Gay would lose his only chance of ever owning it. Just thinking of that made the sweat bead up under the spirit gum that held his false mustache in place.

Hastily saying good-bye, he hurried from the telephone booth to ask the dealer to wait just a few more days. People smiled and stared at him as he passed them in the street. His mustache was drooping down one cheek. Unaware, the old man entered his dingy store.

He clicked the padlocks into place. Making sure no one was looking through the window, he hustled upstairs to his living quarters. He took down one of the books that held his stamp collection and gazed at the special place he had prepared for that certain bit of pinkish-purple paper so dear to his heart. For a long time he stared at the spot.

All the evenings he had spent working on the weapon to kill some unknown monarch half a world away would be worth it when that spot was filled at last. What did he care what they did with the gun after he finished with it? Nothing. It lost all meaning for him once it left his shop and reached the hands of the killer.

He glanced over in the corner of the room where the box stood, holding the lethal camera and its tripod. "Photo equipment. Handle with care," it said on the outside. Handle with care.

From his pocket he took a well-used pipe and a package of tobacco. The cloth bag containing the tobacco was one of the old kind, with little drawstrings on the top. His fingers reached down into the aromatic brown leaves and felt around until they closed on the hard objects hidden within. Bullets, thirteen of them. For some reason he always made thirteen, that unlucky number, and so far they had been lucky for him. The heads felt grainy where he had hollowed them out and inserted a little mercury fulminate. It was a neat little touch he depended on, for the police had never found one of his bullets. They entered the body and exploded; they never came out the other side.

What a mess it must make inside, Mr. Gay thought uncomfortably. He really hated the end result of his work, but it was highly lucrative, and at his age what else could he do?

Often he tried to justify his profession to himself. Think of all the people killed in wars, pestilence, floods, and, oh, the auto accidents. Now, there was a killer! But deep inside he lived with a guilt that gnawed his guts day in and day out. He had known, many years ago, what it was to be merely a statistic himself, a nonentity barely kept alive at the whim of his persecutors. Because of that, he had developed a callous attitude toward living. He had survived the prime persecution of this century, but he often wondered if he wouldn't rather have died.

He sighed deeply and looked around the empty place he called home. He reached again for his stamp books and pored over them with intense concentration, trying to forget many things. There were neat little squares arranged in neat little rows, clean and orderly—the complete antithesis of his personality and the place in which he lived. He cut his fingers on the sharp edges of the plastic holder. With a terrible reality, he looked again at the stamps and saw nothing but colored bits of paper encased in cheap plastic. Suddenly he felt empty. His fingers trembling, he shut the books tightly and put them back on the shelf.

He went to the chest and got out his flannel pajamas, a soft shirt, socks, and underwear and placed them in an old canvas bag, all ready for tomorrow, when he would take the first train in the morning to Washington. Hopefully, this would be the last time he had to go.

Back at group headquarters, Omar was calling Paul in Middletowne to arrange delivery of the gun. Perhaps they could test it on Saturday. Omar always liked to go there on the weekends, when the town was full of tourists, when two more faces would go unnoticed among the transients who filled the streets. It felt so much safer then. Even his own dark features and the pitifully inept disguises of Mr. Gay blended in with the others. Middletowne had been an ideal place to conduct business; it was a town of make-believe, beards and costume, where the quaint, the unusual, had become the commonplace. Murder there would come as an unwelcome jolt of twentieth-century violence.

As Omar informed Paul that they would be arriving on the weekend, Paul seethed inwardly but agreed that they should bring the weapon as soon as they could. When he had hung up the telephone, he reluctantly dialed the number of Andrea's office.

"What's Happening Here, may I help you?"

"Mrs. Wayne, please."

He could hear the usual mad din of the press room. Then a slightly husky voice came over the line.

"Andy Wayne here."

"Paul Hunter here," he mimicked playfully. "I hate to change our plans for Sunday, but something unexpected has come up. We won't be able to make it to the beach," he explained.

"Oh... I'm sorry. Jade was looking forward to another round with Wolf."

"Yeah, well, I can tell you Wolf will be disappointed, too. But, ah... my brother is coming down for a visit, and I'll have to... you know, show him around."

"Why can't he go with us? There's a girl here in the office, Bernadette, and we could make it a foursome. How about it?" Andrea suggested.

"No, I don't think so. You see, he's married… kids. Besides, we'll have a lot of family stuff to talk over, and I wouldn't want to bore you. Do you understand?"

"Sure. Maybe we can get together sometime next week," she agreed, disappointed.

"Please don't be angry. I'd rather be with you, you know that. I'll call you Monday."

"I'm not angry. I understand, really. Good-bye, Paul." She hung up quickly, not waiting to hear anything else. She slammed her notebook across the desk, scattering papers in every direction. Her weekend, which she had struggled to have off, was now shot to hell by some relative who came to see the sights of Quaintsville. Didn't Paul realize how she'd had to beg to be given those two lousy days? Probably not, she decided reluctantly. With a sigh, she picked up the fallen papers, stacked them neatly and strode into Jack Wise's office.

"Hi. Andrea the crestfallen reporting in. I know I asked for the weekend off, but now I find I'm free as a bird; so lay something on me—any old nasty, grueling assignment. I know you must have something particularly obnoxious, because Gage has been hiding from you all day."

Jack Wise laughed in undisguised admiration. "How perceptive you are. I'll rout him out in a few minutes and send him to the Ladies Quilting Society bash. They've got the ballroom at the Holiday Inn, and they're making this giant flag quilt. What I'd like you to cover is the motorcycle speed races on the dunes. Get the riders, some short inside story, the winner, of course. Get right into the whole motorcycle club scene."

"Right into the scene, huh? The way my luck has been going lately, I'll turn on one of Hell's Angels and his 'big mama' will beat up on me," said Andrea disconsolately. She had been back at work for only a week since her fall, and she was still wearing scarves to cover the bruises on her throat. She remembered nothing that had happened that night, but she still had nightmares.

"Would you like Gage to go along? You still look pale, Andy."

"No, I'll manage. When is all this wild fun due to begin out at the dunes?"

"The riders start arriving here on Friday. You might look around the motels and see where they're staying. You might get a prerace interview," suggested Jack.

"I know the routine," she agreed, sounding a little peevish.

Jack looked up at her quizzically, aware that she was feeling really down, and asked, "What happened to that big guy I've seen you around town with a couple of times recently? I thought maybe you were going to be with him this weekend."

"I was, but his brother is coming in."

"Brother? Probably some blonde from his shady past," he chortled. He was only kidding, but Andrea looked back at him unsmiling.

"You know, you may be right, Jack. I know nothing about him, nothing at all."

She turned from the desk, her head bowed in deep reflection, trying to remember anything Paul had told her. It seemed he had mentioned a brother once, vaguely. But what did she really know about him, even now that they were so close? Who was Paul? He seemed to constantly reach out to her, on the verge of revealing something about himself, but then he'd retreat, becoming silent, withholding something. What was it?

She went out to the parking lot and got into one of the Datsuns. Without much interest, she cruised the motel area and saw that a few early arrivals had checked in. Their gleaming bikes were locked with miles of colored plastic chain. She didn't stop. She went over to Buddy's Bar and had a couple of stingers instead. They did little to knock out the despondent feeling that had settled on her after Paul's telephone call.

Gage came in and insisted on buying her another stinger despite her protest. He began to tell her about having to interview the ladies at the Holiday Inn and somehow shifted to his favorite subject—his cold, cold wife. Andrea knew his routine well.

"Why don't you and I forget all this lousy business and drive down and spend the night at the beach. I got this feeling it would do both of us good."

She turned and looked at him solemnly, then got up from the bar.

"I'm leaving, Gage. You're beginning to make sense, and that's very dangerous for both of us. Tell you what you should do. Go home and breathe on your wife's neck the way you breathe on mine. You'll thaw her out in no time."

"Well, I may try it, but meanwhile, think about it, Andy. You and me."

"See you Monday, Gage. Have a good weekend."

"Yeah, sure. You too, Andy."

In New York, Mr. Gay made his train reservations and wondered how he was going to carry the big box marked "Photo Equipment" on board. For carry it he must. He dared not let it out of his sight. At home he practiced lifting it and his small bag. He groaned at his plight.

In Washington Omar was calling Moody's Bar and Grill, making his own plans for the trip. He managed to get Kim on the telephone and asked her to arrange for his old room—number eight—for Sunday night and also to see whether the old Pontiac would be available if he needed it. Moody was glad to rent it out. It was just an old wreck he had taken from some guy over in Hopewell in payment for a big bar bill. He let anybody that needed it borrow it for the day for ten bucks. Kim had told Omar it was twenty and kept the rest for herself, praying that he would never find out. That extra ten, along with the twenty he always gave her, made thirty for the fund to go back to Korea. She had almost saved enough. Soon she and her son would be able to leave.

In the three cities, many different people were making different plans, each touching the other in some way, yet unaware of the connection.

CHAPTER FOURTEEN

Paul heard a car stop across the street and suspected from its sound that it had to be one of those rejuvenated vehicles Omar somehow always managed to eke another hundred miles out of. He looked out the window, and his suspicions were confirmed.

The car, a light-colored Cadillac, perhaps at one time had been light green, beige, or even gray. It had huge whitewalls, almost oval in their softness. It probably got about five miles to the gallon, with an equal amount of oil. Omar gave the automobile an affectionate pat on the long hood as he rounded the front to come across to the house. Mr. Gay struggled to open his door; Omar finally went back and wrenched it loose with a grinding twist.

As Mr. Gay tottered down the walk carrying a canvas overnight bag, Omar, with the help of a screwdriver, unlocked the trunk and took out a large box. *Mr. Gay is really getting old,* Paul thought, as the old man neared the door. *He should take his cut and get out of this business.*

Paul opened the door for him to enter. "You look tired," he said. "How about a cup of tea?"

"Oh, my, that would be welcome. You would be surprised how fast he can drive an old car like that! It shook me to pieces." He removed for a moment the dark glasses he habitually wore, at least in Middletowne, and gazed into Paul's eyes, asking for sympathy. His eyes were brown and watery, with dark circles underneath. Without the glasses, his nose appeared to be more prominent. His brown synthetic mustache covered his small, drooping mouth. At last the real Mr. Gay was almost revealed to

Paul. As if sensing this, Mr. Gay shoved his glasses back on in a hurry and again sublimated his true personality.

"You brought the other camera this time, then?" asked Paul as he went into the kitchen and put the kettle on.

"Yes. Omar is bringing it in now," murmured Mr. Gay, settling wearily into a chair. He leaned his head back, and his wig was pushed down on his forehead. He looked like a pathetic clown.

Omar edged carefully through the door and placed the box on the floor. He took his knife from his boot and slit the tape across the top. He stared eagerly into the box, his face crinkling with pleasure, his white teeth flashing in a grin.

"Aieeee! Is beautiful! *Wahelo, zahelo!* You sure this one is gun, old man?"

"I'm sure," said Mr. Gay solemnly. "Take a look, Paul. It belongs to you now."

Paul lifted the camera and tripod from the box and handed it to Mr. Gay, who unscrewed the end of the adjusting handle and turned it over so that Paul could have a closer look. The forward end was a silencer; the short connecting piece, the barrel of the firing section.

"Of course, it is now immobile, welded into a solid part. Here is the chamber, with space for two bullets. That's all you said you would need. See, one is in place and the other will revolve upward as soon as the first is fired." Mr. Gay droned on, as if describing an air conditioner or some commonplace piece of household equipment. Paul marveled at the way he was able to look at the weapon dispassionately—one more piece of work well done and out of his life into the hands of a consumer. He noticed how Omar hung on Mr. Gay's every word. His dark, slim fingers reached out to caress each part as Mr. Gay described its function. He was thrilled, fascinated to be a part of such a wonderful thing. Finally, the old man grasped the tripod and looked into the sight. He turned to them, ready to prove the efficiency of the complex mechanism. His finger sought the shutter release, and an almost inaudible click sounded in the quiet room.

The three men sat silently, impressed. Paul swallowed carefully, his throat tight, and found to his surprise that his palms were covered with cold sweat. It had dawned on him that this was murder in a different form—cold, premeditated, unlike the others. The alley at Marrakesh and the field just outside of Adana in Turkey seemed long ago and drastically remote from this present situation. The men he had hunted and killed then had all been conspiring in one way or another against the lives and safety of the government or against the people of his own country. To him it had seemed justifiable, even patriotic. But this—this was murder, taking away the life of someone he knew very little about. And the reasoning that had inspired him to join Omar's plan of revenge now seemed much less important. As he sat there in the small living room, he noticed the other two men also lost in their personal thoughts, somehow mesmerized by the soft click of destruction.

Suddenly, outside in the backyard, Wolf barked and broke the silence.

Omar clapped his hands and laughed maniacally. "You have kill the lamp, old man!" he shrilled, jumping from his chair.

Mr. Gay lowered the camera and joined the laughter quietly.

The pot in the kitchen had begun to boil, and Paul left the room to fix tea. He looked through the window at Wolf, who was racing up and down near the fence. He then saw a cat sitting on top of a tool shed. It licked its paws, yawned in boredom and casually ignored the loud noise of the dog below. *Some survive by their wits,* Paul thought.

Mr. Gay came into the kitchen and gratefully accepted the cup of tea.

"Have you ever created a weapon like this one before?" Paul asked.

"No, never in a camera. This was a new challenge for me. But there have been others even more ingenious. I once made a gun inside of a wheelchair. It was a perfect vehicle for conversion, being as it was made of aluminum tubing. You can see the advantage? It had numerous controls on the sides. No one suspects a poor crippled fellow. It was used at a parade…" His voice dwindled uncertainly, and Paul guessed instantly that something had gone terribly wrong.

"Was it a clear hit?" asked Paul, aware that Mr. Gay suddenly looked very ill.

"The mark was hit, yes. He was riding in an open convertible. Just at the moment our client fired the second shot, however, a child—it was a little girl—ran forward with a bouquet of flowers for the man in the car. She was hit in the back."

The two men gazed at each other. After a moment Mr. Gay said softly, "I told you this story because it may tend to make you more cautious. There will be crowds where you are going. Be careful, careful of the little children."

Paul heard the warning and marveled at the strange inconsistencies that made up Mr. Gay's personality.

"You *know* that the guns you make are not toys. They are used to kill, and you are legally as much a part of the final act as if you did the job yourself," said Paul.

"All these years I have tried to stand aloof from that fact. I considered the guns… ah, special tools for special jobs. I was able to do this, you know, divorce myself from their real purpose until the day of which I just spoke. Perhaps God, if indeed there is one, wanted me to know exactly what it was that I was doing. I was there at that parade that day as a spectator, watching, enjoying the music. Then the shots rang out. First the man, then the child, fell before my eyes. I saw a nurse wheeling an old man away from the scene. It was *my* wheelchair. I *knew that chair*."

"And did they get away in the crowd?" asked Paul.

"Yes. No one, the police—no one—ever guessed what had really happened or where the shots had come from. Except me, and *them*, of course. I never saw *them* again."

"An incredible thing. The guns became real to you."

Until then they hadn't noticed Omar standing just beyond the kitchen door. He was listening with interest, but then the smoke of his cigar permeated the room. His shadow passed silently across the door, and within a few minutes the sound of the record player broke the silence. The familiar wail of Oum Khartoum filled the house with a sad, intense message, and Omar joined in with impassioned fervor. When they joined him in the living room, his eyes were closed. He was smiling. He had enjoyed Mr. Gay's story. He considered that job a huge success.

The camera stood menacingly on the coffee table. Resignedly, Mr. Gay pulled it toward him and, over the din of the music, began again to enumerate the various features and how they worked. Paul listened carefully. And for once Omar turned the volume down low and tried to follow the conversation. Omar would have to remember everything that was said, for if Paul were unable to complete the mission, he would have to give instructions to Meda, the stand-in. Omar had told Paul about Meda, but Paul had never met her. She had seen him, though—the one time he had come to group headquarters in Washington.

Mr. Gay took out the tobacco bag and pipe and passed them to Paul, who looked at the bullets and put most of them back in the bag. A few he put in his pocket.

"Have you found a secluded area where you can try this weapon? It's a bit heavier than the other but well balanced. I don't think you'll have any trouble."

"It does feel different, and here the neck strap is too high. I'm much taller than you. There, that's better. Still heavy and awkward, though."

Lengthening the strap, Paul thought about Andrea and tested its strength with his hand. It was surprisingly strong, and she was small. Andrea—he wondered what she was doing while he sat planning a murder. Blue smoke hung over the room, and the music seemed to drone on endlessly. Omar appeared to be asleep, and Mr. Gay sat, lost in thought. Paul felt suffocated. He crossed to the window and drew the drapes slightly apart to catch a breath of fresh air. When he was with Andrea, it always seemed brighter. When he was with these two, it seemed dark. He wondered if there were any truth to that theory about people creating auras?

For a minute he allowed himself to consider Andrea in his world. Would all that spark go out of her forever if he told her of his past? And could she love him enough to run away with him, away from this town, these people, and the things he had come here to do?

"You didn't answer," murmured Omar sleepily.

"What?" asked Paul. He turned back to the room.

A smile played about Omar's lips as he thought, *Paul's thinking about that dead girl.* He knew that Paul must have been very sorry when the girl didn't come back.

"Mr. Gay, he want to know where you can go to play 'boom-boom.' He want to find out if the gun hokey-dokey so he get his money," reminded Omar, laughing.

"Oh, yes. Well, there is a place, a rather isolated strip of beach at the edge of some dense woods. We can go in the late afternoon, just before the tide comes in. There will be enough light, and when we leave, the water will come up and cover the area to the woods, erasing our footsteps, as if we had never been there."

"That sounds very good," concurred Mr. Gay. "Will you need me?"

"I'm afraid so. Somebody has to stay in the car as a lookout. All you'll have to do is sit there. If anyone stops, pretend to blow the horn accidentally but loud enough for us to hear. Then drive away. Do you understand?" instructed Paul.

Carefully, he picked up the camera and placed it back in the box. It reminded him of a giant black-widow spider in hiding.

Meanwhile, down on the sandy dunes where the motorcycle races were taking place, Andrea tried to find a cool spot away from the blazing sun. The motorcycles raced by, throwing up sand everywhere. She could even feel it in her eyelashes. She wished that she hadn't volunteered for this job. She could have been sitting in a nice cool ballroom talking to sweet old ladies about their bicentennial flag if she had just kept her mouth shut. But then, probably not. Gage, smart boy, didn't do pictures. She wondered where Paul was. He and his brother were probably sitting in a cool bar somewhere, swapping family stories while they waited for dinner, perhaps sizzling steaks. Everybody was doing their thing. *And I must do mine,* she admitted to herself. Wearily, she threw the heavy pro bag over her shoulder and walked slowly back toward the sidelines.

She stayed until the races were over and then interviewed the winner, a thin, wiry guy of about nineteen who had no front teeth and seemed very proud of it.

"You're looking at my teeth, ain'tcha? I left them on a beach in Carolina when I's only fifteen years old. That's how long I been bikin'. Hey, take a picture of me with this trophy so I can give it to my mother."

Andrea snapped a few shots, and then he waltzed away with a girl on each arm.

It was nearly dusk when she found the Datsun and crawled in. She turned out to the road that led to the big new highway but then changed her mind and swung over to a less busy road. She wanted to think about the events of the day without having to worry about keeping up with traffic.

As she drove along, she realized that she was near the beach Paul had taken her to that day. She searched for the opening in the trees that led to the path through the woods.

With surprise, she noted that someone else knew about their spot, for there was an old Cadillac parked directly across the opening in the trees. It obscured the path. As she drew abreast of it, she noticed that the car was occupied by an old man who wore sun glasses and sat low in the seat on the passenger side. There was something odd about him, but she couldn't figure out what it was, because he turned his head away and pulled his hat down over his forehead.

She drove past and forgot the incident as she listened to the news and weather on the radio. Another hot day scheduled for tomorrow.

When she reached Middletowne, she picked up a pizza, then headed home. Jade met her at the door, making hungry sounds. Andrea stripped off her sandy clothes and put her feet into a pan of cool water. What a day! She then turned on the television.

The smiling face of the winner of the races appeared on the screen. "Congratulations," said Andrea, raising her tom collins. "I'll get the pix out to your mother tomorrow, maybe Monday. And skoal to you, too, Paul, wherever you are."

Jade came over and laid her jaw against Andrea's knee and looked up at her.

"You always know when I'm lonely, don't you, little friend?" Andrea took a pepperoni from the pizza and put it into the dog's mouth.

CHAPTER FIFTEEN

She squeezed her eyes shut tighter and waited, but the telephone next to her bed kept ringing.

"Andy?" said the familiar voice.

"Who else? Yes, it's me, but I'm asleep, Jack."

"Dance just called and said somebody drove into College Lake. You're closer to it than Gage, so get over there and see what's going on."

"Oh, my God, give me a minute to get my head on, will you?"

She sat up and looked through the blinds. It wasn't even dawn. "What time is it?" she stalled.

"Don't know exactly, maybe six, something like that. People don't pick their time to die, Andy. We work when the news happens."

"I'm going. If I don't check in, say, in an hour, send somebody up here to pick up the cycle film. If Fischer comes, tell him to lock the door when he leaves."

"You're a good kid, Andy. Now, jump to it."

"Remember that on payday—a little old bonus or something?"

There was a belligerent silence from the other end, but Jack Wise did not say no.

Andrea hung up the telephone and struggled out of bed to the bathroom, where she took a cold, fast shower. She dressed quickly, then went out to where the Datsun waited at the curb. It was still not quite light, and as she got into the driver's seat, she realized that the car was beginning to feel more like home than her apartment.

It was only about a mile to the wide creek that flowed inland from the river to form a lake behind the red brick buildings of the college. It was, in its way, deceptively treacherous water, looking serene on the surface, but dangerously deep below. Over the years, its waters had claimed a number of lives—those unaware of its depth and occasional erratic currents. And now College Lake had quietly received another victim.

As she neared the spot, Andrea could see the blinking red lights of the police cars by the side of the road. She edged the Datsun in behind them. Angrily, Colby Dance started to shout at her to move on into the line of cars that had slowed down to catch a glimpse of the scene. She flipped the press sign down just as he recognized the familiar car and hurried over.

"Hi, Andy. Didn't realize it was you. Where's that old ugly Gage this morning? This is an awful thing for a little lady like you to see. Sometimes they swell all up—"

"No lurid descriptions, Colby. I'll make up my own. Can I go down?"

"Sure, but stay clear. They'll be bringing the ambulance down as far as they can."

She got out and headed down the bank, stopping on the way to take a couple shots of the tire tracks that cut deeply into the grass to disappear ominously in the water. She noted that they had been made by a big, heavy vehicle, wide tires with very little tread. A very faint V was visible.

Andrea joined the police on the bank. Two men in wet suits were wading into the water. Beyond them, a large, oily circle lay widening on the surface of the lake.

"Good morning, Chief Ransome. What do you have so far?" she asked the large man in uniform, who was directing the operations.

"Good morning, Andy. The divers say there is one body in the car. They've taken equipment down to cut the door away. We'll have him out shortly."

"One body? Male or female?" She took notes as he spoke.

"Male."

"Local plates? Somebody we know, Ed?"

"I don't think so. The car has Maryland plates. We're checking them out. License number has been radioed to the Maryland police." He shook his head ruefully.

She looked up at him. "Something unusual about that?"

"Sorry, I can give you nothing more at this time, but you can stick around. They'll be bringing the body up shortly."

She moved among the small group of local police and asked more questions, trying to piece together the opening facts from several sources. It seemed that two college track men running across the bridge had spotted the tire marks and the oil spill and were able to discern a large, pale shape beneath the water. She got the names of the two boys, who were still there waiting on the bank, but they could add no more to the story.

One of the divers surfaced and threw a rope to a policeman on shore. Bubbles exploded in the oil as the door broke free and the air inside the car traveled upward. The policemen gathered together as the line became taut. Guided by the two divers, a large, unwieldy bundle, looking like old, wet rags, was carefully reeled in. It was the body of an old man.

Andrea reluctantly walked forward. In her job she had viewed many dead bodies, but death in any form had never become commonplace for her. Unlike some policemen to whom every dead body was automatically classified as a stiff, she still was able to see the person who had once lived and breathed, and something in her quietly mourned the passing.

As the reporters crowded forward, a patch of hair slid down the dead man's forehead. A sodden mustache covered his mouth. Two women watching from the bridge screamed and covered their eyes. The young rookie standing next to Andrea made a retching sound, turned quickly and ran to the edge of the woods, where he lost his breakfast.

"What the hell! What the hell! It's a damn hairpiece and a fake mustache," said Ed Ransome. A corpse in disguise. This drowning was turning into something not quite kosher, and already he disliked it. He visualized reams of reports clogging his desk, late hours at the station.

Flash equipment exploded as the gruesome sight was fixed on film.

"Could we have a shot with the hair in place, the way he might have worn it when alive? It may help to aid with identification," suggested Andrea. The chief nodded.

Because none of the police stepped forward to fix the hair, Andrea reached over and arranged the pieces. She stepped back and raised her camera, focusing on the face of the dead man. Through the sight, the features stared back in sharp focus. She gasped. Quickly, she snapped off several shots and turned to find Chief Ransome.

"Ed, I know you know something about that car down there. What make is it? Come on, now, Chief, I may have something to tell you that will help."

"Cadillac. Big old one. Maryland plates... from 1969," he admitted reluctantly.

"From 1969?" she repeated, not convinced.

"That's why it's taking a while to trace the owner. Deke and John are going through the man's pockets to find anything to identify him. It's my guess that he had the car stored somewhere and decided to take it out for one last ride. It was his last ride, all right. The brakes failed, or the steering went out on him."

"Ed, I don't think it happened that way. I think I saw *this* man in *this* car, parked on the side of the road, on the old highway yesterday. I noticed him because of the mustache. It looked just as weird when he was alive."

"Go take another look. I want a positive identification!"

Dutifully, she went over and looked again. The poor fellow lay there staring upward, somehow vulnerable. She bent over and closed his eyes. "No doubt in my mind. I saw this man yesterday."

"Where on the old highway?" demanded Chief Ransome.

"I'm really not sure, exactly," she hedged, "but I believe it was between Middletowne and the turnoff from the new highway."

"You mean to tell me that he has been driving a car with *those* plates in *my* town and nobody on *my* force picked him up? What has that traffic bunch been doing?" he demanded furiously.

Deke came up the hill waving empty hands. "Nothing on him but a dirty handkerchief, sixty dollars in cash, no wallet, no driver's license. Oh, yeah, a six-pack of Pepto-Bismol."

Chief Ransome and Deke walked back down the hill to where the body, now wrapped in plastic, was being fastened to a stretcher.

"This is a funny one. He don't seem to have regular fingerprints, just smooth ends like they were burned—scar tissue, no whorls," added Deke as the ambulance took the body away to the morgue.

The chief digested this last bit of information with a sigh. He had only four years until retirement, and over the years had had hardly more bother than parade crowds, lost tourists, the occasional drunk, small potatoes like that. Now he probably had a Mafia boss dropped in his lap—some archcriminal from the underworld. No fingerprints! False hair! *Oh, Lord, let him be a kindly old actor with a penchant for antique cars,* the chief intoned silently. He turned to Andrea, who was following him up the hill to the road.

"I want you to come up to the station and dictate to Virginia what you told me. What were you doing on the old highway?" he asked suddenly.

"Coming back from the races. I covered the cycle races at the dunes. I took the old road to avoid the traffic, and that's when I saw the car—a big white car —and him."

"Alone? Was the deceased alone in the car when you saw him?"

"What? Ah, I don't know. He was sitting on the right side, the passenger's side. There was no one else in the car, but there may have been a driver who stopped, to go… ah, you know?"

"Another person, a driver, who had gotten out to relieve himself in the woods. But did you actually see such a person? Don't get coy with me, Andrea."

"No, I did not see anyone else."

By this time they were standing next to the Datsun, and she turned to ask, "When is the wrecker going down for the car? I've got to check in with Jack."

"Probably be another half hour or so. Get over there and give Virginia your statement for the record. It eliminates the theory that he was a tourist passing through."

"All right, Chief. See you later"

She squeezed the Datsun out from behind the police car and the red-and-white press car that had her hemmed in. With a little metal scraping she managed to break free.

She pulled in at the bank to use its outdoor phone. She dialed Paul's number and waited impatiently as it rang several times. Finally he answered.

"Paul? Andrea. I've got to see you. Can I come over? Has your brother left?"

"My brother? Oh… yes, he's gone. Left last night."

"Well, it's important that I talk with you right away. Be there in five minutes." She hung up without waiting for a reply, then dialed her office.

"Jack, we've got a male Caucasian, about sixty-five. He's not local, so relax on that score. You won't have to pull an obit file on some old friend. The body was in a white Caddy with—get this now—1969 Maryland plates."

"Hey, there's an angle! Anything else?"

"Not at this moment, Jack."

"Well, stay on it. Mr. Fischer went up and got the film, and your dog almost ate him up. And, Andy, we got a problem on that film."

"Can't imagine what the beef is, Jack. I got those bike jockeys coming and going, and I've still got the sand in my teeth to prove it."

"It's the faces, sweetheart. People like to see faces. Goggles we got; helmets we got. Our readers want to see *people,* Andy, not robots. Now, get back to the drowning!"

She hung up and slammed her fist angrily against the side of the booth. She was tired and hungry and overworked. There wasn't even time for a cup of coffee. She had to see Paul now.

She jumped into the car and sped off across town. She had never been to his house before but had driven past it many times since the night they met. She wondered what it was like inside. Did he read? What did he read? As she thought of him, a silly feeling came over her, and she couldn't shake it off. *I've got a crush on Paul,* she admitted to herself, *a genuine stupid kid crush. Look at me, pant, pant, pant. I'll be inside his house, all alone with him. Can I handle it? Him? Me?*

Wolf was prancing near the fence when she parked. She went over and let him out of the backyard. He greeted her joyously, associating her with his true love, Jade.

Paul opened the door and smiled at them quizzically. "You know you're ruining my dog. He's trained as an attack dog, but he's so fond of you he's turning into an old softie." He was joking, but he looked concerned.

"He's a darling dog. I think I'll take him home with me and put that Peke's nose out of joint. Come on, boy." She motioned him into the house. Wolf waited.

"He doesn't come into the house," said Paul.

"Oh, make an exception. He can be our chaperone."

"Chaperone? What an old-fashioned word for a chick like you. Come," he said to Wolf, who had been waiting for Paul's approval.

The dog entered the living room, uneasy yet curious. He cast a beckoning glance over his shoulder to see if Andrea was following. She smiled to reassure him.

Andrea sat down in the easy chair near the window and immediately frowned as she looked at the ashtray on the coffee table. "Cigars, Paul?"

"Oh, no. They belonged to my brother," he answered hastily.

"Oh." *Thank goodness,* she thought. *They don't seem part of Paul's character, but what do I really know about him, anyway? He could have any kind of habit, much worse than an occasional disgusting cigar. What do I know about him? Only that I love him.* She looked away from his inquiring glance and reached to pet the dog.

"What did you want to see me about, Andrea?" he asked.

"Well, it may have absolutely nothing to do with us at all. In fact, I'm sure it doesn't. You remember the beach where we had our picnic, where we were going again before your brother called? Yesterday, I passed there and saw an old white car with a man in it." She hesitated as he started forward, as if shocked. "This morning the same old man was found drowned in College

Lake. It was sometime before dawn. He could have been there all night."

She stared at Paul curiously. His face was ashen, and his hand gripped the sides of the chair until his knuckles were white. He started to get up. "What's the matter, Paul. Are you ill?"

He sank back in the chair, trying to recover his composure.

"As a matter of fact, my stomach is a little queasy. It could have been the eggs I had for breakfast, maybe the butter." He tried to relax.

"That little path to the beach—it's so hidden. Not too many people would know about it. I wondered whether you had mentioned it to anybody you've talked to lately. Someone who would have been there with that poor old man?"

"Of course not. Do you think I'd tell anybody about a place that I consider our own private hideaway? Of course not," he repeated, trying to smile convincingly. She noted something strange about his voice but dismissed it.

"Well, I really didn't think you had, but now that I know for sure, there is no reason for anyone to know our connection with that place. This is a small town, and I'm legally still married to Patch. There would be some nice morsels for some gossips if they knew we had gone down to the beach together."

He looked at her solemnly. "You can depend on me, Andrea. I'll never mention being anywhere near that beach with you. Satisfied?"

"Good. It would only complicate things. Thanks, Paul. Now I have to get back to work."

She stood up to leave and noticed some pastry on the dining-room table.

"That's baklava, isn't it?" she asked. Her stomach growled.

"My brother brought it. He loves sweets. Would you like to have it?"

Paul wrapped the dripping pastry up in waxed paper and handed it to Andrea.

"I hope this isn't what made you sick!" she teased.

"Oh, no, no." For a moment his jaw was clenched.

"I'm only kidding. Thank you very much. I must go now."

As she started for the door, he came up behind her and put his arms around her waist.

"I'm sorry I couldn't see you yesterday. Can we make it tonight instead?"

"Yes, but would it be all right if we stayed in at my place? I'll be on assignment most of the day. You'll have to take potluck for supper. I haven't been to the store lately."

"Don't worry about it. I'll come over at seven and bring dinner with me."

"That sounds wonderful. See you tonight, then."

As he watched her hurry down the walk to the car, he let out his breath. It had been hard to keep his composure when she mentioned seeing Mr. Gay in the Cadillac, harder when he heard that the old man was dead, drowned in the lake. Where was Omar? He should have asked Andrea if there was more than one body, but he was afraid she'd get suspicious if he asked too many questions or took too much interest in the drowning of a stranger. He could get more facts later from the news on television.

Reluctantly, he dialed Washington. A woman answered the phone.

"Let me speak to Omar. This is Middletowne, and it's urgent," he said quietly.

"Oh. Is that Paul? How are you, Paul?" she asked. He knew it must be Meda, wife of the embassy aide. Omar had once described her to Paul as a bitch. He neither liked nor trusted the woman, so Paul proceeded cautiously.

"Would you please put Omar on? If he's not there, where can I reach him?"

"Omar is supposed to be with you. He's certainly not here. What has gone wrong?"

Without answering, Paul slammed down the phone. His head was pounding with unanswered questions. Where in hell was Omar? How did Mr. Gay get into the lake? His thoughts raced back to the events of yesterday. What if Andrea had decided to come down to the beach while he was test-firing the gun? Would Omar have felt the need to kill her to keep her from talking? Immediately, another thought entered his mind, one that had hovered in the background ever since he heard of the old man's death. Did Omar kill Mr. Gay? If so, why?

Paul turned on the radio to get the local news. Reports were still sketchy; the body was still unidentified. The police had raised a 1955 Cadillac sedan from the lake. There was no mention of another body, either in the car or in the lake. If Omar had not drowned and was not in Washington, where was he?

CHAPTER SIXTEEN

The shades of room number eight were tightly closed against the daylight. The dark figure on the bed lay facedown, snoring peacefully on top of the spread. His muddy boots dangled over the foot of the bed.

It had been a long night for him and a very long walk across town. When he left the lake, he had had to run barefoot through the grass to the road so as to leave no footprints. He then had to sneak through the night streets, dodging behind trees and fences, as security cars prowled the town. When he got to the highway, he put his boots on and trudged past the used-car lots to the motel. The No Vacancy sign had been turned on and Calvin was asleep when he slipped past the office and let himself into the end cabin.

Toward evening he awoke feeling very hungry and called Moody's Bar and Grill. "Hallo! I will speak with Kim!" he demanded.

"This is Kim. This is Johnee?"

"Bring me some food. I got the bad headache, and I don't come out to eat all day. Now I am ready to eat. No cheeseburger—make me real food!"

"Listen, Moody don't have no take-out on food, just the beer," she said, biting her fingernails. She didn't like to say no to Johnee. He got very mad when anybody said no.

A string of Arabic curses rent the air, and she cowered, even at that distance.

"I'll bring you something. It'll be good, Johnee. I get off from work at nine o'clock."

Omar scowled into the telephone. His stomach was empty now, and it was only seven. Two hours until she got here with some decent food! But what else could he do? He knew he would have to stay under cover for a while.

"Hokey-dokey. You come, but no cheeseburger."

He pushed the telephone down like an angry little boy and looked around the room. He was sorry he had left the last piece of baklava at Paul's.

His glance drifted to the dresser, and his eyes lit up when he saw the strange object Kim had brought with her the last time she had visited. It was a large reddish-orange chicken with shiny black eyes. It was constructed of very heavy paper and shellacked to a high gloss. Kim had called it a *piñata*, a Mexican child's toy for parties. She had bought it for her son's birthday and left it here so that it would be a real surprise for him when the day came. He recalled something else she had said about it. The toy was filled with candy. Filled with candy! Omar eyed it hungrily and picked it up, looking for an opening. Not finding one, he began to dig into the underside of the paper with his fingernail. Pretty soon he had made a jagged opening about two inches wide. Bits of colored cellophane clung to his fingernail. He reached in and triumphantly brought forth a piece of candy. Several more rolled into his waiting hand. He laughed delightedly like a small child.

He lay down on his bed with the candy beside him and switched on the television set, becoming absorbed in a musical that was playing. He especially liked to watch the girls dancing, dancing with nothing on their legs, sometimes catching a glimpse of a white breast that stirred him.

When the news came on, he got up to change the channel, but then he saw the car and heard the words: "A 1955 Cadillac with the body of Arnold Geistein trapped inside was recovered this morning from College Lake. Geistein was a Jewish immigrant who came to this country after World War II. In 1949 he was thought to have perished in a fire that totally destroyed the rooming house in which he was living at the time. Geistein's body was identified not by fingerprints, but by the numbers tattooed on his inner wrist, put there when he was confined in a concentration camp. The whereabouts of Geistein for more than twenty-six years following the war will remain a secret, taken with him to his watery grave, unless perhaps one of you viewers will recognize his face." The cold fish eyes of Mr. Gay stared from the screen, seeming to bore into Omar.

He quickly flipped the channel and breathed a sigh of relief as music blared forth and a comedienne began to sing a silly song. The face of Mr. Gay stayed with him, however, reminding him of something he had forgotten to do, something very important.

Omar turned away from the screen. What was it? Then it came to him in a rush. Of course, the money! He still had the five thousand dollars, Mr. Gay's payment. Omar laughed silently and pulled the bills from his jacket. He gazed at them almost without interest. What he wanted now was food, women, and wheels. But in the future, ah, there he had plans that would take much money. He wanted someday to return to his village and laugh at all those who had said he would never amount to anything. Those old fools in his village respected money, because none of them had ever had any, not even the mayor. Money would bring him admiration and respect. A clean young girl no man had ever touched before would be offered him as a wife.

At the thought of such a wonderful future, Omar pulled the rest of the candy from the *piñata,* and, rolling the bills like cigarettes, he managed to stuff most of the money inside. He then dampened some of the sticky candy wrappers, wadded them together, and plugged up the opening. The toy looked untouched. The job done, he sighed happily, put the chicken back on the dresser and turned his full attention to the television.

On the screen a dark-skinned girl was dancing, waving a long silver scarf suggestively between her legs. Omar edged closer to the set, and watched avidly as the girl threw herself backward in a spasmodic finish. The camera came in close. Her lips glistened, and her breasts quivered against the silver cloth. Omar gave a groan of admiration. He wished he could meet that girl.

There was a light knock on the door.

"Open the door, Johnee. I brought your supper," said a voice softly.

He opened the door, and Kim stood outside holding a large tray covered with paper napkins. She smiled at him, a timid smile, unsure of her welcome. She was pale. Her bowed legs arched beneath her short white uniform. For a moment Omar compared the girl in the doorway with the red-lipped girl in silver on the television screen. He had a feeling of somehow being cheated. He stood aside and let Kim into the room, where she put the tray on the bedside table and uncovered it for his appraisal. She had taken a lot of pains to make it nice.

Without comment, he began to wolf down the hot chicken and mashed potatoes. For dessert, there was half a peach with whipped cream and a single cherry, borrowed from the bar. She had brought coffee in a paper cup.

As he devoured the food, his eyes devoured another dancer on the screen. She had pale-gold hair and very white skin. She wore little white plastic boots and seemed to be marching directly toward him.

Kim stared at Omar and found herself becoming excited by the raw desire on his face, even though she knew it would never be for her, a look like that!

Omar finished the meal and turned to wipe his greasy hands on the bedspread. To his surprise, Kim had undressed and was waiting, nude. A small, sad smile quivered at the corners of her lips. She was not one of those blatant beauties that had just thrilled him on the screen, but he shrugged philosophically. They were so far away, on some stage in New York; Kim was here, and Kim was real.

"You pretty good kid, you know this?" he said generously. He rubbed his stomach and let out a belch. She looked away, pretending not to hear.

"Why you turn your head like this? In my country is good compliment to the cook, sometimes also make the... wind?" He laughed, happy at seeing the shock in her face.

"Not in my country," she murmured wistfully. She wished desperately to be away from this place, away from strange people, and someday soon she would go. In the meanwhile there was this man, so dark and somehow cruel in his way, but he never beat her, and she loved him a little bit. He filled up her loneliness.

She watched him undress. First he tossed his shirt on the floor. Then he kicked his pants under the bed. He stood in front of her in his undershorts, with his navy cap pushed down on his head. He was wearing muddy boots.

"Oh, please take off your boots," she implored as he climbed into bed. He only laughed.

CHAPTER SEVENTEEN

That afternoon, Paul listened to the radio reports of the drowning, and as he did, he became more and more amazed and puzzled by the contradictions of Mr. Gay. Paul thought of the gunmaker's warning—"Be careful of the little children." It seemed to Paul that for Mr. Gay the hope of the world resided in the very young, the still innocent, who didn't dream about Auschwitz or Dachau. Had the unspoken horror in his past produced this philosophy?

Nervously, Paul paced his living room, going over the events of the afternoon they had spent together. What a fool he had been to take Mr. Gay and Omar to the beach, but it was the only truly isolated place he knew, and it had been necessary to take the old man along to act as a lookout. Andrea must have been going at a normal speed when she saw him, because if she had looked the least bit suspicious, Mr. Gay would surely have mentioned it. They were able to fire the camera gun, and it had worked perfectly. Omar had become frantic with joy as he watched the bullets enter the targets time after time.

Late in the afternoon they had picked up the casings and dragged driftwood over their footprints as an additional caution. It wasn't necessary, because the tide came in while they were there, washing all the way up to the edge of the trees, covering the sand. There wasn't a trace of their having been there. After that, they had walked single file up the path to where Mr. Gay waited in the car. He hadn't said anything about seeing anyone slow down or look at him while they were gone.

That damned car! Paul hadn't even noticed the out-of-date plates. They all could have been picked up that day, with the gun! Omar was crazy, crazy, to have used a car as easily recognizable as that, and illegal plates as well.

The news report explained the car. It had been stolen from a private garage in Chevy Chase. The owner had bought it as an antique, a classic, and was going to restore it in his spare time. He had had it towed to the garage because he thought it was inoperable and was astounded when the police informed him that it was in a lake nearly two hundred miles away. How had Omar driven it all the way from Chevy Chase to Middletowne? He must have known that it was in bad shape when he stole it. And what had happened to Omar when whatever it was went wrong?

But there was another piece of the puzzle, and it was most baffling of all to Paul. In order for the car to have gone into College Lake, Omar had to be driving south out of town instead of north to Washington, where he was presumed to be heading when he left that night.

Something had become clear to Paul, however. The assassination plot would have to be abandoned as too risky. Andrea had seen Mr. Gay and if Mr. Gay and Paul were linked by someone else who had seen the car the short time it was parked across from the house, it would be too hot to handle. Andrea had already indirectly connected him with the car, and she was certainly no dummy. Her business was to ask questions and dig for answers. The old man's death had changed everything.

There was no one in the group in Washington that Paul trusted well enough to tell of his decision. First he had to find Omar, if he was still alive, get some answers and convince him that it would now be foolish to continue with the mission. He would not be forced to mention Andrea's seeing the car. He would point out that since Mr. Gay's picture had appeared on television, someone out of the old man's past might recognize him. That person might tell the police that Mr. Gay was a gunsmith, at the service of professional political assassins. That would surely be enough to start an FBI investigation in Middletowne to find out why Arnold Geistein drowned in the lake. On that score, there was only one thing going for

Omar and Paul. If Arnold Geistein were involved in a caper in Middletowne, his partners would not be likely to dump him in the same town. Investigators would try to find ties to him in bigger cities like Detroit, Chicago, and, yes, New York and D.C.

Paul thought of the camera and the pouch of exploding bullets now hidden in the roof of Wolf's dog house. Even though it was a beautiful weapon, Paul sensed that day on the beach that he would never actually use it. He knew that, for himself, involvement in the scheme was over. He had resolved to tell Omar he was getting out when they returned to the house that day but Omar and the old man drove off immediately. Omar had been acting strangely, as if he were on a high. The old man had simply looked tired and resigned.

About six o'clock Paul fed Wolf, made sure he was secure on his chain and walked downtown to the delicatessen about two blocks from Andrea's apartment. As he selected corned beef, sausage, sweet-and-sour pickles, cheese, wine, and a heavy loaf of black bread, he thought of Mr. Gay, and the face that looked across the counter at him looked like Mr. Gay. The man was sallow, slightly chubby, with a mustache.

"That will be nine sixty-five with the tax." Even his voice had the same accent.

As Paul hesitated, the man shrugged his shoulders and said, "So the corned beef is up again this week? You should see what *I* haf to pay wholesale! These prices, I agree is a crime, but what can I do? It's my business!"

"It's quite all right." Paul put ten dollars down on the counter, picked up the brown bag and hurried out.

He shivered in the warmth of the summer evening, still thinking of the old man. In the morgue, Mr. Gay's body lay cold and stiff in a long metal box, an identity tag fastened to his big toe, waiting for the next of kin who would never come. Paul wished he could go as a friend, claim the remains and give the old guy a decent burial. But, of course, that was impossible.

At the corner of St. George, he stopped and looked up at the window over the barbershop. He saw that the lights were on behind the pale drapes. Andrea was home. The panic and depression that had been with him all day lifted somewhat, and he hurried toward the steps that led up to the apartment.

Jade began to bark frantically even before he knocked, and Andrea met him at the door. The dog recognized him and jumped on his legs to be petted.

"Come in. Oh, it looks like you've been to the deli. I made iced tea, and there's dessert in the refrigerator." She had also managed to clean the apartment, take a bath and wash her hair, which hung in damp curls to her shoulders.

She was wearing a white dress, which showed off the tan she had acquired at the races. Paul's eyes never left her as she hurried about setting the table, pouring the iced tea into tall glasses and lighting two tall white tapers.

"You look very domestic tonight. I've never seen you in this role." He smiled.

"Don't let it fool you. Housekeeping is one of my virtues that comes and goes. Sometimes I cook, entertain, have furious bouts of cleaning, then an interesting assignment comes along and it all goes blooey! The next man I marry will definitely have to wash his own socks—" She stopped suddenly, and her eyes darted to the dresser, where another letter from Patch lay, as yet unopened. She hadn't had time to read it.

They sat down at the table and for a moment just looked at each other through the flicker of the candles. She smiled, and he reached across and held her hand tightly.

"This is nice. I think we should be together, you and I. You know how I feel about you. I tried to tell you that night after the accident on the ferry. I'm in love with you, Andrea."

"Oh, Paul, I... my feelings for you are..." She looked away and hesitated, her glance resting for a moment on Patch's letter. Confused, she turned to the food on the table and became very busy arranging it on their plates.

"Can't we talk later? The food will get cold, and, ah..."

"The food is supposed to be cold, Andrea."

"Well, of course, but the ice is melting. Oh, Paul, I'm not ready to talk about us."

"But we have to. It's very important," he insisted seriously.

She tasted the beef, gave the dog a piece of cheese under the table and carefully sipped her tea, avoiding his eyes.

Reluctantly, he began to eat. He poured the wine, drank one glass, then poured another. She lifted her glass as if to make a toast and saw that he had already finished his. She drank slowly, noticing that he had filled his glass for the third time. She thought about the dessert and went into the kitchen to take the pie from the refrigerator. He sat silently at the table.

"I hope you like Boston cream pie. It's terribly fattening, but it's delicious. So many calories. Look at the chocolate, how rich." She found herself babbling, saying anything to break the awkward, almost hostile silence in the room.

"Shut up!" he ordered abruptly.

"What?" She looked at him in disbelief.

"Stop that damn nonsense. Put the damn pie down and quit talking about it. Finish what you were going to say, about me, about you. I've got to know what you feel."

She frowned, held up her hands as if he were about to strike her and shook her head. *I can't tell him, I can't,* she thought. *The last time I loved somebody, he hurt me; it's left me afraid to openly commit myself to loving anybody that way again.* But she found herself unable to explain this to Paul. She buried her face in her hands.

He came around the table and drew her gently into his arms. She pressed her face into his chest and clung to him tightly. He forced her head back until she was looking into his eyes. She could feel the muscles in his arms, hard, unyielding like iron.

"Tell me. Tell me," he demanded.

"I've told you about Patch," she countered.

"I don't want to hear about Patch. I want to hear about me. Right now. Knowing whether you love me as much as I love you is the most important thing in my life. *I have to know!*" The instant those words were out of his mouth, Paul realized how true they really were. Andrea was the most important thing in his life. Nothing else mattered anymore, not himself or Mr. Gay or Omar with his group of fanatics or that potentate from Uddapha. Even Yasmina was finally laid to rest.

"I care for you very much, Paul. I guess... you've known that all along. I've tried to play it cool, stay uninvolved, but lately I find myself thinking of you constantly." She faltered and tried to pull away, but he held her tighter.

"That's not enough!" The words tore from him painfully.

"What do you want from me?" she whispered.

"Say it. Say it," he insisted.

The candles flickered in the breeze from the window, and down on the street they heard children laughing. They clung together in the dark, their bodies pressed so close together she could feel the perspiration from his shirt soaking into her dress. She pulled away and stood trembling.

"I love you, Paul."

He dropped to his knees and kissed her hands. She touched his head. Embarrassed to find him literally at her feet, she sank down beside him. "Why was it so important for you to know? Does it mean so much?"

"It means everything," he assured her. *It means I am changing my whole life,* he admitted to himself. He realized that, although the direction of his own future depended on Andrea, his decision to abandon the role of assassin had been made even before he had her answer. That decision had been further finalized by the death of Mr. Gay.

Paul suddenly felt almost free. Of course, he'd never be completely free. Omar's group would hunt him down. They would try to kill him.

"Penny for those deep thoughts," Andrea said. There was something strange and frightening about his face.

"Someday I hope I can tell you everything about myself, my past. It will shock you, and you probably won't like what you hear," he admitted.

"Are you married? What is it?" she demanded.

"No, I'm not married. Never have been. I wish it were that simple." He smiled wryly.

"Well, together we can handle anything else, can't we?" she asked innocently.

"I hope so, but, darling, I'm going to need a lot of trust—more than anyone ought to expect from another person. There are going to be lots of bad times ahead. Oh, God, why didn't I just go away and leave you out of—" His voice cracked with emotion.

Unnerved by the passion in his voice, she tried to change the subject, to break the mood that was causing him anguish that he couldn't express.

"Some dessert?"

"Save it for tomorrow. Andrea, let me stay with you tonight."

She embraced him, and for a long time they stood in the dark, just holding each other.

CHAPTER EIGHTEEN

The light from the television reflected on the two nude figures reclining on the bed. They were sharing a bowl of cherries between them, and their lips and fingers were stained red with juice. The man spit the seeds into his hand and handed them to the girl, who put them back in the bowl. The girl was watching the news.

"Oh, I could not do that for anything!" squealed Kim in horrified fascination.

"What you not do?" asked Omar in a bored voice. He was lying back against the pillows, half dozing, indifferent to the events of the day.

"That girl. I think she is a reporter. She closed the dead man's eyes. You know, the man who drowned in the lake."

Omar sat up quickly, just in time to catch a glimpse of the girl on the screen. She had turned away from the cameras and was walking toward a policeman, but even from the back Omar recognized the trim figure, the dark, curly hair. He gasped and clutched his stomach as if in physical pain.

"*L'ah! L'ah!* She is dead!" he burst forth.

"No, not the girl, Johnee. You all mixed up. The man, he's dead," explained Kim.

Omar covered his face and shook his head with disbelief. How could that girl still be alive? He had made sure that night that her body was sliding under the lifeboat. There had been absolutely nothing to stop it from falling into the sea. Yet there she was, alive! It had to be another girl. It *had* to be.

He lay back, chills of fear crawling over him. He had to know for sure whether she was alive or dead. Then an even more terrifying thought wracked his head. He sat up, shaking Kim's shoulder roughly. "That old man. You sure *he dead?*" he demanded, trembling with uncertainty.

"Oh, he's dead, all right. I told you she closed his eyes. Ugh!"

Kim shivered. As a tiny girl, she had seen many dead bodies in Korea, but somehow this one old man seemed more dead, maybe because all around him everyone else was so active, so busy, so alive.

She turned to Omar and kissed him tenderly. "We are going to live a long time and be very happy. Don't worry so much, Johnee."

He lay staring at the ceiling, a frown creasing his forehead. He couldn't understand how his plan backfired when he had gone through it so cleverly. That girl was meant to be dead! Why had she come back like some unwelcome ghost to torment him and to continue to draw Paul away from their important business in this place? The plan had been so simple when it began—just himself, Paul, and Mr. Gay. Now there was only Paul's part left. Mr. Gay had completed his assigned job, Paul would do his part, and the king would be dead. Then the happy ending—get rid of Paul. All the money would then belong to Omar. He would go home and live like a rich man forever. His head grew weary with so much thought, and his eyes felt heavy. He took a sleepy look at the dresser, where the reddish-orange chicken was reflected in the mirror. Its black eyes stared straight ahead, innocently concealing the small fortune stuffed in its paper craw—Mr. Gay's five thousand dollars, the seed money that Omar expected to bloom into a wealthy harvest.

For a while Kim lay beside Omar, listening to his moans of discontent as he tossed and turned in sleep. She wondered what it was that was causing him to worry so much. Then she quietly dressed and slipped out the door without disturbing him. No matter how late she stayed, she always liked to reach home before Micky woke up in the morning.

At dawn Omar roused himself and stood under the shower for a long time, trying unsuccessfully to wash away his troubles. He didn't even notice that Kim was gone. When he didn't need her, she never entered his mind. Her absence in the mornings seemed right to him.

He dressed and walked across the highway to Moody's for breakfast. He asked Moody if the car was available for the day. Laughing, Moody said if Omar could start it, he could rent it, and threw the keys across the counter.

Omar got into the car, and it started immediately. From inside the restaurant, Moody shook his head in wonder. The old wreck never started for him.

Omar drove carefully to Middletowne. He took a circuitous route so as to avoid the area where Paul lived. He wanted Paul to believe that he was back in Washington, and he had conceived a fairly believable alibi about his escape from the car. He was the hapless hero who had tried desperately to save the drowning man, but the water pulled him back toward shore. Oh, yes, it would be something wonderful to tell! Omar knew he had better not make it too good, though, or Paul wouldn't buy it for a minute.

Omar parked on a side street several blocks from his destination and got out. As he approached St. George Street, he wondered where he could wait unseen. He decided the best place would be the cheese shop. It faced her apartment house and would afford an excellent view should she come out and cross the street to go to her office.

He went inside the shop and began to browse around. After a few minutes a clerk began to hover about, then asked him what he wanted. He chose a box of brownies, paid her and left.

He crossed the street to the small restaurant where he had waited before and ordered a cup of coffee. He sat on the end stool, where, by turning slightly, he could watch the people in the street behind him. It wasn't as good a lookout as the cheese shop but probably would serve his purpose just as well. He finished his first cup and ordered another. Just as he was about to take a sip, he caught a glimpse of the girl he had come to verify. The cup clattered to the counter. Coffee ran everywhere.

"Watch it, mister!" said the counterman, wiping it up. "It's hot."

But Omar didn't appear to hear, for coming out of the doorway was that girl, who looked ecstatically happy, and beside her, his arm around her waist, was Paul! That dog! *Il kalib.* The cheat. Omar was furious.

Hot coffee ran over his hands as he stared at the two of them. A jumble of mixed emotions ran rampant through his body. How many times had he told Paul, no friends, stay away from people, and, especially, leave women alone!

Shocked, he realized Paul must have spent the night with her. He noticed the smile on her face, smug like a cat. Omar had seen that smile on other women before. Yes, Paul had slept with her.

Omar scowled and realized he was jealous, jealous in a strange way. He knew deep down that he would never ever have a woman like Andrea Wayne. *I will kill her again!* he decided. *But it will be for Paul. He needs someone to protect him from the power of that woman, especially now that he has been in her bed!*

Omar watched the girl enter the building across the street and saw Paul go into the cheese shop. In a moment he reappeared with a small white bag. *It is good that I did not wait in that place,* thought Omar, feeling a little nervous. What would have happened if Paul had seen him? He watched Paul walk in the direction of his house.

Omar went out to the street to a telephone booth on the corner. He would give Paul fifteen minutes to get home. While waiting, Omar tried to prepare for his tragic role. He dialed the number.

Paul's voice, shockingly close, came over the line. Omar hesitated.

"Hallo, my friend! I have seen much trouble, much unhappiness since I saw you last. You know our dear friend, he die in the water?"

"Where the hell are you? What happened to the old man?" demanded Paul angrily. The beautiful feeling of the morning dropped from him instantly. Paul had detected a false tone in Omar's lament.

"It was terrible, terrible! That old car, she go crazy just as I am driving to this bridge, you see? She no steer; she got no brakes! What can I do? When I see that I can no stop, I try very hard to pull the old man out with me when I jump from the car, but he is heavy. I try, but I no get him. Oh, Allah, take his soul!"

"Why didn't you come straight to me and tell me what happened? And where are you now, Omar?" Paul asked, his voice barely under control.

"Oh, I am so... confuse. My head is, you know. There was nothing you can do for him, nothing for me, so I dry myself and catch the big gray bus to Washington."

You filthy liar, thought Paul. *You killed the old man, and the lie is right there in your voice. I know you're lying, but I'll play your little rotten game for now.* "When will I see you again, Omar? We have a lot to discuss."

"Soon, my friend, very soon. Good-bye." He hung up, then smiled.

Omar took from his pocket one of his cigars and, swaggering with success, lit it. That took care of Paul. Now back to the problem of the girl.

Omar devoted himself to thoughts of Andrea as he made his way back to the old Pontiac. When he reached the car, he opened the trunk, threw the brownies inside and then noticed a can that had been rolling around in the back. It contained ant and roach powder. He read the directions with some difficulty, then placed the can beside the brownies and shut the trunk.

Back at his house, Paul dialed headquarters in Washington. "Let me speak to Omar, please," he said, disguising his voice.

"He's not here. Who's calling?"

Paul hung up the telephone. He went into the backyard, and Wolf came running toward him, barking with enthusiasm. He rubbed the dog's big head lovingly and took the hook off his collar, allowing the dog to run free.

Paul ran his hand under the roof of the doghouse and could tell by the weight of the underpanel that the weapon was still in place. He contemplated moving it to the house or to a locker at the bus station, but the tripod, although retracted, was too awkward to carry inside a bag or suitcase. No one knew where the gun was hidden, not even Omar, and since Paul was the only one that Wolf let into the yard, he figured it was still in the safest place.

There *was* one other person that Wolf had a sort of mutual understanding with—Mrs. Twell, whose backyard abutted Paul's. She often heaped praise on Wolf for protecting her yard from stray cats, which she loathed. Paul wondered if he could trust Mrs. Twell to feed Wolf.

He walked to the edge of the yard and called her name. She appeared almost immediately at her back door, carrying a paper plate of cookies and offered some to Paul.

"Oh, for me? How thoughtful of you, Mrs. Twell."

"Yes, I do miss having a man to cook for these days, but I still like to bake a little something every now and then. I always seem to make too many, though."

Paul bit into a cookie, which had the consistency of a jawbreaker. "Mrs. Twell, I'd like to ask a favor of you. Mmmm, these are delicious," he lied, accepting another cookie from the plate with some reluctance.

"Here, take the whole plate," the old lady said generously, a big smile wrinkling her eighty-year-old face. As she passed the plate over the fence, one of the cookies rolled onto the grass. Wolf eagerly snapped it up, then whimpered at Paul, who patted his head in sympathy. Mrs. Twell looked confused. She never ate cookies herself.

"What was the favor you wanted to ask me, Mr. Hunter?"

"I was wondering if you could feed my dog while I visited my folks for a couple of days," he ventured.

"Well, I suppose I could. He gives everybody else a scare, but I like Wolf." She patted the dog's head. He wagged his tail.

"All you would have to do is push his food under the fence once a day. He likes to eat just before dark usually. You could fill his water bowl, there next to the house, from the hose in your yard. I think your hose will reach, won't it?" he asked.

"Well, let's try it right now."

She hurried back to the house and unreeled the hose to its farthest length. Without warning, she turned the nozzle full blast and aimed at the water bowl. Paul and Wolf jumped to one side, but not fast enough to avoid a liberal sprinkling before Mrs. Twell had the hose under control.

"I hit it first try!" she cackled triumphantly.

And me, too, mused Paul, shaking water from his pants leg and feeling it run down inside his shoe. Wolf shook himself and went behind his house.

"That was excellent, Mrs. Twell. Now I'll go in the house and get his food. Don't give him too much, just his regular bowl."

"How long did you say you'd be gone?"

"Couple of days, that's all."

"Whom shall I call in case of trouble?" asked Mrs. Twell, her brown eyes shining. At her age, this was a tiny adventure for her. No one ever expected anything of her anymore. Taking care of Wolf was a break in the humdrum sameness of her lonely days.

"Trouble? What trouble could there possibly be?" asked Paul cautiously.

"Well, if the doggie gets sick, or the house catches fire. Dreadful things do happen even to those of us who live by the Book, Mr. Hunter."

"You're right. If Wolf gets sick, call Miss Wayne at the paper."

"Oh, my! Is she your lady friend? Such a pretty little thing."

"You might say that, but let's keep it a secret between us, OK?"

"On account of her no-good husband, you mean? I understand. I'll be quiet as a mouse."

Mrs. Twell reached over and patted his arm. Paul laughed self-consciously. The chance of remaining anonymous in a small town for very long was almost impossible. Don't make friends, don't talk to people—he had broken all the rules this time, especially with Andrea.

He went into the house and returned with the bag of dog food. He handed it over the fence. Wolf growled in protest.

"Don't worry, doggie. I won't forget to feed you. Have a good trip, Mr. Hunter."

Paul thanked her, put the dog back on the chain and went into the house. Almost immediately, he went out again, to the telephone booth on the corner near the service station. It was a rather isolated one, partially enclosed on one side by the wall of the building.

He faced the dial and, simulating some numbers, actually dialing others, he reached the private party in Washington. If the number had not been changed, he would recognize the voice that would answer somewhere in a private study on Embassy Row.

A man answered quietly with a simple "Yes?"

"Elliott? This is Paul Hunter. Please do not hang up."

"I'm sorry, you have the wrong number."

"Oh? I was told you are an old friend of Mary's."

There was a silence; then the man spoke hesitantly. "You were the one who was interested in the flowers she used to raise?"

"Yes, but they're all dead now."

Only one man besides Paul knew anything about Paul's most difficult case, the one with the code name of Mary, Mary, Quite Contrary. It had been a hit involving a drug dealer in Turkey, who was shot to death in a field of poppies. At the time, Paul wasn't sure the hit was clear; the man had fallen, but might have been only wounded. To be sure, Paul set the fields on fire. No one came out. A corpse was found, but it was too charred to be identified, and since none of the villagers were missing, only a perfunctory investigation was made. Paul had never been able to forget that violent night.

The man at the other end sighed, then said, "I thought you were dead."

"Officially, I am."

"Then, you are never to call here again."

"You know that I would not use this number if it were not vitally important. I must see you. Are you still in 213? Can I see you there?" asked Paul anxiously.

"No, not in 213." His laugh was without mirth. "In the vernacular of our odd profession, let me say this, the television overloaded the circuit. You could infer that this caused the air conditioning to break down."

Paul smiled. He gathered from the man's words that a television crew on location had photographed the building, and now all secret information had to be discussed somewhere else. The site was too hot to continue.

The voice softened somewhat, yielding to the urgency in Paul's voice.

"If it is truly of importance, if our national security is involved, then come see me as just a friend. Tomorrow night we're having a few embassy people to dinner. Use your own name, and I'll tell my man to let you through the gate. We can discuss it."

"I'll be there about eight. Good-bye, Elliott."

Paul hung up the telephone and walked slowly toward the service station as if to look at the tires on display. In the reflection of the glass, he cased the area behind him for unusual movement in the street; but if Omar or any others of the group were in Middletowne, they weren't in evidence. But where was Omar, and why had he lied about Mr. Gay?

Paul returned to the booth and dialed Andrea's number. No one answered. There was no time to try to find her and tell her he was leaving town, but he found himself hurrying toward St. George Street anyway. When he reached the corner, he could see that the windows over the barbershop were dark. One of the Datsuns was gone from the parking lot behind the office of the newspaper.

Unhappily, he turned away and strode back toward his house to pack for the trip to Washington.

CHAPTER NINETEEN

"These were on your desk when I came in," Bernadette said, pointing to a slightly dirty white box next to her typewriter.

Andrea looked at the box with disgust and opened it with the tips of her fingers. "What is this, somebody's idea of a joke? They look as if they've been taken apart and pushed back together."

"Maybe they're homemade and stuck to the pan," suggested Bernadette.

"No, they look like the ones from Le Fromage, but all crushed up."

"They smell funny, too—like gasoline." Bernadette wrinkled her nose.

"Well, where did the damn things come from?"

"The College Boy Delivery Service. The guy said they had been left with five dollars. Nobody knows where they came from. Oh, yes, there was a note with the box. Here."

Andrea took the piece of paper and read it, then read it aloud to Bernadette. "Mi drling. yr the gril four me is persenform yradmira."

She looked at the paper with curiosity. "What the hell is it, code?"

She handed the note to Mr. Fischer, who was hovering around pretending not to listen. He was so used to computer type that he could decipher anything. He glanced at it, interpreting immediately:

"My darling, you are the girl for me. Here is a present from your admirer."

He sniffed and looked aghast at the crushed brown mess in the box. What kind of person would send Miss Wayne a gift like that? Although he disapproved of almost everything Andrea did—her occasional curse word, her "tough" clothing, her disregard for authority—secretly he admired her a great deal.

"This was sent by a very illiterate person," he said. "Perhaps a misguided soul who fell in love with you and didn't know how to express himself properly. Possibly he made them himself—"

"—and they stuck to the pan," insisted Bernadette.

"That's very romantic, Mr. Fischer," said Andrea, "but what did he flavor them with? Did he run out of vanilla and throw in just a dab of gasoline? Smell that stuff!"

He bent forward and sniffed, turning slightly green.

"Besides, how many men do you know who whip up brownies? Men don't do that."

"Billy Perkins was in my home-economics class," stated Bernadette, nodding her head.

"Is good old Billy around Middletowne? Maybe he made these," joked Andrea.

"Billy died," said Bernadette. Andrea sobered up immediately and apologized. Then she dropped the note and the box into the wastebasket.

"If you're throwing them away," said Bernadette, "I may as well feed them to the birds. I eat my lunch on that bench in the parking lot, and they always flock down looking for crumbs."

Andrea turned to the notes on her desk, taken at the town-council meeting she had attended the night before. But her thoughts kept veering off to Paul, a much better issue than the proposed extension of city streets in Middletowne to adjoin the new highway. Idly, she found herself dialing his number. She sat listening to the telephone ring, inventing excuses to see him. Her mind delved into fantasy. *Hold me, let me touch your face, I love you, Paul. Oh, Lord, I do love you.* The telephone rang on. *If he answers, I'll dump the minutes of the town council and meet him at my apartment on my lunch hour.* The phone rang on.

Finally she hung up and tried to concentrate on work, but her thoughts stayed with Paul. *I've got to shape up or I'll never get a line done today,* she admitted to herself. She went to the coffee machine and got a cup, hot and black, and started to type. By digging in, she was able to put fifty lines of copy about the council meeting on Jack's desk by one-thirty. Then she went across to Buddy's Bar and had them make a chicken salad to go. On her way back, she saw one of the Datsuns in the parking lot. She got in and, before she even knew it, was halfway to Paul's house.

Pulling up to his house, she saw that the drapes were drawn across the front windows, giving it an empty appearance. She heard Wolf barking in the backyard, so she got out of the car and went around to the fence. Wolf bounded across the yard and leaped for joy when he saw her.

A little old lady came out of the house in the next yard. "Toodle-oo! Toodle-oo!" she yodeled cheerfully.

"Hello," replied Andrea.

"Mr. Hunter went off for a few days. I'm in charge. I'm taking care of the dog," declared the tiny woman with more than a hint of pride in her voice.

"Did he say where he was going?"

"I believe he's visiting his people. They live 'off' somewhere. You're Miss Wayne. You *are* the paper lady, aren't you?"

"The paper lady? Oh, yeah, I work for the paper," she admitted.

"I thought you were her... ah, she?" The older woman nodded her head as if she were party to a deep conspiracy and beckoned to Andrea to lean closer. "I think Mr. Hunter is sweet on you," she confided, winking.

"Oh, I certainly hope so!" Andrea blurted. Then she laughed at herself.

"He said to call *you* if his house burns down while he is gone. That's how I know."

"I'm sure Paul appreciates your help. If you need anything, call me either at the paper or at home. I'm in the book."

"I surely will," said Mrs. Twell. "And good luck on your paper work. I saw you on the television with the drowned man."

"Yes, that was a tragedy. Well, good-bye," said Andrea, heading for the car.

She drove back to the office slowly, nibbling the chicken salad on the way. When she reached the parking lot, Bernadette ran toward the car screaming hysterically.

"Oh, Andy, help me! Something's wrong with the birds! Oh, it's awful, awful. They're falling down all over." She began to cry helplessly, her eyes wide with fear.

Andrea stepped from the car and looked about with amazement. Pigeons, robins, jays, and grackles were staggering about, unable to get off the ground to fly away. Wrens and sparrows already lay stiff on the asphalt.

"The brownies! Bernadette, did you feed those brownies to the birds?"

Bernadette didn't answer. White as a sheet, she fell to the pavement.

Andrea screamed and ran toward the back door of the office. "Jack! Gage! Oh, somebody, come quick!"

In a moment the parking lot was filled with people. They crowded around, wondering, looking at the birds. Jack Wise carried Bernadette into his office and sat her in a chair. He rubbed her hands to aid circulation, and slowly she came around. When she did, she began to cry.

"Those little birds. I killed them, didn't I? The cake was poisoned."

Andrea leaned weakly against the desk. In a moment she regained enough control to reach for the telephone. "Get the police over here right away," she said into the receiver. "Oh, I'm sorry. This is Andy Wayne at the office of *What's Happening Here*. There's been an accident."

Within minutes she heard sirens wailing, and Colby Dance burst through the door. "What's the trouble here? I was over at the college when Andy called."

She led him out to the parking lot where, unable to speak, she sank to her knees on the asphalt, surrounded by the dead birds. By this time, few of them, even the hardiest, were still moving. She gestured hopelessly.

Colby looked about him in astonishment. Tourists were huddled close to the buildings; little children cried loudly. All about the parking area, bundles of feathers lay stiffening in the hot afternoon sun. It was unlike anything he had ever seen.

"These birds," said Andrea in a small, shaky voice, "were poisoned. Bernadette fed them brownies while she was eating her own lunch. Of course, she had no idea..." She faltered, feeling ill.

"That they were poisoned?"

Andrea sat down on the bench suddenly. She looked up at Colby, seeking answers.

"The brownies were meant for me, Colby. Someone left them on my desk this morning. Why would anybody want to kill *me?*"

CHAPTER TWENTY

The three-story gray stone residence on Embassy Row was lit up across the front and all the way down the driveway to the gatehouse. It was imposing, dignified, a fortress of a house without any visible warmth.

The man who lived there was known to many and yet well known to none. He lived two distinct and separate lives and had done so for twenty years. On the surface, he had a normal job. He was also, however, involved in an underground network, an agency that was so discreet the CIA itself could only guess at half its activities. The government, moreover, denied that such an agency even existed.

As Paul entered the drive in a rented car, a liveried gateman met him. "May I see your invitation, sir?" he asked, smiling.

"I don't have an invitation, but I'm a guest of Mr. Winston. My name is Paul Hunter, and if you check with Mr. Winston..."

The man's smile disappeared when he heard the words "no invitation." He tipped his hat and stepped back into the gatehouse, where he consulted a list. Not seeing the name, he picked up an intercom and spoke briefly. Evidently he was unable to reach Elliott right away, because Paul could see him waiting for an answer.

Another car drove up behind Paul's, and for some reason a chill passed over his shoulders. It was his built-in radar, and it had saved his life many times in the past. Had he been in another country, he would have driven away without hesitation. Here, though, there was no reason to believe that he was not safe. In the rearview mirror he studied the people who had just driven up. Paul didn't recognize either of them. They looked like embassy types, aides or secretaries, not top echelon.

The driver was a swarthy man, slightly fat, impeccably dressed in dinner clothes. The woman beside him was overdressed, with a diamond choker and large earrings. As she lit a cigarette, Paul could see she had a narrow face, heavily made up. Her hair was pulled back into a tight chignon at the nape of her neck. She was turned toward the man and seemed to be talking excitedly.

The gateman hurried over. "Sorry to make you wait, sir. You are to go directly to Mr. Winston's study, which is the end door facing east on the left hand side."

Paul nodded, and the man stepped aside. He drove all the way to the rear of the house and parked. As he approached the study door, he noticed that the people in the car behind had not followed him into the drive. They had, in fact, backed out, then driven rapidly off down the street. Were they party crashers turned away because they had no invitation? Not likely, dressed like that, Paul thought.

As he stood pondering, he heard a cough.

"Come in, come in," called a familiar voice from the study door.

"Hello, Elliott, it's been a long time," said Paul.

As they went inside, Paul could see that the years had been kind to Elliott Winston, despite his harassing business. His hair was slightly tinged with gray. His physique was still firm and lean at sixty-four.

"You shouldn't be here at all, you know, but if you felt brave enough to break the rules, I felt that I must let you come," he chided quietly. Then his eyes narrowed, and his tone was not as sweet as before. "It's not the money, is it? Didn't we settle enough on you at the break?" He eyed Paul suspiciously.

Paul turned away angrily. "You know Goddamn well it isn't money."

"Well, it has happened before with other people," replied Winston.

"And did the gentleman have a nice funeral, or was there enough of him left after the 'jump'?" asked Paul, surprising the older man.

Elliott Winston's face remained undisturbed as he leafed through some papers on his desk. He seemed to enjoy making Paul wait. Finally he clasped his long fingers together and gazed at Paul inquiringly, as if it were *he* who was waiting for Paul.

"Shall I just jump in, or do you want to hear all the prior details to the decision that brought me to you?" asked Paul.

"Spare the details. How does this concern the government?"

"Very well. King Hassan of Uddapha is coming here shortly. You know there has been talk in the press, opposition to the deal he is alleged to be trying to sell the president—you know, trading oil money for real estate."

"Yes, yes. I read the papers. Go on."

"There is an assassination plot against the king, and I... I'm in the middle of it."

Elliott Winston sat forward, his cool composure dropping from him at each word. He waved his hands for Paul to proceed. His eyes were alert as Paul related the bizarre scheme. Paul minimized his relationship with Yasmina, saying only that he had been a friend of the Shaifi family. And he did not mention knowing Andrea Wayne.

"Daddy, Mommy is getting mad at you. People are already here," said a young voice on the other side of the study door.

"Yes, yes, darling. Tell her I'll be out shortly." Winston's voice had softened noticeably.

The tall, thin man paced back and forth. For the first time Paul saw a look of indecision on Winston's face. "Three days! My God, man!" he exploded. "Why didn't you contact us sooner?"

"What do you mean, three days?" asked Paul with surprise. "The king will be here in three days?"

"It's the best kept secret of all my years in Washington. I, myself, was told the date only last Monday. We half expected something of the sort, and the Uddaphans must have, also. He's not even popular among his own people, you know. Now we have their security problem dumped in our laps while he's in this country. What do you think we can do, Paul, without blowing it wide open?"

"I think I can handle it myself. Omar and his group have no reason to suspect that I'm not still with them all the way. They picked me carefully; they know I've killed before. Somebody had to have access to your files, Elliott. You had better check that service record you fed into my air-force file. If they could put it together, how safe are the rest of us?" Paul hesitated, upset and angry.

"But this is not the immediate problem. I'm sorry it happened, of course, but what concerns us now is the king. I think you are part of the solution, but not all of it. We can leave absolutely nothing to chance."

"I can carry the plot all the way through as planned but abort the killing at the last minute. This is the only way we can risk it and clean up the group afterward without rousing suspicion. If they for a moment suspect *me*, some kamikaze type will rush into Middletowne and take over the job himself— sacrifice for the good of the people—and, of course, someone else will be sent to take care of me."

"Don't tell me that you couldn't master another disappearing act the same way you did nearly eight years ago in Europe and the Middle East. Even we couldn't find you for three months that time. You survived. Not many of us do."

Footsteps approached in the hall, and they ceased talking immediately.

"Please, Daddy, Mommy is steaming. You'd better come."

Abruptly, Winston unlocked the study door, and a beautiful young girl of about fourteen peered in. She stopped when she saw Paul and smiled. Self-consciously, she pressed her hands down on her dress, which was cool and flimsy with low-cut neckline.

"Did Mother pick that dress?" asked Winston gruffly.

"No, she was too busy, so I charged it at Hecht's. Isn't it gorgeous?"

She was talking to her father, but she was looking at Paul. On the way out, she threw her father a kiss.

"My daughter, Kara. She's fourteen, going on thirty."

"A very lovely child," emphasized Paul.

"I have to attend this damn dinner, but you must stay. Come and eat. We'll break away as soon as possible. We'll talk the rest of the night if necessary. This thing is top priority and must be handled tonight. My God, can you imagine what might happen if a king from the Middle East were killed in the States?"

"All the Arab countries would probably sever relations, at least temporarily. And, of course, there is the danger that black gold would stop pouring in. That would make a lot of cold tails, even in Washington. But what we're really discussing here is a man's life."

Elliott Winston fixed him with a stare. "Since when did that become important to you?"

"Since I came back to my own country. My years abroad were another time, another place. This is now, and this is not espionage. It's murder. If you don't want to touch it, Elliott, I can bow out and blow the whole plot to the CIA. Let them take it."

A woman's voice, well modulated but angry, was heard on the other side of the door.

"Yes, my dear, we're coming right away. Come, Paul. You're staying."

They went out into the hall, where Winston introduced Paul to his wife. She was a tall, pale woman with jet-black hair. She smiled icily, and Paul smiled at her in return.

"I believe that two of your guests turned away at the gate at the last minute. I hope it didn't ruin your seating arrangement, Mrs. Winston."

"Not at all. My secretary and her husband are filling in, but it was terribly upsetting. How did you know?"

"They were waiting at the gate at the same time I was."

"Oh, I see. Well, I was not in the mood, anyway, to put up with Ahmed and Meda and her incessant talk about Paris, which everyone knows is passe. Perhaps their child got sick."

Paul digested this bit of news and felt a little more relaxed. Perhaps he was being overcautious. He stood in the door as Winston moved off to greet his other guests.

Kara flitted over to Paul's side and stared up at him with admiration. "You're awfully tall, aren't you? I have a thing for tall men. There's this boy at school who is just crazy about me, but he's not even six feet."

She clung to him for the rest of the evening and managed to switch her place card next to his at dinner. That infuriated her mother and bored Paul immensely.

After coffee and brandy, Elliott and Paul returned to the study.

"My God, I'm sorry to have put you through that, but it was scheduled before your call and there was nothing I could do about it. Kara didn't... ah, manage to talk you into anything, did she? A date? She can be very persuasive, damn it!" said Elliott.

"No. But now can we get back to discussion without interruption?"

"Of course. There will be stepped-up security from all branches in Middletowne. There are seven different police departments in the general area. Good coverage for a town of that size. The government people will send their own down from Washington. The Uddaphans bring their own security. So the place *should be* tight as hell."

"That's true. But the town is wide open—fields, parks, lanes. There's enough space there to bring in a cannon."

"Tell me this. Did you truthfully believe that you could get the king and get out alive?" asked Winston.

"Yes."

"You are one strange man, Paul Hunter. I, too, believe you could have pulled it off. Thank God you're on our side now."

Paul had nothing to say.

"I'm not naïve enough to think that there isn't something you want from me. If you do abort this mission, what is it that we can do for you?"

"I want cover. Cover me as if I were still acting for you. Tell them that you were aware of the whole plot from the beginning and I was undercover for you. I don't want to survive this caper and have to face conspiracy charges. That's what you can do for me."

"I can't do that! You are in with those fanatics up to your neck."

Paul leaned across the desk and grabbed Winston's arm. They stared angrily at each other. Paul released his grip, laughed casually and stood up. He walked to the door. "Good-bye, Elliott. Nice seeing you again. Sorry we can't do business."

"Wait! Goddamn it, wait! Let's see if we can work something out." Winston grasped Paul's shoulder. "Think of my angle. I've got no record that you were working on this."

"Records, Elliott? Everybody knows you work out of your sleeve. I want your word on this. Cover for me or go to the other departments and let them handle it their way. I've given you enough to go on."

"Maybe I can fake a few records just in this case. We can work together, Paul. Now, come and sit down, and let's hash this thing through."

"The first thing to do is reschedule everything—delay the plane, delay the motorcade. The Uddaphan party will be screaming, but let them scream. We'll throw the whole thing off about two hours. Killers don't like to wait around. This will shake them up if they bring in a second, backup assassin."

"I don't think they will," said Paul. "It was never discussed at any time. They knew my record and trusted me with the job."

"You know, you could be put away this minute for your involvement thus far."

"But you need me, Elliott. I have all the pieces."

"And damn it, you're holding out a few, aren't you?"

Paul had deliberately not told Winston about the weapon. The only other person who knew about the camera was Omar, and even he didn't know where it was hidden. Avoiding the issue, he finally said, "It would make it easier if we had something definite between us."

"I'll have to use the telephone in another room."

"I'll go with you while you talk."

"Very well. I guess I taught you never to trust anybody—even me," conceded Winston. Paul followed him out of the room and down the hall.

Sometime later, Paul came out of the house and walked to his car. He turned on the ignition and drove slowly to the gate. The gateman tipped his hat and said good night as he turned into the street. Again Paul felt that chill and looked at the dark, silent streets suspiciously. All was quiet.

As Paul's car passed, a man and woman stepped out of some shrubbery across the street from the gatehouse.

"Now that you've seen him again, are you sure, Meda?" the man asked.

"Yes, it is him. I only saw him once at headquarters. I would not forget a magnificent blond in a room of our own people. Praise Allah, I was behind the door when I saw him. He did not see me, but I will remember him always." The woman smiled.

"Why is he here at Winston's?" the man asked. "Why in Washington at all?"

"I don't know, but I don't like it. I'll contact Shaifi at once. Come, Ahmed. This may be serious."

CHAPTER TWENTY-ONE

"You had a very close call, Andy," said Chief Ransome. "The lab managed to get enough crumbs together to find out the cause of the death of those birds. Those brownies were loaded with an ant and roach powder that contained a chemical that affects people as well as insects. It's a good thing nobody ate any. We're trying to check the source of the powder, but it's not handled by any local stores."

"I feel sorry for the birds, and I don't think Bernadette will ever get over it."

"That girl! Why did she put the box and note in the incinerator instead of just dropping them in a trash can?"

"She always does that with her lunch papers. How was she to know that the box would become evidence?" defended Andrea.

"Well, it would have been something to go on. I tell you, Andy, we don't have a real clue in this case. Hildy, at Le Fromage, can't remember any particular customer that bought brownies that day. They made and sold thirty-five dozen before noon. And the fellow who runs College Boy Delivery Service had deposited the five bucks in the bank by the time we got to him."

"Don't worry so much, Ed. You're making too much of this. It could have been some crank who took offense at something I wrote in the paper. You remember that article I went after about drugs at the college a while back? Some kid kept calling Jack and telling him that if he didn't fire me, he'd blow up the building. We didn't think it was serious, and it wasn't. The kid was scared stiff and bluffing. He didn't want to lose his source of supply."

"This is a little different. If you had eaten those cookies, you would have become sick, possibly died. This is direct contact, not just phone calls, and you should take it seriously. Do you know anyone who could stay with you for a few days until we can get some sort of lead on this?"

"Maybe," she answered hesitantly, thinking of Paul.

"Any chance of Patch coming back?" he queried. "I always liked that boy."

"I got a letter that indicated he may be heading this way. He was having trouble with the van, though. In any case, he is not coming back to *me*, because he knows I've started a divorce action."

"Somebody else in the picture, Andy?"

"Yes, there is," Andrea admitted, giving no details. She picked up her bag and cameras and walked to the door. The chief followed her out to the parking lot, where Gage was waiting for her in the Datsun.

"Heading off to a story?" asked the policeman.

"We're on our way to the launching of the new aircraft carrier at the shipyard. Andy will do the pictures and I'll write it," said Gage.

"Well, take care of this girl, Gage. And be careful what you eat. Oh, yeah, Andy, do you still have that gun you got the permit for about a year ago?"

"Sure, it's at home somewhere."

"Why don't you carry it with you?" he suggested, frowning slightly.

"With all this other stuff? Oh, come on, how would I carry the thing?"

"Think about it. Somebody out there doesn't like you. The world is full of crackpots. I'd advise you to start carrying it. It could save your life, Andy."

She paled as she realized Chief Ransome was not mincing his words. He really believed that she was in danger from some unknown source. She looked at Gage, who was trying not to act as alarmed as he felt.

"You're trying to scare me, and you're doing a good job of it. I'll be careful, and I'll find the gun. God knows I hope I never have to use it."

"By the way," the chief said casually, "you haven't had any other… ah, incidents out of the ordinary lately, have you?"

"What do you mean, out of the ordinary?"

"Phone calls? A freak accident, maybe?" he guessed.

"No," she said. Then she remembered her fall. That certainly was a freak accident. She still couldn't recall exactly what had happened that night, but she attributed it to the wet deck and her new sandals.

"You do remember something, don't you?" The chief sensed a change.

"No, it's nothing. Let's roll, Gage. We're going to be late. 'Bye, Ed, and don't worry."

Ed Ransome stared after the Datsun as they drove off. He was sure Andrea was keeping something to herself. Could she be protecting someone, and why? Maybe she had received a threat from some irate reader opposed to something she wrote in the paper. He decided to go over to *What's Happening Here* and scan her copy for the last couple of months. He'd hate for anything to happen to that girl.

Andrea was very quiet all the way to the shipyard, but Gage didn't notice. In confidence, Jack Wise had assigned him to work with Andrea on everything until something broke on the brownie caper; that meant sticking close during all working hours. He was pleased to be Andrea's bodyguard and wished there was some way to stay on the job after hours as well. Sleep on her couch, maybe? He couldn't say a word about the arrangement, because Andrea knew nothing about it. He shot a glance in her direction, but she seemed to be deep in thought, staring out at the highway as he drove along.

I know I felt a blow on my head before I touched the deck, she was thinking. *How was that possible?* Andrea felt her palms beginning to perspire as she reviewed that night on the ferry with a different purpose in mind. An accident, or was it planned? Paul was asleep in the car on the lower deck. I was the only one on the upper deck except for Captain and Mrs. Gandy. I *was* alone. Paul *was* asleep. Anyway, why would Paul— Oh, it was too ridiculous to suspect Paul! She groaned at the thought.

"What's the matter, baby?" asked Gage anxiously. She looked pale.

"I have this awful headache, but I'll be OK," she said truthfully.

"Nerves, it's nerves. You've really been pushing it lately. Lean on old Gage. I'll carry this one today. You whack off a couple of straight shots and I'll do the rest. When we're through with this big splash party, let's go get a steak."

"OK," she agreed meekly. She pushed the ominous thoughts of that night to the back of her mind. Today, she had to concentrate on her work. Unconsciously, she pulled out some thin tissue and began to polish her lens.

Gage smiled. He hoped he had been able to get her mind off whatever it was that bothered her. At least she agreed to dinner. He supposed that was progress.

As she swirled the tissue around and around, it seemed to be saying, *Paul, Paul, Paul.* She gazed from the window at the passing countryside, but his face was superimposed on the image, the eyes so dark and blue, that small scar on his forehead.

The day went by uneventfully. It was an assignment they had both had before, and Andrea knew the exact protocol of the launchings. Only the speakers and the lady with the champagne bottle were different each time. She knew just where to stand to get the best shot, and with Gage handling the words, it was a walk-through. They finished up by four-thirty, and instead of driving back to Middletowne, Gage headed for the ocean.

Children were playing on the sand. Far out at sea, a freighter moved across the horizon like some toy boat pushed along by an unseen hand. For the moment all of Andrea's troubles seemed remote. She was glad Gage had brought her to this place. They stood on the boardwalk overlooking the beach and silently enjoyed the scene.

"Won't Natalie expect you for dinner? Shouldn't you call?" Andrea suggested as Gage took her by the arm and they headed toward the Pier Restaurant.

"She told me this morning she had a dinner meeting. In fact, even the kid has a meeting with his stamp club. I'd be eating alone as usual. They don't give a damn whether I'm home or not."

"Oh, come on, Gage. I'm sure they both love you and all you need is to communicate with each other. Marriage takes a lot of effort." She added to herself, *effort on both parts, not just one.*

"That woman hasn't tried to 'communicate' with me in years. Now she's got the kid acting the same way. You know, like I'm of no importance to them."

Andrea turned, looked up at him sympathetically and squeezed his arm.

"You're a good guy, Gage. Things *will* get better. Now, let's forget all the tears and strife and have fun. Sing me no sad songs on this occasion. Where's that steak?"

"I agree," he said. "What kind of wine would you like?"

"How about Lambrusco? And don't let me forget the bones for Jade."

"Oh, gosh, you're going to make me ask for a doggy bag again. You know they think we go home and make soup for a whole week, don't you? OK, OK, for you I'd go around gathering the bones from other people's plates, you know that, don't you?" He looked at her fondly, wishing that things were different between them.

The dinner was better than expected. They dawdled over the last of the wine, and it was after ten when they drove back to Middletowne to Andrea's apartment. Gage insisted on going up to make sure everything was as usual.

A sleepy-eyed Peke met them at the door, yipping halfheartedly, but shut up immediately when she smelled the steak bones, which Andrea put down in the kitchen.

"While I'm here, why don't you check out that gun that Ed was talking about? He seemed to think you'd be safer with it," suggested Gage, reluctant to leave.

Andrea went to the bedside table and unlocked the drawer. The revolver was there, safety on, and loaded. She felt strangely relieved.

"To tell the truth, I thought maybe Patch took it with him when he left. He took a lot of stuff—the radio, for instance, and a television. Lucky he left the cameras or I'd have followed him and beat his socks off," she said vindictively, then laughed.

"Well, I guess I have to go now. I do, don't I, Andy?" Gage grinned.

"Yes, you do, and thanks for a wonderful time. Good night, Gage."

CHAPTER TWENTY-TWO

The clock down at the old church chimed twelve, the sound sadly hushed in the drizzle that had begun to fall. The streets were gray in the misty damp, and a chill in the air signaled an early fall. A thin yellow cat turned over a barrel behind the cheese shop, sniffed in vain for crumbs, then crawled inside and fell asleep.

From far off, a bell was ringing in Andrea's dreams. She kept opening doors in empty houses and finding no one there. The bell persisted until it became a reality. Groggily, she reached for the telephone and pulled it under the covers.

"Umm? Who is it?" she managed, her eyes still tightly closed.

"The big dog is barking and barking!" said a frightened little voice.

"Dog? What dog? Who is this?"

"This is Mrs. Twell, Mr. Hunter's neighbor," she whispered worriedly.

Andrea forced herself to listen. She recalled that Mrs. Twell had looked to be about eighty and was all alone.

"I thought I saw a light in the house, not a real light but more like a flashlight, kind of here and there like someone moving about inside, maybe a burglar," the old lady continued, a tremor in her voice.

"Maybe it's Paul—I mean, Mr. Hunter. He probably came home," Andrea said hopefully.

"Why didn't he speak to the dog?" asked Mrs. Twell.

"I don't know. If you're uneasy, why not call the police?"

"Mr. Hunter told me if anything went wrong, I was to call *you*, Miss Wayne, and that's what I'm doing!" The old lady's voice got stronger with a touch of determined righteousness.

Andrea rubbed her eyes and sat on the edge of the bed. The telephone dangled from her fingers. Jade waddled in and looked at her with half-closed eyes. Finally she answered, reluctantly, "Don't worry, Mrs. Twell. I'll drive down and check on the dog. You go on back to bed now. Good night."

She lay back on the bed and fought off overwhelming drowsiness as she tried to decide the best thing to do. She could call the police herself, but on the other hand, if it were Paul... *Oh, hell. Get up and go down there yourself,* she thought. She dialed Paul's number, but there was no answer.

From the closet she took a pair of jeans and a light turtleneck sweater and put them on. She then put on a pair of sneakers and ran her fingers through her tousled hair. Her bag lay on the night table, and as she picked it up, she thought of the revolver in the drawer.

She unlocked the drawer and gazed down on the gun, lying there like some toy. She had never fired it, but she had carried it in the glove compartment for several months during the drug investigation. Carefully, she picked it up and double-checked to make sure the safety was on before putting it in her bag.

The chill from the rain settled on her shoulders as she crossed the street to the parking lot to get the Datsun. The engine sputtered twice, then started up.

When she reached the cemetery, she drove slowly past Paul's house, which was totally dark and quiet. The drapes were drawn exactly as they had been before. There was no light behind them, of any kind. No sound came from the backyard, and Wolf was nowhere to be seen. *Probably asleep in his doghouse,* she thought, beginning to feel angry.

She parked near the gate to the cemetery and sat in the car, observing the house. *That old lady has a good imagination,* she decided. Andrea was about to start the car, when a truck passing on another street momentarily slanted a light on the front door. Suddenly she sat forward, alert and wide awake. The door was open! She stared at the opening, wondering if someone was looking back at her from the other side. The hair on her neck rose, and her hands were cold with sweat as she reached for her bag. She pulled it over her shoulder and felt the hardness of the gun inside.

Minutes passed. Her eyes never left the door. Another light scanned the house from an adjacent street, and she could see that there was no one standing behind or near the crack in the door.

Slowly she got out of the car and walked toward the house, her hand inside her bag. She looked from one set of windows to the other, then back to the door, but there was no movement of any kind. The stillness was unbelievable. No cars passed. Even the night birds in the cemetery sat silent in the trees.

Finally she went around the side of the house, avoiding the shrubbery, and tried to whistle for the dog. Her lips were so dry only a feeble little sound emerged. Weakly, she leaned against the fence and called out in a low, soft voice, "Here, boy. Come on, Wolf. *Here, Wolf!*"

She cleared her throat and called a little louder, but there was no sign of the dog. The doghouse stood in deep shadow under the trees, too far away for her to see inside it. The long chain glistened in the grass.

She stood there for a minute trying to think of a logical explanation. Maybe Paul had come home and taken the dog inside the house to stop him from barking. That had to be it. Still, she looked back at the chain that led nowhere and called again. She remembered that Paul *never* took Wolf into the house and was upset on the one occasion *she* had brought him in. Then, why didn't Wolf come when she called?

Across at Mrs. Twell's house, a single dim bulb burned behind an old-fashioned window of frosted glass, a narrow pane perhaps in the bathroom. The old lady had probably gone back to bed now that the dog had stopped barking.

Andrea retraced her steps to the front of the house and looked through the open door. Stealthily she pushed it flat against the wall. At least there was no one lurking behind it! She ran her fingers against the wall, found the light switch and flipped it on. Andrea gasped in surprise and stepped inside, forgetting caution as she looked about in dismay. The room was ravaged, torn apart.

The back of the couch was slashed, but the seats were intact. The rug was pushed against one wall, leaving the floor dusty and bare. A myriad of heavy footprints had scuffed the surface. The chair back was slit. A record cabinet had been pushed away from the wall; books had been thrown on the floor; the contents of the hall closet had been pulled out. A large camera on a tripod lay on its side near the closet. It had been opened, and a roll of film lay tangled on the rug. Andrea winced at the sight of the exposed film. *Twenty frames shot to hell,* she thought angrily, then laughed shakily at herself.

She made her way to the dining area and looked in the kitchen. All the cabinets had been flung open, and even the refrigerator door was ajar. The light inside flickered, on the verge of going out. Maybe that was what Mrs. Twell saw from her window. Like a flashlight, she had said. Andrea closed the door, not thinking of fingerprints.

Backing out of the kitchen, she returned to the living room and looked for the telephone. She couldn't remember exactly where it had been connected the one time she had been there before. She looked under the couch cushions and around the rug. Where was the damn thing, she wondered. Maybe it *wasn't* in the living room at all.

With a sinking sensation, she stared down the dark hall. Carefully, she inched forward and turned on the hall light. She peered into the first bedroom. The mattress had been pulled from the bed. An empty closet stood open, its hangers moving gently in the air.

The bedroom at the end must be Paul's and the telephone was in there, next to the bed, she guessed. All she had to do was walk down there and open the door. Her throat closed with fear, and her heart beat rapidly as she inched her way toward the door.

She pressed her ear against it, listening for any sound from the other side. She imagined she heard heavy breathing, then realized it was her own. Clamping her hand over her mouth, she listened again and heard nothing.

Her hand gripped the gun inside of her bag, and she pressed the safety off. Her fingers felt wet against the cold steel.

Suddenly she kicked the bedroom door, and as it sprang open into the room, she flattened herself against the hall wall and waited. Nothing moved. She stepped into the room and turned on the lamp, which was lying just inside the door. As in the other bedroom, the mattress had been pulled off, the closet stood ajar, but the clothing and linen were heaped in piles, a pattern that appeared in the other rooms as well. Someone had been looking for something large, it appeared.

What on earth could Paul have hidden that somebody wanted badly enough to tear a house apart like this? Her eyes went to the table near the bed. No telephone there. She'd have to go back to the living room and hunt for it, or, better still, go home and telephone the police from her apartment. At least, she knew where *her* phone was.

She turned off the lamp in the bedroom. In the darkness she heard the sound of a car stopping in front of the house. She hesitated as she heard the car door being eased shut, a kind of subtle click, as if the driver were acting very cautiously. She ran to the bedroom window and saw a figure coming toward the house.

Her heart was pounding frantically. *I can't reach the front door before he does,* she reasoned. Oh, God, where *was* the back door? She couldn't remember. She couldn't move. In a panic, she managed to slip into the closet and pull the door shut behind her. Her hand was trembling, but she was holding the gun pointed toward the door.

Softly, someone entered the house. Then a cautious search, from room to room, began. Doors opened and closed with quiet clicks. Then there were footsteps, coming down the hall toward the bedroom where she waited, paralyzed.

She sensed someone on the other side of the door, and her chest ached with the agony of suppressing a scream. Perspiration poured down her back. *Oh, God,* she prayed, *help me now. Give me the courage to do whatever I have to do.* Her wet hand grasped the gun.

Suddenly the closet door swung open. She closed her eyes and squeezed the trigger. Just as she heard the muffled explosion, she opened her eyes and saw Paul standing against the wall.

The bullet tore through the bottom of her leather bag and landed with a thud in a pile of clothing on the floor. Blue smoke filled the closet, where she stood choking. Tears ran down her face.

Paul approached her carefully. "What are you doing here?" he asked, his voice surprisingly steady.

"Mrs. Twell called. The dog was barking. It was all… like this." From somewhere a voice was coming, mouthing the words, but they didn't seem to belong to her. Through the tears, she gestured feebly at the mess strewn everywhere.

"Who are you?" demanded Paul. He held his own gun pointed toward her. He wanted to believe her, but he couldn't trust anybody.

She looked at him with shock and whispered, "I'm Andrea, Paul."

He stared at her small figure huddled on a pile of his clothes on the closet floor.

Could he believe her? There was one thing that made him believe she was exactly what she seemed, an innocent bystander caught up in an intrigue of which she was totally unaware. She had directed the gun at the floor. If she were an agent, she would have waited until he was in her sight, then fired, not downward but at him.

He had recognized the Datsun and guessed that it was Andrea inside the house, but when he saw the wreckage… He decided to give her a chance to explain how she came to be in the house. What was it she had said? "The dog was barking." Somebody had called her because Wolf was barking.

He pulled her to her feet roughly and steered her down the hall and out through the kitchen to the back door. He cut off the lights as they went through the rooms.

The yard was dark. The trees and shrubs glistened in the soft, persistent rain. There was no moon. Blindly they made their way across to the doghouse, where Paul looked briefly inside, gave a muffled exclamation, then followed the chain to the low-hanging bushes at the corner of the yard. He commanded Andrea to stay where she was, and, picking up the chain, he followed it, crawling on his knees. She heard him cry out, a piercing sob of anger and pain, and she ran toward the sound. Paul crawled out of the bushes and pushed her away with hands covered in blood. He motioned her to go back.

"It's Wolf!" His voice cracked with grief. "He's been stabbed to death. That damn son of a bitch. Wolf knew him. He may have thought he was a friend and let him in."

"Who, Paul? Who would kill a nice dog like Wolf? For God's sake, please tell me what's going on! I'm calling the police. I'm going to find the phone and call them right now!"

Paul came after her and pulled her back. He shook his head. "No, no, don't call the police. You've got to trust me to handle this. Go in the house and make some coffee, and I'll be in as soon as I can. I've got to bury Wolf. I can't leave him like that."

She hesitated, then turned back to him saying, "Do you want me to help?"

He looked at her oddly, not exactly understanding what she meant.

"Do you want me to help you bury the dog?" she repeated.

He shook his head. "Go into the house, please."

She turned and walked slowly back through the yard, while he turned toward the doghouse. He ran his hand under the roof, but the weapon was missing. Somebody had informed on him, and Omar had managed to get here and find the gun while he was driving back from Washington. He would have to call Elliott or find Omar before— Two days, only two days—it was impossible.

He looked down at the blood on his hands, and it suddenly seemed horribly symbolic of his life. Blood on his hands. Hastily, he wiped them on his shirt and turned to the ugly task ahead.

Inside the house, Andrea rummaged among the things in the cabinets and found two cups and saucers and put water in the kettle to boil. She poured two snifters half full of brandy. They both needed it. Her head was pounding with tension, and she flinched when she heard the shovel hit against a stone. Why, oh, why? Who would kill a dog?

There was a muffled ring from the living room, and she followed the sound to find the telephone under a pile of couch pillows.

"Hello?" she ventured cautiously.

"Oh, it's you, Miss Wayne. Is everything all right over there?"

"Yes, Mrs. Twell. Mr. Hunter is home. That was the light you saw," she lied.

"Well, tell him I fed the dog every day. I took good care of the dog."

"Yes, I'll tell him." Andrea hung up and sat there thinking, *How ironic.*

When Paul came in, he found her still sitting in the living room in the dark, tears running down her cheeks. Gently, he lifted her and held her.

"Come on, darling. Let's go into the kitchen. I have a lot to tell you. It's going to be a long story, and most of it you won't like and won't understand. But first I must know if I can trust you never to divulge a word I tell you."

"I suspected that you were not just another GI student from the beginning. I couldn't help but notice the way you avoided people, hated crowds and kept to yourself. But I fell in love with you anyway, not knowing anything about you. Nothing you can tell me now will change that."

He looked away and began to talk rapidly. He began with his meeting with Omar. As his own part in the assassination plot unfolded, she looked at him in disbelief. Her eyes grew wide as he told her about Mr. Gay and that he thought Omar had killed the old man by pushing the car in the river.

"I was there when they brought him up. I even told you about it! Oh, Paul, why didn't you tell me then? How could you go on, thinking that this Omar had killed him? Now he's gotten Wolf, and if he's stolen the gun, he doesn't trust you anymore. Don't you realize that you may be next?"

"I couldn't tell you anything at that time. Surely you know that. I was in the whole thing up to my neck! I'm begging you to try to understand. And you are right about Omar, of course. I've got to find him."

"I'll help you. Just tell me what he looks like. I can get into places in this town where nobody else can go, believe me. Wait a minute! This Omar, does he have long, black, curly hair and sometimes rides a motorcycle?"

"Yes, but how do you know him?" asked Paul, his voice sharp with surprise.

"I took his picture sometime last summer."

"You what? That's impossible. He goes absolutely crazy when anybody tries to take his picture. He smashes the camera, anything. How did you manage to take it?"

"I had my long lens on. He was sitting on his motorcycle, not looking my way. I thought he had an interesting face. I have a good one of you, too," she added. Momentarily Paul paled, then began to laugh.

"We thought we were being so careful. You are in a dangerous business, a very dangerous business," he warned.

"I know that. Just last week somebody sent me a box of poisoned brownies."

"Poisoned brownies? Did they find out who sent them?" Paul demanded. He tried to recall if Omar could have seen them together. Omar was constantly warning him about women. Had he found out about Andrea? Trying to poison her was exactly the kind of crazy trick Omar would attempt. *My God, Andrea!* Paul shuddered.

"No, they didn't find out—that is, not yet."

He stood up and put his arms around her, cradling her head against his shoulder.

"Oh, darling, if I hurt you in any way..." he said painfully.

"I'm all right, Paul. Don't worry about me. Please tell me what I can do to help you. Is there anything else I should know?"

"Yes, it's about the weapon. The gun's concealed in a camera with a tripod attached."

"A camera on a retracted tripod?"

"The tripod contains the silencer," he added, not admitting that the idea of the camera came from watching her work.

"Damn! Can my little paper scoop the whole nation on this thing once it's over? I mean, the whole story. Oh, of course, not about you, but about the people in Washington?"

"No!" he shouted angrily. He grasped her hands and held them tightly. "You must never even mention my name. There is so much you don't know about me, and there will be people searching for me when it's all over. Andrea, if I get out of this alive, someday when I'm clear and free of my past, I'll come for you. Until then, it would be better if we stayed apart. Right now, I'm in deep trouble with everybody, even the ones I trust. And those who trust me can't possibly know what will happen."

"Well, regardless, I'm already in this with you, and even if I weren't, you know I'll be covering King Hassan's visit. Just this morning Jack Wise got a call asking whether some foreign correspondents could use our darkroom in the next two days. It was the news team from Uddapha."

"So it's really begun. The waiting will be over." Paul sank down wearily, rubbing his hands across his eyes. He looked dispassionately at the wreckage of the house.

"You need sleep. There's nothing you can do tonight. In fact, it's almost dawn. You'll be able to think if you get some rest. I'll fix the bed."

Paul came and stood in the doorway of the bedroom. He had removed his coat, and his leather holster crossed his shirt. Andrea looked at his gun.

"I never really knew you before tonight. Is your name Paul Hunter, or is that just something you call yourself?"

"That's my name."

"Well, at least that wasn't all a lie."

"And my telling you I love you wasn't a lie, either. I love you now, Andrea."

She didn't answer, just moved toward the door to leave. He held out his hand as she tried to pass. She attempted to pull away, but he pressed her against the door. She felt the cold steel of the gun on her cheek, shocking in contrast to the heat of his body.

His mouth found hers, and his kisses poured over her mouth and down her neck. He picked her up and carried her to the bed. She closed her eyes as she felt the weight of his body. He breathed a kiss into her ear, whispering, "When this is over, my darling, we'll be together. I promise you." He tasted salty tears on his lips and realized she was crying. Her arms were around his neck, drawing him close; her lips parted, seeking his. "Love me, love me," she whispered.

CHAPTER TWENTY-THREE

Jack Wise scowled at Andrea as she came through his office door. It was after ten o'clock, and she had missed an important briefing. She was wearing jeans and an old turtleneck sweater that looked as if they had been slept in. And her eyes were puffed, with dark smudges underneath.

"Where in hell have you been? We had a briefing at nine o'clock! Now you come in here looking like something the cat dragged in, and I suppose you want me to go over the entire procedure just for you!"

"Never mind, if you don't want to. Why don't you fire me?" she said grumpily. She plunked down in the office chair, staring at him sleepily.

"You look like hell, you know. Where have you been all night? Where's your bag?"

She almost laughed, thinking, *What if I told him I shot the bottom out of my bag and spent the whole night in the arms of a paid assassin?* Then she sobered knowing he'd believe her. He really would. He knew she never lied to him about anything; he was like a father to her.

"A friend of mine died last night," she improvised, thinking of Wolf. Wolf had been a friend, better than some of the usual kind.

"Who?" he asked suspiciously. "Someone who lives in Middletowne?"

"No, it was somebody you don't know." She looked genuinely sad, and he softened.

"Oh, well... I'm sorry," he muttered. He sized her up, noting the dejected way she slumped in the chair. Her mind was obviously miles from the office. He didn't quite buy the story about the dead friend, but from her appearance it must be something equally serious. Not since Patch left had she come to the office in such a deep depression.

"Do you need to take the day off? It's a very bad time. The inn is full of people with the Uddaphan party. Mr. Fischer is going nuts with these foreigners stopping by to use our darkroom, and I expected you and Gage to get out there today and meet those people, talk to them, get some good pictures," he pleaded desperately.

"I'm here to go to work, don't worry about it. Just let me go home for five minutes and change my clothes and get my equipment."

"All right! Here's a rundown of the schedule, and here"—he threw a plastic square on the desk—"here is a special pass that you must display at all times, pinned right where security can see it or you won't get in anyplace. I've never seen so many police here before. I hope the press can get within twenty feet of the king. They've even put a cordon on the press people."

"That's good to know," said Andrea fervently. He looked at her strangely. She added, "Well, we wouldn't want anything to happen to the king, would we?"

"Hell, no! It would blow the lid off this town. Everybody who lives here or works here would be affected. Nothing would be the same if anything went wrong during one of these official visits."

"Oh, God, I wish the damn thing was over." Her hands shook, and she shoved them deep into her pockets so he wouldn't notice.

"Soon, Andy, soon. Now, let's get down to work."

He briefed her on each point of the visit over the next twenty-four hours, until the events were engraved on her mind. She took the special pass and looked at it. A cheap piece of plastic, but it would get her into places that other people couldn't go, places where people could hide—church towers, basement boiler rooms, underground parking areas, private places in public places that few knew.

She stood up to leave, and Jack grabbed her hand tightly. "Are you really OK, Andy? You look like a gal with big problems."

"I'm all right. Sorry about being late."

As she reached the door, he asked, "Did Ed Ransome ever catch the person who sent you those brownies that killed the birds? He came over here and read your copy from the last three months, trying to find something inflammatory in it."

"No kidding. Did he uncover anything?"

"No more than the borderline bias that creeps into every writer's material no matter how hard they try to remain neutral. There was nothing overtly incriminating, but we never know how anything we print will hit some people personally. Some trivia can trigger an unbalanced mind and cause it to read things that aren't even there," he mused aloud.

"So it's probably not connected with the paper."

"No. Some jilted lover from your past, more likely."

"Sure, there are hundreds of those," she joked without humor.

"I can see at least one from here." Jack nodded in the direction of Gage, who was lounging on a desk, waiting for Andrea to come out of the office.

"Oh, no! He's not waiting for *me!*" she objected fiercely.

"Yes, he is. I'm the boss here, and I say he goes where you go. I think you're involved in some kind of mess that you're not talking about, and it would help if he went along. Besides, you're assigned to do pictures only. Now, get the hell to work!"

As she reached the door, she asked, "Do we split the by-line?"

"Get out of here. Think it would look good on your application to the *Post*? I know Graham called you after that drug story."

"That was six months ago, at least. I'm still here, aren't I, Jack?"

"Yeah, I guess so. But, for me, Andy, stick with Gage."

She could see it was hopeless to argue further, so she walked out into the main office. She would start out with Gage and then dump him so as to do some investigation on her own.

She went to her desk and, carefully moving some reference books, took out the photograph underneath. Under the scrutiny of a magnifier, the man looked younger than she had thought at first—maybe twenty-eight—black-haired and vital. So this was Omar Shaifi, who had the weapon now—a killer of innocent dogs, and probably of people, too. She thought about the note that had come with the brownies, and she could almost see this man laboring over the right words in his primitive English, that stupid attempt at an anonymous love letter. Why had he tried to do that to *her?* She memorized the face in the picture, then tore it up and threw it into the wastebasket next to her desk. She'd know him if she found him, and she was determined to find him if he was here.

Gage walked over to her desk and looked her over carefully. He said nothing about how she looked. "Are you going to work today?" he asked. "If you are, we'd better get crackin'. This ain't no desk job, honey." He gazed down into her wastebasket curiously. She pushed a Kleenex box off the end of the desk, scattering the pieces of the picture as it fell into the basket. When she retrieved it, the picture was pushed out of sight.

"What was that picture I saw you tearing up just now?" he asked.

"A shot of the city council. I thought I could crop one of the heads out for another feature, but they were too close together."

"Oh." At the words "city council," he lost interest. She sighed in relief.

"Jack says to stick with you today and tomorrow during the king's visit. Hey, do you have one of the work wagons? There was no car in the lot when I came in this morning."

"Yes, I kept it last night," she answered without explanation. "And now I have to go over to the apartment and change and pick up the cameras. Meet me in the lot."

He was waiting for her when she came back in a pantsuit. She carried a new bag.

"Now you look sharp."

First on the agenda was an interview at the Hilton with a public-relations man for the royal party. Then there was another interview, in the outside kitchen of Marlborough House, with the Middletowne press bureau. Andrea sat through each one, bored and aching to get on the streets.

Never had she seen so many dark-skinned people from the Middle East in town, not even during the visit of the shah of Iran. They seemed to be everywhere—in the halls of the buildings, in the foyers of the hotels, on the streets. For the most part, the men wore western dress—white shirts, dark suits, neat ties, and gold jewelry. Only a few of the older men wore the loose white robes, the burnoose.

At an interview at the inn at noon, the robed men pointedly ignored the questions of any female reporters. They were obviously disdainful of women and preferred to answer only the men. Gage was writing furiously, while Andrea found herself pushed into a corner. One very old Arab man pinched her gently on the arm, smiling through his gold teeth.

"*Salaam aleikum*," greeted Andrea, hoping desperately it sounded right. It was the only Arabic phrase she knew.

He acknowledged her greeting and grinned. "Kane-tuck-y Fry Cheek-in." It was the only American phrase *he* knew, and he had pronounced it with remarkable success.

Andrea stepped back uncertainly. Had he actually said Kentucky fried chicken? She took several pictures of the old man. *Now, what caption is going on this one,* she wondered, *"Arabian visitor says it's finger lickin' good"?* She motioned to Gage, mouthing, "Get his name from the interpreter," and pushed through the crowd to the corridor outside.

Where was Omar Shaifi? Was he hiding, waiting somewhere far from Middletowne, or was he here, disguised in the mob of his own people? Was he wearing a robe? Who would know?

She walked down the corridor, glancing from side to side. Out on the lawn she could see the security men from Washington with their little gold insignia in their lapels. Several uniformed state police stood in assigned positions near the various doors. She trembled suddenly, glimpsing the familiar blond hair and broad shoulders of Paul as he walked with two other men near the pool. He was wearing a light-gray suit. She realized she was seeing him as he really was, no longer the student who had happened to walk into her life, but one of them, one of those agents she had looked upon with something akin to amusement. Suddenly they no longer seemed amusing.

She stepped back out of sight but continued to gaze at Paul. She felt an odd thrill of excitement, thinking how he was last night. *Oh, Lord, let nothing happen to him. I do want him so very much.* For a moment he seemed to look directly at the glass door where she was standing. There was no sign of recognition from him.

She turned and went back down the corridor to find Gage, who was coming frantically from the opposite direction. "Where did you go to? You're supposed to stay by me. Now, let's get out of this madhouse and find some lunch somewhere. How about your place?"

"All I have is dog food, and Jade won't let us have any," she stated.

"Well, come on. We'll try the east side of town. It's too crowded around here."

They drove until they got to Moody's Bar and Grill. Reluctantly Gage pulled in. There were few cars in the parking lot, and he figured they would be served quickly. Andrea looked around doubtfully.

"Don't turn up your nose. We'll just have hamburgers," said Gage.

"And quite possibly ptomaine," muttered Andrea as they entered the dining area.

"I can help you?" asked a small Korean waitress. "Good chicken, good hamburger. Hot dog no good!"

"Two burgers, please, and two coffees," ordered Gage.

"Have any of the Middle Eastern people come in here today?" Andrea asked. The waitress didn't understand what she meant.

"You know, dark skin, curly hair," said Andrea, trying to describe them.

"That sounds like my boyfriend. His name is Johnee Hopkins. He looks like what you say, very good-looking! Oh, sometimes he's mean, but most times sweet. You know the men!" She glanced at Gage, as if teasing him. Then she continued, "My Johnee, he just ride away on his motorcycle, maybe five minutes ago."

Motorcycle! thought Andrea. Could it possibly be... Oh, no. She said his name was Johnny Hopkins. Of course it wouldn't be him. There were lots of guys riding motorcycles.

"You like some pie? Only have apple," said the girl. Gage shook his head, and she marched off to the kitchen humming a little song.

Lots of dark-haired men ride motorcycles, Andrea thought desperately. But the thought would not leave her mind that she was close to something. Omar Shaifi was miles away by this time, and she wished she could shake off this silly feeling. Still, it persisted, and when the waitress returned and placed the burgers and coffee before them, Andrea was so deep in thought that she just sat there, not moving.

Gage looked at her, wondering what was on her mind. "There's a little green worm crawling out of your hamburger," he announced in mock horror, staring at her plate. "My goodness, there's another, and here comes one now—will you look at the little rascal? He's wearing a green hat!"

Slowly Andrea came out of her reverie and smiled at him. She picked up her fork and made little jabbing motions all around her plate. "OK, now they're all dead. Do you want his hat?"

Gage laughed and they began to eat. When they finished, Andrea picked up the check and dropped a tip on the table. She draped her cameras over her shoulder. As they went back to the car, she turned to Gage and suggested, "Since we can cover twice as much if we each take separate sides of town, why don't we split up?"

"We've been through all that before, Andy. Jack told me to stick with you."

"OK, but I'm going in some pretty odd places."

"Why? You're bound to have some reason. You *are* acting strange, and I think it has something to do with those poisoned brownies. I believe you think you know who sent that box and you're looking for him. Well, I think that's important, too, Andy, but can't it wait until after tomorrow?"

She looked at him thoughtfully. He was awfully close to part of the truth without knowing the terrible facts. "Well, I guess you have found out that I'm on to... ah, certain things that point to one person. Yes, I *am* looking for him, to turn him over to the police."

"Who do you suspect? Do I know him?" asked Gage excitedly.

"No, and I can't identify him, because I'm not sure myself."

"Come on, Andy, you're grasping at straws! You better put all this aside until we get the story on the king all tied up. Then I'll help you. We'll go after anybody you say. It's a guy, isn't it?"

"Yes, it's a guy," she muttered resignedly, getting into the car.

The afternoon was open to find side stories that tied in with the king and his party. Despite Gage, Andrea decided to go ahead with her search for Omar. Doggedly, she walked into hotels and motels, went into boiler rooms and through secret passages. She surprised wine stewards, cooks, and garbage men, unused to seeing anyone invade their private areas. Gage stalked grimly behind. He had never walked so much so fast in his life. It was as if Andrea were trying to cover every out-of-the-way nook and cranny.

"Look, we haven't written a line all afternoon," he complained. "Now I want to get back on the streets, Andy!"

"If you can't keep up, go back to the office," she replied curtly.

He gave her a sidelong glance and continued to plod behind her as they walked through the crowded Green, past the cannons, toward Marlborough House. Curious visitors were standing, observing the activity of the security, hoping to see some minor official in the vicinity that they could tell their friends about when they got home.

Two security men were standing, very bored, at each end of the fence, and a Virginia state trooper dozed in his car in front of the house. Two mounted police from Richmond trotted briskly by, conscious of being admired by the small crowd.

Andrea looked up at the stately brick mansion. The sun was shining on the windows, and she could see someone pass behind the drapes inside. She leaned forward intently, then hurried over to one of the security men.

"Who's inside the house?" she asked.

"Just a woman and man from the inn. They're checking the silver, linens, last-minute preparations to make sure everything is right for the royal party," the man answered.

"May we go in and talk to them? Take some interior pictures?" asked Andrea. She wanted to get inside the house and check it out for herself.

"No, ma'am. Sorry, it's absolutely off limits."

Within a few minutes the couple came out of the house. Gage hurried over to talk to them, trying at last to get some related story to placate Jack Wise. It was Andrea this time who followed along, disconsolately checking her camera, prepared to do backup pictures for the interview she knew Gage was after. She had hoped they could get into the house, just on the off chance Omar had slipped in before it was made secure.

The man talking to Gage was very blasé—serving kings was his business—but his wife was a bit nervous. She kept adjusting her long white muslin apron and touching the lace of her starchy mobcap. She laughed as Gage plied her with questions about her job. Andrea took their picture, standing by the door of Marlborough House. In the background, cotton was growing in the yard, an incongruous touch for a house in the city.

Gage closed his notebook, and Andrea thanked them for the picture. A sudden sound, muffled from being far across the Green, startled Andrea as she put her camera away.

She turned quickly toward it. It was the sound of a motorcycle. All she could discern was that everything seemed black—the driver's helmet, his clothing, even the bike itself. And, of course, the rider wore goggles. Even at this distance she could see that the rider was dark and young. She began to run across the Green, but the cycle was too far away and going fast. She stopped and Gage caught up with her.

"What the hell are we running for?" he puffed.

"Quick, where did you leave the car?" she asked.

"Over behind the press building, don't you remember?"

"Three blocks away," she despaired. "Let's go back to the office. There's nothing more I can do. It's no use, it's hopeless." She sounded near tears.

They began to walk down the cobbled street, back past the house and the two agents lounging near the fence. One of the men stifled a yawn, bored with the quiet job of having to protect celebrities.

CHAPTER TWENTY-FOUR

Andrea awoke with a start and turned to answer the telephone ringing near the bed. She was surprised to find she had slept well despite the trouble on her mind that had made getting to sleep so difficult. As she reached for the telephone, she realized with a tinge of cold fear that today was the day.

"Hello."

"Hello, darling. It's Paul. Did I wake you?"

"It doesn't matter. I'm so glad to hear your voice. Oh, Paul, I kept hunting until late last night, but if Omar Shaifi is hidden anywhere in this town, he's found someplace that I don't know about. What are you doing? Have you found anything?"

"No, I haven't located Omar. There's so much security around I can't believe they'd be crazy enough to try to go through with it. This morning I saw two men on the roof of Marlborough House with rifles. However, we've made plans for any attempt, but I can't tell you about them. I probably won't see you today, darling. Be careful."

"Please let me be with you today. I promise to stay out of the way."

"It's impossible. There's something I must do alone." His voice sounded steady, yet reserved. Hesitantly, he added, "No matter what happens today, remember that I love you. I always will love you."

The phone clicked, and she heard the hum of the dial tone. Fear gripped her as she repeated his final words over and over in her mind. *He didn't say goodbye,* she thought helplessly.

She put the telephone on its cradle and lay back on the bed. Her whole world seemed black and ugly, like the rain outside. She lay there unwilling to get up and face the terrible uncertainty of the day. She found herself praying for Paul to come out of this day alive.

She noticed Jade waiting anxiously at the door to go out, and reluctantly she got up. She opened the door; Jade fled down the street to the nearest plot of grass. The phone rang, and Andrea left the door ajar, knowing the small dog would come immediately back up the stairs. She lifted the phone and was not surprised to hear Jack Wise on the other end.

"Don't bother to check in this morning. Go directly down and follow it all the way through, and get me some nice ones. Remember those press awards are coming up."

"Sure, Jack," she managed unenthusiastically. "See you later."

She tried to remember the sequence of events as outlined for the press. King Hassan would arrive at nine o'clock in Middletowne from the airport, which was about fifteen miles away. He'd go straight into residence at Marlborough House without stopping for interviews. The order had come yesterday— no interviews, much to the anger of the press. But the planned carriage ride through the restored area was still on. Andrea thought that that was peculiar in view of what she knew from Paul. Of course, maybe the king himself was still unaware that there was an assassination plot against him. Maybe security was tight enough so that it could be handled without danger. It *was* a short ride, and most dignitaries insisted on it, not so much to see the town as to let the town see them.

Carefully Andrea checked her cameras, making sure she had plenty of film in the two she was going to use today. She reloaded the gun and placed it, safety on, in the bottom of her bag among her extra lenses and filters. She drank a quick cup of coffee and fed Jade, who had returned as expected. She put on a dark-brown top and matching slacks and pinned the special pass to her raincoat.

She gazed at the pass. Until now her job had seemed rather exciting, even important at times in its fast-paced attempt to get the news and make the public aware of things that were happening everywhere. It had been fun chasing down a story, getting to know people with carefully worded questions. But now there was Paul, and all this seemed trivial compared to her need for him. Funny, it had never been that way with Patch.

As she got ready to leave, she looked around the apartment, as if looking at it for the last time. Jade whimpered, her round eyes wide. The little dog had always been able to sense changes in Andrea's moods, and this one frightened her. Andrea stopped to scratch her soothingly behind the ears, but the Peke's body felt tense beneath her hand.

"Everything will be all right, babe, don't be afraid."

She locked the door and went slowly downstairs into the rain.

"The motorcade has finally appeared, and the crowd that braved today's downpour to catch a glimpse of King Hassan of Uddapha will soon be able to see the controversial monarch and welcome him to this quaint little city, which has entertained so many famous visitors in the past. The crowd seems good-natured about the delay in time, more than two hours behind the original schedule. Americans and many people from the Middle East line the streets to see the king, who, it is rumored, will bargain oil for land in the United States."

Over the drone of the commentator's voice came shouts from the crowd—some enthusiastic, some fiercely negative—as the line of limousines rounded the corner and rolled slowly to a stop in front of the big brick mansion. People surged forward, but a cordon of Washington agents shoved them roughly back behind a rope barrier. Both visitors and townspeople were alarmed and surprised by their insistence on keeping everyone so far away, especially after the long wait in the rain.

"Well, I never!" sputtered one elderly lady, poking a policeman with her umbrella. "I saw our own beloved Eisenhower as close as I am to you, my good man! He was much more important than this king, I can tell you! What do you mean, grabbing my umbrella like that?"

"Leave the old broad alone, turkey!" shouted a young college student. He was carrying a sign that said, "America Strike Back. Use Love Power, Not Oil, to Keep Warm!" His friends joined in, deriding the police, visitors, almost everybody.

In front of Marlborough House, security men ran back and forth as the limousines waited. Soon many black umbrellas appeared from inside the house to enable the royal party to go up the walkway without getting soaking wet. Some minor officials went first. Then the crowd hushed as the tall figure of the king, in long white robes covered with a black raincoat, appeared from the third car. He was followed by a tiny woman in a long flowered dress, also covered by a raincoat. She swept hurriedly into the mansion without so much as a glance or wave at the disappointed crowd.

The two security men on the roof stood ready at each end, scanning the angry crowd, which was already dispersing. The press people, in their privileged spot near the fence, were staring in disbelief at the closed door.

"Hell, I could have stayed home and phoned this one in," said one reporter. "Did you get a shot?" "The umbrellas covered their heads." "Which one was the king?" "I got a shot of his feet." "How do you know they were *his* feet?" The comments rumbled about Gage and Andrea as the door shut firmly behind the royal visitors.

Gage shook her elbow. "C'mon, let's get out of the rain. We can go back to the office and dry out. I can get about three lines out of this fiasco! Is the carriage ride still on, or has that been fouled up, too? Why was there such a long wait at the airport after the plane landed? Did you know the lounge was literally sealed off out there? They didn't have this much heat for Hirohito!" He continued to gripe as he tried to hurry Andrea through the crowd.

"I'm going to stick around for a while, Gage. Maybe I'll interview some of the protest groups over on the Green. They're always good for copy when all else fails."

"Are you nuts? In this weather? C'mon, Andy."

"No, I'm staying. You go ahead."

"Well, OK. Meet you here in about, say, an hour?"

Whistling tunelessly, a copy of *What's Happening Here* covering his head, Gage strode off down the street through the fast-disappearing crowd.

Andrea looked around the area, peering at the people in the rain. *If they are here today, let me find them before they find Paul,* she prayed silently. *What a foolish optimist I am,* she mused as the water fell inside the collar of her raincoat, *to think that I could spot a killer, when Middletowne is full of agents who haven't turned up anything. But still I have to try,* she thought, *for Paul.*

She walked over to where the college students were waiting with their signs. One big one stated, "King Hassan Knows How to Oil a Ford," and on a more serious note another asked, "Will the Gaza Strip Be Another Vietnam?" She talked to them for a while and marveled at their youthful energy, undampened by the rain.

There were a few brave souls still waiting, among them the newspeople from Uddapha—four men and one woman, identified by their yellow plastic pins. Two of the men had used the darkroom at the office, but Andrea didn't recognize the woman or the other two men. The woman looked very chic despite the dampness. Her face was almost covered by a Garbo-type hat, and her slim figure was enhanced by a trench coat that appeared to have been made in Paris. *They must get paid more than we do,* Andrea thought, feeling slightly jealous.

She looks interesting, Andrea decided. *I wonder if she speaks English. If she is over here on assignment, she certainly must know enough to be understood.* Andrea started to walk to the end of the fence where the group was huddled, but she got only a few steps in their direction when she heard Gage call out behind her. He ran up to her side.

"Hey, Andy, are you OK? Jack told me to get my tail back down here. Do you know that he is still worried about you being alone?"

"Oh, he worries entirely too much. I'm perfectly all right. I was just going down there to talk to the Uddaphan newspeople. Hey, wait a minute. Something's happening at the house. One of the aides is opening the door," observed Andrea, suddenly interested.

"Probably checking this miserable weather," growled Gage unenthusiastically.

"No, it's more than that. He's looking for the carriage, and here it comes around the corner! My God, they're going through with it!" Her voice was shaking. She clutched Gage by the arm, her face white with fear.

As the door opened wide, Andrea started running blindly toward the house. A bewildered Gage tried desperately to keep up with her. Others surged forward, trying to get nearer to the gate. Andrea got there first, but two burly security agents shoved the oncoming crowd, and she, being in front, took the brunt of it and fell backward, losing her footing. She sank to the pavement as the crowd pushed around her, ignoring her as they tried to get nearer the gate. Gage managed to pull her to her feet just as the king appeared in the doorway. She struggled forward, trying to call out a warning.

Up on the porch, black umbrellas were opening, shielding the people in the doorway from the view of the crowd. Eager photographers popped flashes anyway. The members of the press had turned and were now pushing toward the carriage. Some people were slipping on the cobblestones, falling against the others. Security paid them no attention, determined as they were to keep everyone at bay. Police formed a cordon all the way down the walkway from the house to the street, where the carriage was waiting. Andrea felt herself pummeled by bodies, but she lifted her camera and squeezed the shutter release, hoping the focus was nearly correct. The act was mechanical. She was no longer able to speak or call out. She was encased in a paralysis of fear.

She kept taking pictures, toward the doorway, into the crowd, along the line of the multitude of uniformed troopers who seemed to have appeared from nowhere. And then, through the mist and haze, she saw the long white robe of the king. Head down, covered again by a black raincoat, he was coming down the walk with his wife right behind him.

She focused on the bobbing, hurrying figures. They reached the street safely.

Andrea shoved fiercely for a position near the carriage. She reached the edge of the street and began to raise the camera to her eye, when she caught a sudden movement in the crowd. She froze in horror. The king had entered the carriage and was about to be seated when she saw it—the camera, affixed to the tripod. It was identical to the one she had seen in Paul's house that night.

It was in the hands of the Uddaphan newswoman. She had pulled it up from the confines of her raincoat and held it high in front of her. Her eyes were glittering; her face was a contorted mask of righteousness; her red lips were mouthing some unheard message of revenge as she pressed the trigger. The mute shot passed wildly over the heads of the people, who were totally unaware.

Andrea pushed forward, screaming as loud as she could, but it was too late. No one heard her in the noise of the crowd. The woman fired again, this time into the carriage. The king turned, as if expecting danger, half rose from his seat and flung his hand forward. As the shot hit its mark, blood spurted from his hand and sprayed all over his white robes. A scream of fright rose from the shocked crowd.

The horses, wild-eyed at the sound, reared up frantically, trying to disengage the carriage. Andrea was so close, the big green wheel almost rolled over her foot. As the horses reared, the king's headdress slipped to one side. The hair was blond and thick. At that instant, the terrified horses broke away from the crowd. The carriage reeled from side to side.

"Paul!" screamed Andrea. "Oh, God! It's Paul!"

Sobs tore from her chest, and she beat people away with her camera. As they edged back, she was able to get free and run toward the far side of the Green. She knew those horses well, and she realized that even in their fright they would follow through on a pattern that fear would not change. They would run the familiar route from sheer habit.

Her feet slipped in the wet grass, but she stumbled on, past the old trees and the cannon, until she was almost on the other side. There was a thundering rush of sound to her right, the clatter of a horse's hooves plowing through the soft grass. A mounted policeman had seemingly appeared from nowhere and was riding wildly down the incline toward the carriage.

"Thank God, he'll be able to stop the horses," Andrea gasped, turning toward the policeman. She glanced up at the rider, and he stared down at her in equal surprise. A scream froze in her throat. She threw up her hands and rushed forward.

The horse reared and plunged backward. Under the shiny black visor of the cap, black eyes flared; white teeth flashed in a surprised grimace. It was Omar Shaifi, the man she had been hunting for two days. He pulled the reins tightly, and a mirthless peal of laughter rent the air as he got the horse under control. He uttered something obscene and dug his heels in the horse's ribs to kick him into action, but Andrea had seen the long, thin knife in his hand and knew he was on his way to finish off the assassination.

She could hear the wheels of the carriage approaching behind her. She sprang toward Omar's horse, grabbed the bit in her hand and twisted it cruelly. The horse pulled sideways and stumbled to its knees in pain, while the rider landed on his back on the grass. Andrea collapsed in exhaustion.

A stream of curses filled the air as Omar lay on the ground, bellowing in rage and indignation. Then his body coiled forward like a snake about to strike. He got to his knees, with the knife clutched in his hand. Murder was in his eyes. The knife rose in his hand.

"You die. You die," he intoned. He managed to struggle to one knee, and they stared into each other's eyes, each seeing death only moments away.

Omar crept forward, coming closer. Like a robot, Andrea felt her own hand move, go deep into her bag. She withdrew the gun, flipped off the safety, and fired point-blank. A tiny black hole appeared between Omar's eyes. Blood spurted suddenly from the hole and ran down his face. For one second a look of disbelief appeared in his eyes; then they turned glassy, and he fell.

From nearby there were sounds of running and voices shouting. Rough hands grabbed Andrea and pushed her into a car, which sped across the Green. She gazed in alarm at the agents on either side of her. She felt a pinprick in her arm. Then, everything went blank.

CHAPTER TWENTY-FIVE

Sun filtered onto her face, but Andrea didn't move. A certain smell drifted into her nostrils. It was sharp, antiseptic, cloying. She could taste it on her tongue. It was a hospital smell, and she realized with annoyance that she must have been brought here while she slept.

Someone was holding her hand. She willed her eyes open and saw a stranger sitting by her bed.

"Where am I?" The words came out wrong, fuzzy. Her mouth was incredibly dry.

"You're in the hospital. After all the excitement yesterday, you must have passed out from the shock. Do you remember what happened?"

She looked at him cagily, remembering that she had not passed out. Somewhere on her arm would be the mark of a needle, but right now she wouldn't look and give him the satisfaction of knowing how much she remembered. Suddenly she thought, *yesterday!*

The word took a long time to come out. "Yesterday? Here all night?" she managed.

"Do you remember what you did before you passed out?" he urged, reaching to press the bell for the nurse.

"Sholla man. Gimme walla. So dry," she said drowsily, closing her eyes.

She heard the rustle of nylon nearby, the swish of the door opening and closing, and then her bed was elevated slightly. A low voice murmured, "You want her to wake now, or shall I give her another—?"

"No, not necessary," a man answered.

"She wants water. Can she have water? I think she can answer questions now."

"Sure. I'll tell Dr. Lancaster that she's awake." A female voice was speaking.

With great effort, Andrea opened her eyes and sat up. The man came into focus. He gave her a glass of water and a plastic straw, a red one, bent in the center.

"Where is Paul? Is he hurt? Is he in this hospital?" she demanded. She tried to get up, but her head throbbed and the room spun crazily. She realized from the cold draft across her derriere that she was wearing one of those idiotic short gowns that tied only at the neck in the back. She stuck her feet back under the cover. Shaking, she sank back on the pillow.

"Now, who is Paul, Miss Wayne? Is he a friend of yours?" the man asked stupidly.

She looked back at him with undisguised contempt and spit out angrily, "And who the hell are you? Do you think I'm some kind of idiot? I remember now! You were with Paul yesterday. No, not yesterday, the day before. You were walking with him near the inn, on the lawn near the pool."

The man half smiled in surprise. He and Paul had been together about five minutes; yet this girl had managed to see them somehow in that short period. There was only one thing to do, and that was take her even further into confidence and hope that she had the integrity to handle the situation.

"I'm Agent Wilson. Paul is not here. I heard that he did suffer some kind of, ah, accident, but he has been moved out of town to another destination and is quite likely being treated—"

"Mr. Wilson, I also know that Paul replaced the king. There was a long layover at the airport. I remember my partner, Gage, saying that the lounge was sealed, and I believe the change was made right there. King Hassan never came to Middletowne, did he?"

"Actually, no. I believe the whole party was secretly moved to one of our planes and returned to London. But, Miss Wayne, you must understand that you are involved in an extremely delicate international incident. For your own sake, and Mr. Hunter's, you are to remain in custody for a certain period of time and speak to no one about this entire affair. We hope you intend to cooperate with us."

"What about the man I killed? Do you think you can just sweep that under the table? People saw me—not close, of course, they were all chasing the carriage—but I'm sure some of them were near enough. And what happened to the body?" she asked, her eyes wide.

"We put him in the back seat. We acted as fast as we could. But the story you must stick to, and the one we told the press, is that the man was a maniac who attacked you."

"Well, that is true. He was a maniac," she agreed.

"But all the rest, the plot against the king—you must never acknowledge such a thing existed. Stay with the story that the attack on you was one isolated, unfortunate incident that just happened spontaneously. And as far as 'King Hassan' is concerned, he suffered a minor wound, was treated here and has been flown back to Uddapha."

"But where is Paul? I want to see him!"

"That's impossible at this time."

"That's what you think. Where are my clothes?" Andrea attempted to get up.

"Get back in bed, Miss Wayne. There are two policemen in the hall to prevent your escape, and to keep out the curious," the man said, looking deadly serious.

"Escape? My escape? What are you talking about?" she asked, unbelieving.

"Homicide. You committed a homicide. You're under guard, Miss Wayne."

As Dr. Lancaster came through the door, Andrea looked through to the hall. She could see a blue uniform at the edge of the door. Wilson wasn't kidding. She sank back against the pillows weakly, trying to think the situation through. It was all coming too fast. So much had happened. She felt she had to sort things out. The doctor held her pulse and gazed down at her with a sympathetic little smile.

"When can I get out of here, Doctor? Or should I ask *him?*" she asked hopelessly.

"I think all vital signs are normal. Another day ought to do it. Why don't you just take this time to relax? You've been through a harrowing experience. Probably could use the rest. Hospital food here isn't so bad, either," comforted the doctor.

He looked toward the agent, who nodded his head in agreement. Another day! She withdrew her hand from the doctor's and turned toward the wall, ignoring them both. She heard the door shut, but the scrape of a chair told her the other man was still there. She closed her eyes, but she couldn't get back to sleep. A cart rattled through the hall and stopped with a clink of dishes outside the door.

"Dr. Lancaster ordered a meal. Come on, now, Miss Wayne. Let me see, it's Andrea, isn't it? If you eat, you'll feel a lot better."

She sat up and looked directly at him. "You're right. It may help to counter the effect of the drugs, too, don't you think?"

The man didn't answer, just brought the tray and slid it onto a metal stand that spanned the bed. It smelled delicious, and Andrea realized it had been a long time since that hamburger at Moody's bar. She was struggling with a custard dessert, when Mr. Wilson was called into the hall.

He reappeared almost immediately and asked, "Do you want visitors? It may be easier if you don't see anybody just yet. I can always say you're sleeping."

"Who is it?"

"Two college students who live in your apartment building."

"Oh, sure, Matt and George. Yes, I want to see them. Oh, gosh, I *have* to see them!" she said, suddenly thinking of Jade, locked in the apartment.

"Well, remember to be careful what you say. You *do* want to see Hunter again?"

"Send them in," she said soberly. "I know what to say."

Wilson left the room as Matt and George came in.

"Hi, beautiful. We're smuggling in a nurse's uniform so you can break out of this dump," confided Matt in a stage whisper.

"Great idea. I was having an awful time tying sheets together. They won't reach the ground," she kidded in return.

"That's funny. You're on the first floor," observed George.

They stood uneasily by the bed, as if they were too embarrassed to know what to say.

"Have you seen Jade? Please use the key I gave you and get her out."

"We already have her. We took her over to our place as soon as we heard… you know. Did you know that rascal can jump onto the coffee table from the couch? She got a bag of potato chips and ate the whole thing!" swore George, shaking his head.

"Well, I'll buy you a bushel. Be sure to take the milk and bread. You guys eat it."

"When will you be coming home, Andy?" they both asked.

"Tomorrow, I hope."

"Well, you do what the doc says. Stay as long as you like, but, of course, when you do get home, the potato-chip bill will probably be enormous," admitted Matt.

He squeezed her hand, and for a moment their eyes met. Then he looked down, as if he didn't quite know how to tell her he was sorry about what had happened on the Green. After all, the man outside had instructed them not to mention it. George leaned over and gave her an awkward kiss on the cheek, saying, "See ya tomorrow."

Just as they reached the door, George turned abruptly and pulled a packet of mail from his pocket. He put it on the side of the bed.

"Almost forgot your mail. Thought there might be something there you'd like to see as soon as possible. It looks official. Be good, Andy."

"Yeah, you, too, guys. Kiss the mutt for me."

Andrea looked through the pile of letters and discarded the junk mail. She opened a long white envelope very carefully and read the legal print down to the bottom line. There it was, Patch's signature. He had signed after all. He had signed the divorce papers.

Suddenly she felt more alone than she had ever felt before. Now Patch was gone, and Paul was… where? She didn't even know. Her head began to ache, and she was overcome with a strange tiredness. Her throat hurt. Tears streamed down her face as she hugged her pillow.

When Jack Wise tiptoed into the room sometime later, she was asleep. She was curled up like a child, her face was unnaturally flushed, and her hair felt damp to his touch. He kissed her cheek and left quietly, his heart heavy at the sight. He didn't understand exactly what had happened. He only had a feeling that this was one story Andrea would never write.

CHAPTER TWENTY-SIX

Andrea sat at the apartment window and gazed down into the street. She sat hunched like an old person, a sweater wrapped around her shoulders, a lukewarm cup of tea in her hands. These days it seemed she could never get warm enough, and yet it was not really cold. She had lost weight and appetite. Many nights the face of Omar Shaifi appeared in a recurring nightmare. His eyes were always wide with surprise. Vivid red blood streamed from his head. His mouth began as a dark hole. Then the hole became an abyss that Andrea fell into. At that point, she would wake, trying to call for Paul.

Across the street, near Le Fromage, she could see the young man in a plaid sport coat and navy pants, standing bored and waiting patiently. He had been there ever since she came home from the hospital. She knew there was a second one on this side of the street, but she couldn't see him from the window. She sighed, wondering how much longer this isolation must go on.

She had not been allowed to go back to work for the past two weeks. All her friends and visitors were cordially but firmly turned away. She looked wistfully at the familiar brick building across the street and wished she were back at her desk, arguing with Jack, teasing old Gage, bedeviling Mr. Fischer in the lab. The only ones she was allowed to see were Matt and George, because they lived in the same building.

At night she went down to eat in the little restaurant, with the two men on guard. They also accompanied her when she walked Jade late at night. One evening she walked all the way to the Green, and another time she went to the little green house across from the cemetery. The house, of course, was silent and empty. There was not even an echo of the big dog's bark to remind her of those days so recently past.

Mostly, she sat at the window, waiting for something to happen. Once it did. The week before, two more agents came to Middletowne and took her on a car trip to a tiny courthouse in Fairfax County, where a very solemn judge presided at a hearing into the murder of Omar Shaifi. It was like being in a play, only she hadn't been shown the script. Her lines had been assigned by the "director," her lawyer, a man she had never seen before. He had actually given her a written statement to read—to *read*, not even memorize—about self-defense and unprovoked attack by a person of unsound mind. It was basically the truth but completely void of any reference to Omar's involvement in the assassination plot on King Hassan. Obediently, she read the statement, and the judge dismissed all charges, technically allowing her to go free. But the two men took her back to her apartment, and she still remained under guard.

This day, as she sat by the window, the telephone began to ring. This, in itself, was peculiar, because she had tried to call outside and found that it had been disconnected almost two weeks ago. She put the cup of tea on the windowsill and picked up the telephone.

"Hello," she answered, her voice flat, disinterested. It was probably one of *them*.

"Andrea Wayne? One moment, please."

There was a faint click. *I'm being recorded,* she thought, slightly amused.

"This is Elliott Winston. I have a message concerning Paul Hunter. You must keep this information totally confidential. Are you prepared to follow instructions without divulging any part of them to any person—" he began.

She interrupted anxiously. "Yes, of course. Please tell me about Paul. Is he all right? When can I see him?"

"You must give me your word that it will be strictly confidential," he persisted.

"Absolutely! You have my word. Now, please," she begged.

"Paul Hunter is in a military hospital near Washington, D.C. He wants to see you as soon as he can and is being very difficult with us about it."

"How badly is he hurt, Mr. Winston?" she stammered, gripping the telephone.

"I won't withhold anything from you. His left hand was shattered by the bullet from the woman's gun." Here he paused, as if reluctant to say more. "The doctors couldn't do anything to save it. His hand has been amputated."

She sat in stunned silence, unable to speak. *Oh, my darling, I'm so sorry.* Faintly, she heard Winston's voice still speaking and strained to hear the words.

"In view of what I have just told you, do you still wish to see him?"

"When can I leave?" she asked without hesitation.

"You can take the six A.M. plane to Dulles Airport. There you will be met by our man, Agent Wilson, who will pick you up and take you directly to the hospital. Can you be ready to go by tomorrow morning, Miss Wayne?"

"I'll be there."

"Good. And, Miss Wayne—thanks from all of us involved in this sometimes very ugly but necessary business. You may have saved Hunter's life. Good-bye."

"Good-bye," she said softly, barely paying attention to his words.

Her hands were shaking as she hung up the telephone. The agony of waiting was almost over. Tomorrow they'd be together. She whirled around the room to silent music. Oh, God, it was good to feel alive again!

When she finally fell into bed that night, happy but exhausted, she lay for a while just looking through the open blinds at the moon. It was almost full, similar to the night she had stumbled down the hill and into Paul's life. So much had happened since then. She dozed off wondering what was yet to come.

At 5:30 in the morning, the small airport was nearly deserted. A taxi deposited Andrea and the young agent in the plaid sport coat at the doors. He carried her bag into the terminal, and she found a seat overlooking the airfield. She turned to the man.

"Are you going with me?" she asked, wishing desperately to be free of constant surveillance.

"No ma'am. My job is to see you safely on the plane. You'll be met by another man at Dulles."

"Well, I feel that I should thank you. I know it becomes a boring job," she offered almost apologetically. He smiled, the cloak of reserve slipping momentarily as he seemed to regard her as a person in her own right, not as a job.

"I kind of enjoyed the nights we walked the dog. That's a nice town you live in," he confided. "I think I'll take my wife there sometime. She'd really enjoy it."

Silently they sat together in the terminal, watching the clock. Down at the far end, Andrea noticed two other early travelers waiting. One was an Oriental girl, vaguely familiar. With her was a small boy with big black eyes and shiny black bangs. They were surrounded by old suitcases tied with string and several shopping bags bursting with clothing and household goods. The boy was an especially beautiful child.

Andrea took out her camera and turned to the agent beside her. "Would it be OK if I go down there and take a picture of that little boy?"

"I'm sorry. Your flight is due in, in just two minutes."

"What a shame! He looks so cute sitting there holding that big, red chicken. I believe it's called a *piñata,* isn't it?"

"I think so. There's your plane coming in now. Good-bye, Miss Wayne."

"Good-bye."

They shook hands like two conservative old friends, and, with a smile, Andrea turned and went through the gate toward the waiting plane.

The Search for Scheherazade is a sequel to
A Matter of Revenge

CHAPTER ONE

The No Smoking sign flashed on and the soft voice of the stewardess intoned, "Fasten your seat belts, please. We will land at Dulles International in ten minutes."

The beautiful young girl in the third row aisle seat leaned over the man seated next to the window to look down at the panorama of Washington, D.C. The chalk white buildings, the vivid green grass and the too blue water all had the unreal appearance of a model created by a meticulous architect, and as many times as she had flown over it, Kara Winston still felt a thrill of excitement when she first glimpsed the dome of the Capitol, especially now that she had been overseas for several months.

"Look, there's the Lincoln Monument and the Washington Monument. Did you know it was once called "Cleopatra's Needle?" she exclaimed." I didn't realize that I would miss Washington so much!"

The man next to her got a heady whiff of French perfume and smiled at her as she leaned over him. "How about dinner with me?" he asked hopefully.

"Sorry, I couldn't possibly. I'm meeting my father in the VIP Lounge as soon as we land. But thanks."

"Does your father work for the government?"

"Yes, he does. He is very dedicated to his job. He was never home when we needed him, and that's why Mother divorced him and now we live in Paris."

She picked up a wide-brimmed lacy straw hat and placed it straight across her brow, her blue-green eyes peeping out mischievously. "Isn't this hat divine? From a terribly expensive boutique. Tres chic, n'est pas?"

"Charming!" he agreed. "How old are you, sweetheart?"

"Nineteen," she lied glibly, recalling the martini she had ordered earlier. She took a mirror from her purse and inspected her makeup carefully. She had reapplied it twice since they left Orly and the sophisticated image that smiled back at her pleased her ...and it would please Daddy.

The sprawling complex that was Dulles International Airport came into view as the plane circled to land. It taxied smoothly to a stop about a hundred yards from the terminal and cut its engines, as the boxlike transport buses rolled out onto the field to pick up the passengers. As the bus on which Kara rode neared the terminal, she glanced up at the waiting crowd but saw no sign of her father. She knew how he detested crowds but she couldn't help feeling disappointed. He would be in the Lounge. He had promised. In just a few minutes she would run up to him and give him a big kiss, and he would gaze down at her with all the love he had stored up over the last few months since they had been together at Christmas. She breezed through customs and left her luggage in a temporary holding area to be held until after she met her father. He would probably want to take her to lunch at the restaurant on the lower level. Now all she had to do was locate the VIP Lounge. She looked to her right and to her left and as she hesitated, unsure which way to go, she was approached by a slim, dark-skinned man in a chauffeur's uniform and a shiny visor cap, who seemed to have recognized her. Nervously, he flashed her a smile, showing white even teeth, and bowed from the hip.

Angrily, she stared back, knowing that her father must have sent him.

"Mees Weenston?"

"Yes?"

"Your father, he send me to meet you. He no can come heemself so he send me weeth a limousine. You will accompany me, please?" In his voice she heard certain desperation and oddly, there seemed to be something like fear in his wide dark eyes. He swept off the cap and held it respectfully to his chest.

She hesitated. "Damn it! He promised he'd be here!" She put her hands on her hips and stared about the airport, hoping that she would see her father appear suddenly, full of smiles and apologies.

"He is…immersed with the business but he say to tell you he will meet you at his home within the hour." The chauffeur, relieved to have delivered the message, then motioned to follow him to the door that led to the parking lot.

"Wait a minute, what about my luggage?"

"If madam geeve to me the ticket I will come back and gather them for you You weel wait for me in the limousine. Air-condition. Cool, I assure you and is much comfort." He nodded and smiled his nervous smile.

The lobby was extremely warm. Hot air seemed to burst into the lobby of the terminal each time someone came through a door. Kara took off her hat and fanned herself, remembering other Julys she had spent in Washington in sweltering summer weather. Waiting in an air-cooled limousine sounded infinitely better than wasting time by the ramp, so she shrugged and put her hat back on.

"Very well. Let's go. I will kill Daddy for this!"

The chauffeur sighed with relief and led the way out of the building, down a long concrete ramp on the far left side away from the parking lot. He scurried ahead, glancing back frequently to make sure she was following him, and beckoned to her to descend to what appeared to be a delivery area under the ramp.

She spotted the long black limousine at once, the type her father always used to send for her at school when she and her parents lived in dubious harmony on Embassy Row before the divorce. As she approached the car, she became aware that it was not empty and she stopped short, turning to the chauffeur for some explanation. She had no intention of sharing the limousine with a stranger.

"Who is that?" she demanded.

"Oh, I do not weeesh to spoil the surprise! He is a jeweler sent by your father with a little what is, uh, welcoming home present. He only wishes to please you. Do not offend him," begged the little dark man.

"Is he from Cartier's?"

"That may be the name, yes," mumbled the chauffeur.

"Presents. Always great with the presents and not with himself, that's Daddy's style," said Kara with more than a trace of bitterness. "And he even went to the trouble of sending a cable promising to meet me."

"So sorry," murmured the chauffeur sympathetically. He touched her elbow, urging her toward the car. "It is much too hot for a person of such delicacy."

She stepped inside, removing her hat to allow the cascade of long, blonde hair to fall against the cool gray leather seat, then turned to scrutinize the man in the shadows. He was dark like the chauffeur with a heavy, powerful physique concealed under a three-piece cream colored suit. His face was broad; his upper lip adorned with a mustache, and his curly hair was black tinged with gray. On his fingers were magnificent gold rings, set in diamonds, rubies and emeralds and Kara thought he was a walking advertisement for his own merchandise. She wondered what he had brought for her selection, but for the moment, he sat silently, staring at her with barely concealed admiration. She turned away, slightly wrinkling her nose with distaste. The car was filled with the scent of his cologne and there were other smells about him, perspiration and a sharp, medicinal odor, something odd, vaguely reminiscent of a hospital corridor.

The door of the car still stood slightly ajar and the chauffeur stuck his head forward to introduce her to the man inside.

"Mees Winston, this ees…" he began, faltering uncertainly.

"Oh, never mind!" she snapped, handing him the tickets for her luggage. "Run, pick up my bags before they are stolen. You simply can't trust anyone these days." She glanced at him sharply as he took the tickets and continued to stand by the door. She turned toward the jeweler.

"You have something for me?"

"Indeed I do, my little princess," the man answered, smiling. He raised his hand in a sudden motion to the chauffeur.

Kara found herself caught in a vise-like grip as the chauffeur pinioned her arms to her sides. The man inside the car produced a large white piece of cotton soaked with ether and placed it over her nose and mouth! She attempted to scream but it had happened so quickly that instead, she choked and inhaled, causing the ether to take effect immediately. Her eyes rolled upward, then closed, as her body went limp against the back of the seat. The chauffeur, alarmed, stared down into her pale face and released his hold on her arms.

"Is she dead?" he gasped, speaking Turkish. He leaped backward to get away from the acrid fumes and covered his nose with his hand.

"No, Mejid, only sleeping for a while," the other man assured him in the same language. "Now go quickly and retrieve the luggage."

"Perhaps I am caught!" the chauffeur said, hesitating.

"Hurry up, you fool, before her father leaves the lounge to find out why she has not arrived. It is not safe for us to remain here."

Trembling, Mejid ran off toward the terminal and several minutes later the frightened man returned, staggering under the weight of three pieces of luggage, which he thrust into the trunk. He got behind the wheel and took off through the parking lot, glancing behind frequently to see if they were being followed and keeping carefully within the speed limit until he reached the highway. Only when they were in the flow of the racing traffic did his eyes seek those of the man in the rear seat. Looking into the rear view mirror, he asked, "Are you sure she is not dead? She does not move!"

"Of course not, Mejid. All has gone as planned."

The heavyset man leaned over and smoothed the silk skirt over Kara's legs. His eyes feasted on the pale oval of her face, noticing the dark lashes, the rather short nose and her slightly parted mouth, small, like a rosebud. She was much more beautiful than he had anticipated that a daughter of Elliott Winston's would be. It was a shame to cover such beauty, but it must be done. He reached into a small drawstring bag at his feet and removed a long, black diaphanous garment, which he draped over the flowered print of her dress. With one hand, he lifted her head and with the other tucked the black cloth over her hair. He pulled the edges together, leaving only her eyes uncovered.

"Now you look like one of us, little flower," he smiled.

Mejid stared straight ahead, nearly petrified at the chances they were taking in this vast strange country, so unlike their own. From time to time, he took his eyes off the road to consult a map on the seat beside him. He had managed to drive all the way to Dulles with only one brief detour but he had to be twice as sure of the road going back now that the girl was with them. He sighed at the thought of so many miles to go before they arrived at the small island where the girl was to be confined until her father paid the ransom... a ransom not of money, but of many lives.